EVIL IN CARNATIONS

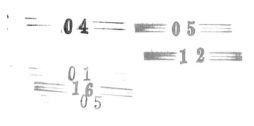
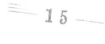

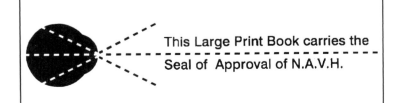

This Large Print Book carries the
Seal of Approval of N.A.V.H.

A FLOWER SHOP MYSTERY

Evil in Carnations

Kate Collins

KENNEBEC LARGE PRINT
A part of Gale, Cengage Learning

GALE
CENGAGE Learning

Detroit • New York • San Francisco • New Haven, Conn • Waterville, Maine • London

GALE
CENGAGE Learning™

LIBRARY OF CONGRESS CATALOGING-IN-PUBLICATION DATA

Collins, Kate, 1951–
    Evil in carnations : a flower shop mystery / by Kate Collins.
        p. cm. — (A flower shop mystery) (Kennebec Large Print superior collection)
    ISBN-13: 978-1-59722-930-2 (pbk. : alk. paper)
    ISBN-10: 1-59722-930-X (pbk. : alk. paper)
    1. Knight, Abby (Fictitious character)—Fiction. 2. Florists—Fiction. 3. Speed dating—Fiction. 4. Large type books. I. Title.
PS3603.O4543E85 2009
813'.6—dc22   2009003820

Published in 2009 by arrangement with NAL Signet, a member of Penguin Group (USA) Inc.

To all my friends in Key West — Jennifer at 7 Artists, Mary at Mary O'Shea's Glass Garden, Nanci and Sandi: I thank you for your continuing friendship, support, and encouragement, and also for the inspiration for some of the art I describe in my books. You know what I'm talking about.

To my husband, Jim; my children, Jason and Julie; and my sister, Nancy: I know it's a cliché, but I couldn't do this without you. Thanks for brainstorming, reviewing, editing, inspiring, spreading the word, and generally putting up with my crazy schedule.

To my editor, Ellen, who continues to amaze me with her insight: I thank you for keeping my plots on the right track.

To Abby and Marco, Jillian and Nikki, Grace and Lottie, and all those other little people who chatter constantly in my head (and sometimes drive me up the wall):

Well, let's keep those stories coming, people! Don't make me come in there!

To my readers, whose excitement keeps me charged up for the next adventure: I hope this book will make you eager for more.

CHAPTER ONE

Monday, January 31st

"Isn't there a law that says public hallways have to be lighted?" Marco complained. "Now there are two bulbs out. How are you supposed to find your key in the dark?"

I stopped rummaging through my duffel bag to whisper, "You'd better keep your voice down or you'll wake the neighbors."

In a complete change of mood, my hunky, ex–Army Ranger boyfriend swept aside my hair to press hot kisses against my neck. "You didn't seem to mind waking the neighbors yesterday, Fireball."

"I didn't *know* those neigh . . ." *Oh, baby.* His kisses were sending tingles to erotic zones I didn't even know existed . . . and I thought he'd found them all. Hard to believe that less than a month ago, I was certain Marco and I were history.

Where was my key? I really had to get a smaller bag.

"Why don't we go back to my apartment," Marco murmured in my ear, "and extend our vacation another day?"

Now, there was an offer that was hard to refuse. Who wouldn't want to prolong a romantic weekend with a hottie like Marco Salvare? He was all man, all the time, a guy who was both tough *and* sensitive, who could cook up a mean omelet and take down a killer all in the same day.

Besides, after our seven-hour red-eye flight back to Indiana from Key West, I wasn't exactly looking forward to putting in a long day at the flower shop — I don't do well on only a few hours' sleep — but as Bloomers' owner, I couldn't ignore my responsibilities either. So as much as it pained me, I had to decline.

Abandoning my key hunt, I wound my arms around his neck and gazed up at him, his sexy brown eyes barely visible in the darkness. "I really, really wish I could, Marco, but you know how hectic Mondays are. And besides, Lottie and Grace are expecting me. But it's a nice thought." Almost too nice to let go.

"Yeah, I figured as much."

Reluctantly, I released him to start rummaging again. "What time is it, anyway? Is it six o'clock yet? I still have to unpack, shower. . . ."

Marco ran his hands over my shoulders and down my arms, his body close to mine, the seductive aroma of his spicy aftershave calling forth sweet memories of our weekend. "How about that?" he murmured in my ear. "I was planning to shower, too."

My fingers closed around the key at last and I pressed it into his palm. "You know what they say: Two can shower as cheaply as one."

"I think we should test that notion right now." He started to unlock the door, then paused. "Nikki will be asleep, right?"

"Déjà vu. You asked me that same question last Saturday night."

"And the answer was?"

"Nikki is depressed and dateless. She'll be sound asleep until noon."

"*Sound* asleep . . . as in, nothing will wake her?"

"Except for smoke alarms."

"Then we'll have to be careful to not set them off."

"Like we almost did Saturday night?"

"Like we almost did *twice* Saturday night." Marco tilted my chin and kissed me, a deep, hot, stirring kiss that made me glad there were no smoke alarms directly overhead.

Somehow he managed to unlock the door,

back me inside, drag our bags in with his foot, close the door, *and* lock it without breaking our kiss. I dropped my peacoat and purse on the floor and we began fumbling at each other's clothing, still kissing hot and heavy.

All at once, someone pounded on the door, shouting, "New Chapel police. Open up!"

With a gasp I jumped back as though I'd done something illegal. Our watchcat, Simon, who had just come around the corner to greet us, arched his back menacingly at the disturbance, then changed his mind and fled the scene, his claws skittering on the hallway tile. Some protector he was.

"What's going on?" Marco exclaimed, buttoning his shirt as he started for the door.

"Could it be Reilly playing some stupid joke? But how would he have gotten into the building without our buzzing him in?"

Marco peered through the peephole, muttered about the bulb being out, then flipped the switch for my front hallway light and opened the door, leaving the chain in place. "It's not Reilly," he said quietly, so I ducked beneath his arm to peer through the crack.

Two men in blue uniforms stood outside, neither of whom was our buddy, Sergeant Sean Reilly of the New Chapel Police

Department. One cop appeared to be in his mid-thirties, about five years older than Marco. The other had a boyish build, a smooth baby face, and a belligerent stance that young cops often adopt to make them seem experienced.

Quickly, I backed out of sight. What had I done this time?

"What's up?" Marco asked nonchalantly. Men in uniform didn't intimidate him. He'd served on the New Chapel police force for about a year after his Army Ranger days — until all the rules and regulations, as well as a vindictive watch commander, got to him.

"We're looking for Nikki Hiduke," a mature voice said.

Nikki? That was novel.

"What business do you have with Nikki?" Marco asked.

"Is she here or not?" a tenor voice demanded. The younger officer was clearly unwilling to divulge any info. He probably had no clue he was talking to an ex-cop.

"She might be here," Marco replied coolly.

Just to be sure, I looked around and spotted Nikki's keys on the table.

"Is it all right if we step inside?" the deep voice asked politely. "You might not want the neighbors in on this."

Yikes. That didn't sound good.

Marco unchained the door, pulled it open, and stepped back to allow them to enter, putting me in full view. Out in the hallway, Mr. Bodenhammer, the building superintendent, tried to get a peek inside before Marco shut the door, solving the mystery as to how the police got in.

"How's it going, Pete?" Marco said, obviously recognizing the older cop.

"Business as usual. That's why we're here."

"Are you Nikki?" the rookie asked me. He was definitely new to the force, because only a newbie would see my bright red hair and freckles and not know who I was. Not that I was a celebrity or anything. More like the town's trouble magnet.

"I'm Abby Knight," I said. "Nikki's my roommate."

"You're the florist, right?" the cop named Pete asked.

It was such a pleasure to hear myself labeled as something other than "the troublemaker who flunked out of law school" that I nodded eagerly. In a college town like mine, being a flunk-out was the equivalent of being the village idiot.

"Yeah, I thought that was you." To his partner he added, "She's the one keeps sticking her nose into police business."

"Excuse me," I said, taking exception to his remark. "I helped solve a few murder cases by sticking my nose into police business. And I'll have you know that my dad was a sergeant on the police force before a drug dealer's bullet put him out of commission."

"Abby," Marco said quietly, laying a hand on my arm as though he feared I might take a swing at the guy. Although I measured in at a mere five feet, two inches, Marco knew that I knew how to throw a punch.

At that moment, Nikki came around the corner sleepily rubbing her eyes, her spiked blond hair sticking up more than usual. She'd tied her purple robe tightly around her tall, slender body and stuck her feet into giant dark purple slippers, making her long legs look like cocktail picks capped by kalamata olives.

"What's all the noise about?" she asked with a yawn.

Marco glanced around in surprise, then gave me a pointed look, obviously remembering my comment about the smoke alarms. Okay, so she was awakened by smoke alarms *and* police raids.

"Nikki Hiduke?" The younger cop tried again.

She squinted at him, unable to see anything without her contacts but blurred shapes. "Yes?"

He showed her his badge, which she had to bring up close to her face. "Would you get your coat and come with us to the police station, please? We have some questions we'd like to ask you."

She looked from one to the other in confusion. "In my pajamas?"

I knew Nikki wasn't completely awake or she would have asked a far more pertinent question, which was exactly what Marco did: "You want to tell us what this is about?" he said.

I stepped in front of Nikki in a valiant act of self-sacrifice. "And why does she have to go with you to answer questions? Why can't you talk to her here?"

"We need to talk to her," the rookie said immediately, thumbs hooked in his thick leather belt, "down at the *station.*"

"I got that part the first time," I said. "But what about? She has the right to know."

"I don't hear *her* asking," the rookie fired back. He was starting to get on my nerves.

"Nikki, ask them why they want to talk to you," Marco instructed.

As she opened her mouth to speak, the rookie said, "She's wanted for questioning in a homicide."

14

At that, Nikki and I both opened our mouths, but only to gasp. I turned and met her shocked stare, and she gave me a look that said, *I don't have a clue what's going on.*

"Do you know a man by the name of Jonas Treat?" Pete the cop asked her.

"Yes," she answered. The name rang a bell with me, but I couldn't place it.

"He was murdered during the night," the rookie announced, looking very pleased for having that information.

Nikki gasped again. I whispered to her, "Is Jonas Treat the guy with the Ferrari from the speed-dating event?"

She gave me a quick nod.

"How was he murdered?" Marco asked the cops.

"You know I can't give you that information, Salvare," Pete said. "You're a civilian now."

"Nikki doesn't need to go down to the station to answer your questions," I told Pete. "She met this man only briefly last Thursday night at a social event. Tell them, Nikki."

My roommate merely put a hand over her mouth, as if in shock.

"Nikki," I urged, "tell them."

"Yes," said the younger cop, with a sly gleam in his eye. "And while you're at it, tell us where you were last night."

Bewildered, I glanced at her and noticed that her face had taken on an ashen hue, as though she might throw up. What was going on?

"Nikki, you don't have to answer any questions," Marco said quietly. "Just state that you want your lawyer present."

"Were you with a man named Jonas Treat yesterday evening?" Pete asked anyway.

When she merely stared at them, I whispered, "What's wrong with you? Tell them no."

She closed her eyes. "I'm sorry, Abby."

Sorry?

"Okay," Pete said, stepping toward Nikki. "Get your coat and let's go."

Suddenly I got it: Nikki *had* gone out with Jonas — in spite of my best efforts to warn her away from him. "Oh, Nikki, you didn't!"

"I couldn't help it, Abby. Jonas was —"

"Nikki," Marco snapped, causing her to jump, "don't say another word."

She looked perplexed. "I was only going to say he was —"

Marco put up his hand to stop her. "*Anything* you say can be used against you. Abby is going to call Dave Hammond and have him meet you at the station." Marco turned toward Pete. "Is it okay if she puts on some decent clothes first?"

"And my c-contact lenses?" Nikki asked, visibly trembling.

The younger cop tapped the face of his watch. "We'll give you five minutes. I'll be right outside your door, so don't even think about sneaking out a window."

As if Nikki would ever do that. Now, me, that was a different story.

"I told you that speed-dating thing was a bad idea," Marco murmured in my ear.

My stomach knotted as I watched poor Nikki lead the young cop through our small living room, heading for the hallway. Just before stepping out of sight, the rookie turned to give me a glare, as though I might be plotting her escape.

"Abby, you want to make that call now?" Marco asked.

I raced off to use the phone in our tiny galley kitchen, huddling in the far corner by the refrigerator so as not to be overheard. At Dave's answer, I said, "Hi, it's Abby. I hope I didn't wake you, but the cops are taking Nikki down to the station for questioning in a murder, and —"

"Slow down, Abby; I just woke up. Your *roommate* Nikki? The girl who looks like Bambi?"

"That's the one. Nikki met this guy at a

speed-dating event a few days ago, Dave, and apparently went out with him last night — against my advice, let me just say right up front — and then he was killed sometime after that, and now the cops think she had something to do with —"

"Abby! Take a breath before you pass out."

I followed his advice and gulped air. "Will you meet her at the police station, Dave? Quickly? Before the cops pressure her into answering questions?"

"I'll be there as soon as I can. Make sure you instruct her not to talk to anyone."

"I will. Thanks, Dave. You're a champ."

Dave truly was a champion attorney. During my year of law school, I was fortunate enough to clerk for him, an experience that taught me many invaluable lessons, such as what a good lawyer was supposed to be like — and it wasn't filing a bunch of trivial motions with the court in order to rack up huge client fees. Thank goodness for that now, because who knew what Nikki's legal costs would be if Dave ended up having to defend her in a murder case.

I pressed my fingers to my temples, forcing my thoughts to stop right there, because surely it would never come to that.

CHAPTER TWO

Marco stood beside me, rubbing my neck, as the cops filed past with Nikki in tow.

"You'll be fine," Marco told her. "Dave will be there soon. Just don't answer any questions or make any statements until you talk to him, okay?"

Nikki gave him a nod but didn't say a word. Her face was so pale and pinched that I wanted to weep. She had been my best friend since third grade, yet suddenly I felt as though I barely knew her at all. Why had she ignored my advice? Was Jonas's charisma so strong that he could make her forget my warning?

"Wait!" I cried, bringing the parade to a halt. "I need to have a minute alone with Nikki. May I? Have a minute? Please?"

The rookie was ready to tell me to take a hike, but Pete relented. "One minute."

I pulled Nikki away from them to whisper, "Did Jonas ask you to go out while we were at the speed-dating event?"

"He hinted that he might call me."

"So you gave him your phone number? Nikki! You weren't supposed to give out personal information."

She sighed unhappily. "I know."

"Damn it, I told you he was trouble. Thanks for listening!"

Nikki looked down, her jaw muscles tightening.

I gripped her arm and forced her to look at me. "Did anything happen on your date? Did you have an argument or did he get too aggressive? Did he hit you or take advantage of you?"

She gave me a hurt look. "No! Why are you asking me that?"

"I need to know if there's anything else you haven't shared with me, anything you did that could cause the cops to think you had a hand in his death."

"I didn't have anything to do with Jonas's death, Abby," she replied in a sharp whisper. "We went to dinner. That was it."

"You're sure?"

She nodded.

"Okay," Pete called, "let's go."

Impulsively, I threw my arms around her and gave her a reassuring hug, then stepped back, blinking tears from my eyes as the cops led her away. As soon as the door had shut behind them, I went to the window and waited for them to appear on the street below.

"I can't believe this is happening, Marco. Nikki is the sweetest, gentlest, most non-murderous person I know. Who could possibly think that she's capable of ending someone's life?"

"Everyone is capable of ending someone's life, Sunshine," Marco said in a matter-of-fact voice, coming to stand beside me.

"I'm not. Nor is Nikki."

"You wouldn't shoot someone to defend yourself? Or to protect a loved one?"

"I'm not talking about *that* kind of situation. My point is that even if Jonas had acted like a jerk to her, Nikki wouldn't kill him. She'd get up and leave."

"Maybe he threatened her in some way."

I stared at him in surprise. "Are you saying she might be guilty?"

"Abby, come on. I'm just saying you don't know the circumstances."

"That's why I asked to talk to Nikki just now. She said straight out that they went to dinner and that was it. If there was anything else, she would have told me."

Marco rubbed his jaw. "For the cops to come in like gangbusters at six in the morn-

21

ing, they had to have strong feelings about Nikki's role in the murder — either some convincing evidence came to light or they received a tip — because they only do that to catch people unawares and scare them into revealing something incriminating."

"Well, they've made a mistake this time, because I'd stake my life on Nikki's innocence. Not so much on her intelligence, however. Do you know anything about Jonas Treat? I know he's got money, but all he said at the speed-dating event was that he developed land."

"You've probably seen his ads on billboards for that new development he's putting up, Chateaux La-something. He's quite a controversial figure — or was, I should say. He always managed to get the County Plan Commission's approval even when there was public opposition, and was a cutthroat salesman — not a guy you'd want to do business with."

"Or date, which is exactly why I told Nikki not to go out with him. I knew Jonas was trouble ten seconds after meeting him, but obviously Nikki doesn't trust my judgment as much as she says she does. You know how close she and I are — or at least I thought we were. Is it possible to be friends with someone and not know she doesn't trust your judgment?"

Marco put his arms around me and rested his chin on my head, letting me know there really wasn't any need to remind him how important trust was to me. It was his lack of trust in my judgment that had caused our recent split and nearly allowed a murderer to escape. "We were out of town this weekend, don't forget. Nikki probably didn't want to be a pest. She knew this was an important time for us."

"She also knew I didn't trust Jonas. So why did she trust him and not me?"

"Because she's lonely and vulnerable, and that makes her perfect prey."

"She should have taken my advice," I said, sighing miserably.

"Yeah," he said with a sigh, "I know how it feels to have someone ignore your advice. I warned you not to go with her to that speed-dating thing."

"Hey, how about some coffee?" I said, slipping out of his arms. "I can brew a pot in five minutes."

Marco pulled me back. "No coffee and no dodging the issue."

Or his penetrating gaze. With a resigned sigh I said, "I'll admit I ignored your advice that one time."

"*One* time?"

"Going with Nikki was the only way I could get her to agree to attend the event. Otherwise she wouldn't have —"

"Met Jonas?"

With a groan, I rested my forehead against Marco's chest. "You're right! It's my fault she met Jonas. It's my fault she's down at the police station right now sitting in that cold, bare interrogation room. What if they arrest Nikki, Marco? What if she's indicted for murder?"

"Dave won't let that happen. Nikki will be cleared and back home before you know it." Marco glanced at his watch. "It's almost seven o'clock. We'd better skip the shower-for-two so you're not late for work. I'll be available by cell phone if you need me. Let me know what happens, okay?"

I gave him a hug. "Thanks, Marco. And thanks for the wonderful weekend in Key West. It was just what we needed."

"Are we back on track now?"

"I'd have to say yes to that. How about you?"

Instead of replying, Marco reeled me in for one last, long, steamy kiss. "Want something else to think about, Fireball?" he murmured, nuzzling my ear.

Something *else?* Wait. Was I supposed to be thinking? "Bring it on, Salvare."

"How about picking a place for our next weekend getaway? And weren't we talking about looking into scuba lessons, since we had such a great time snorkeling?"

Those plans would do the trick.

As I stood in the shower ten minutes later, however, my plans for a second dream weekend were all but forgotten as remorse crowded in. I tried to convince myself that Nikki's predicament wasn't entirely my fault — after all, she *had* chosen to ignore my advice — yet I just knew that somehow I'd failed her. What I needed was a sit-down with Lottie and Grace, my employees and mentors at the flower shop. They always had good, commonsense advice — and, on Mondays, breakfast as well.

Holding on to that thought, I stepped out of the shower, only to hear the phone ringing, so I wrapped a towel around my body and ran to answer it.

"Abby," Dave said, "the police are coming back for the clothing Nikki wore last night. She said they're in her laundry basket in her closet. Would you pull that basket out for them, and would you also pull out her black high-heeled ankle boots?"

"Sure, Dave. How's Nikki doing?"

"I'll talk to you later."

Obviously Dave wasn't in a position to say more, probably because the detectives were present. But just the thought of a forensic team poring over Nikki's clothing, looking for evidence, gave me a knot in my stomach the size of a soccer ball.

I dressed hurriedly, then ran to Nikki's room to gather everything. The same two cops came for her belongings, thanked me, and left without another word, so I brushed my teeth, made sure Simon had food and fresh water, grabbed my cell phone and purse, and took off for Bloomers.

My flower shop is located on one of four streets surrounding the courthouse in my hometown of New Chapel, Indiana. A variety of businesses populate the square — gift, clothing, and shoe shops, banks, law offices, a hardware store, a deli, a travel agency, and Marco's Down the Hatch Bar and Grill, located two doors from Bloomers. It's an area chock-full of old-world charm — brick sidewalks, Victorian light posts, and, unfortunately, parking spots with a two-hour limit.

I parked in a free public lot around the corner from Bloomers and hurried to my shop, always cheered by the sight of the old-fashioned redbrick building with its bright yellow frame door centered between the two big bay windows. As soon as I stepped inside, I heard Grace in the coffee-and-tea parlor preparing her special brews for the day, and Lottie in the tiny kitchen all the way at the back of the building, clattering utensils as she whipped up her famous scrambled-egg breakfast, a tradition she had started years before to make Mondays more tolerable.

Lottie Dombowski was a big, bold, brassy forty-five-year-old woman with four sons, seventeen-year-old quadruplets Jimmy, Joey, Johnny, and Karl (she'd been expecting triplets), and a husband who adored her. She'd owned Bloomers until her husband's medical condition, combined with health insurance that stank, caused a financial setback that forced her to sell.

That was where I entered the picture. Having been booted out of law school, rejected by my fiancé, Pryce Osborne II, and at odds with my parents about where my life was going, I used the last of my grandpa's trust money as a down payment to buy the charming but struggling little shop, and all at once my life had direction — downward, into the black hole of debt.

Desperate to draw in more customers, Lottie and I cleaned out a storage room on one side of the shop, turned it into a Victorian-inspired coffee-and-tea parlor, and staffed it with an authentic British tea maker, Grace Bingham, who had just retired as Dave Hammond's legal secretary. The combination of flowers and hot beverages improved our bottom line, but we were still far from where I wanted to be, which was independently wealthy. In my dreams.

As I locked the yellow door behind me — we wouldn't be open for business until nine o'clock — Grace poked her head out of the parlor, looking as elegant as ever. Today she wore a dark brown tweed wool skirt and a tan sweater set accented with silver trim and silver buttons, setting off her short, stylish silver hair.

"Good morning, dear," Grace said in her charming British accent. "How are we today?"

"Wiped out. I could really use some —"

"Coffee? I'll pour it right now, dear. Go tell Lottie she can serve breakfast anytime."

I was going to say *advice,* but then I realized I was famished and on the verge of a hunger headache, so I let it go. Not only that, but we had a ritual on Mondays: Eat first, share news after. So I paused to breathe in the fresh scents of roses, orchids, eucalyptus, gourmet coffee, and freshly baked scones, and, thus fortified, headed toward the curtain at the back.

The shop, as I called our display room, started at the large bay window in the front, dressed now with silk floral arrangements for the winter. There was a counter with a cash register, a telephone, order forms, and other essential items; wall shelves; two antique hutches filled with flower arrangements and other gift items; and swags, wreaths, and sconces on the walls. A wicker settee framed by two tall potted dieffenbachia in a back corner sat beside a glass-fronted cooler stocked with colorful fresh blossoms.

Next to the cooler was a doorway hidden by a purple velvet curtain. Behind the curtain lay the true pearl in the oyster, my workroom, the place where magic happened, where I was surrounded by sweet-smelling blossoms, fragrant dried flowers, colorful pots and vases, and all the supplies we could stuff onto the shelves that lined two walls.

Following the aroma of scrambled eggs, I dropped my peacoat on the back of my desk chair, glanced at the spindle that held our orders — there looked to be at least ten slips of paper — then skirted the big worktable in the center and headed for the little kitchen. A tiny restroom was located in the back, as well as a door that led down to the basement storeroom, where we kept our larger supplies.

Standing with her back to me, Lottie was dishing eggs from her skillet onto cream-colored plates. She had on her usual winter outfit — jeans and a bright pink sweatshirt — with turquoise-colored barrettes holding back her face-framing brassy curls.

"Smells wonderful," I said, taking a seat at the tiny strip of counter we'd nailed to a wall. Three stools were tucked beneath it, providing just enough room for us to sit and eat.

"Toast will be up in a minute, sweetie. After breakfast, you'll have to tell us what you did over your long weekend."

It wasn't going to be easy to tell, not only because of Nikki's trouble and the loss of a life, but also because Lottie and Grace didn't know about my trip to Key West with Marco. Since we'd gone to heal our relation-ship, nothing more, we'd decided to keep our romantic getaway a secret. The last thing we wanted was for my parents or Marco's big Italian family to get wind of our miniescape and start planning our nup-tials.

Also, I'd been a little nervous about

Lottie's and Grace's reactions. When it came to matters of the heart, they tended to treat me as though I were seventeen instead of twenty-seven. Nikki was the only person I'd told.

"Here's our coffee," Grace sang out, sweeping into the room with a tray filled with a coffeepot, three cups and saucers, a pitcher of cream, and a bowl of sugar cubes.

Lottie handed out our plates and took a seat. "Happy Monday," she said, then grabbed her fork and dug in.

For the next few minutes the only sounds were of utensils hitting plates and coffee cups clattering onto saucers, as we downed the fluffy eggs, crunchy toast, and aromatic coffee. At last, with cups in hand, we sat back with satisfied sighs.

"So," Lottie said to me, "tell us about your weekend. Did you go anywhere new, see anything exciting, do anything fun?"

Just thinking about what had happened to Nikki that morning brought back a knot of distress that nearly canceled out all the good effects of my trip. "Yes to all the above, but first I need to tell you that the police took Nikki to the station an hour ago to question her about a murder, and it's my fault she's here."

Their cups halted in midair. Their eyes

opened wider than I thought humanly possible. Then they started firing questions, until I called, "Wait! One at a time, please."

Lottie held up her hand to go first. "Who was murdered?"

"A guy named Jonas Treat," I said. "Nikki went on a date with Jonas yesterday evening, and, according to the police, that made her the last one to see him alive."

"Good heavens!" Grace said. "That poor sweet girl must be terrified. I hope you called Dave."

"I called him immediately. He's there with her right now."

"Wait a minute," Lottie said. "Are you talking about Jonas Treat the land developer?"

"Do you know him?" I asked.

"Not personally," Lottie said, "but I know several people who do. You know who he is, Gracie. His nickname is Treat the Cheat. Remember the assistant manager over at Tom's Green Thumb? Robin, I think her name is. Remember her telling us about her fiancé, the guy who led her on for a year, letting her make wedding plans for a date he never intended to keep? That was Jonas Treat."

"Yes, of course," Grace said. "Poor Robin. What a travesty that was."

"Yep, Treat the Cheat. He also tried to skin my friends Bob and Shirl on a land deal a couple of months ago," Lottie said. "I shouldn't say this, but it doesn't flabbergast me that someone went after Treat. But Nikki? Not a chance."

"However did Nikki meet this deplorable person?" Grace asked.

"At a speed-dating event," I said. "Jonas was all over her, trying to dazzle her with his suave act. You've seen his type — star-quality handsome, egotistical, a slick dresser, and stocked with so much charm you'd expect to see him dangling from a bracelet."

"I met a man like that once," Grace said. "A handsome devil on the outside, but inside a person whose soul was missing."

"Remind me how that speed-dating thing works, just in case any of my boys ever want to go to one," Lottie said, stacking plates to take them to the sink.

"The registrants are split into groups of nine guys and nine girls. Then, every nine minutes a new guy comes to the table. The two people ask each other questions, decide if they'd like to meet again, and if so, check each other's name on their lists."

"What happens if one of the guys puts a check by your name, but you don't put a check by his?" Lottie asked.

"After the event," I explained, "there's a mixer for the attendees. Then the event organizer culls the lists for matches. Only if both people check that they want to see each other does she then give out the contact information. That way, if you don't want the guy calling you, he doesn't get your number. In fact, the rule is that no one is allowed to ask for personal information. Jonas broke that rule to get Nikki's number."

"Nikki broke the rule, too, don't forget," Lottie said. "She gave him her number."

"Couldn't he have looked up her number in the phone book anyway?" Grace asked, using her hand to sweep the crumbs off the counter into a waste can.

"No last names were given out," I said. "That was a rule, too."

"What if you see someone who isn't on your list but you want to get to know him?" Lottie asked. Both women seemed to be stuck on the details, missing the big picture, which was my role in it.

"There's a mixer afterward for just that purpose," I said.

"What was the event organizer's name?" Grace asked.

"Carmen Gold. Anyway —"

"I don't think I've ever met her. Is she

from around here?" Grace asked.

Trying not to lose patience, I replied, "The Cloud Nine franchise operates out of Chicago. So what happened —"

"I don't understand who'd want to bring speed dating here," Lottie said to Grace. "We're not a big city. How many young people do we have?"

"It wasn't held in New Chapel," I said. "It was held in Maraville, near the interstate highway to make it easy for people from other counties to attend."

"Speed dating, instant food, instant coffee, instant messaging . . ." Grace clucked her tongue disapprovingly. "Why must everything be done in a hurry?"

Everything except getting to the point of this conversation, apparently.

"Whatever happened to church socials?" Lottie asked. "That was a great way for young people to meet."

"Abby," Grace said, "you still haven't explained why you feel to blame for Nikki's situation."

The big picture at last! "I talked Nikki into attending the event. I even sweetened the deal by offering to go along to help her screen the guys. Because she didn't trust her own judgment when it came to dates, that cinched the deal. And then, last night, the night Jonas was murdered, I wasn't home to verify Nikki's alibi."

"Ah," Grace said. "Now it becomes clear."

"To be fair," I countered, "if Nikki had listened to me, she wouldn't have gone out with Jonas, but that's water under the bridge now, because I was the one who set the ball in motion."

"Abby, dear," Grace said calmly, "you're mixing metaphors. Put the ball down, come out from under the bridge, and tell us how this came about."

I blew out my breath. Where to start? "I suppose I should go back to when Marco asked me to go to Key West." I paused to gauge their reactions, but there weren't any, so I continued. "That's where I was this weekend — in Key West."

Lottie and Grace glanced at each other but still said nothing.

"With Marco," I added, in case they hadn't gotten it. "We went together."

"What are you trying to tell us?" Lottie asked. "Did you elope?"

"No! We're not even engaged. We just wanted to reconnect."

"They went to *reconnect*," Lottie said, exchanging a look with Grace.

They both turned to study me. I braced myself.

Suddenly, Lottie began to whoop — "Woo-hoo!" — then threw her napkin into the air. Even Grace got into the spirit and clapped. Genteelly, of course.

"Well, dang it, sweetie," Lottie cried, grabbing me by the shoulders and giving me one of her big Kentucky squeezes, "it's about time. Me and Gracie thought you two were never gonna get back to the way you were before. We were afraid you wouldn't open your heart ever again."

"I always applaud your cautious nature, dear," Grace said, "on the rare occasion you exhibit it. However, in matters of the heart, sometimes one must throw caution to the wind."

At that she rose and took hold of her sweater as though it had lapels, a sure sign she was about to share a quote. She seemed to have a never-ending supply of them. "As Bertram Russell once said, 'Of all forms of caution, caution in love is perhaps the most fatal to true happiness.' "

I blinked at them, wondering if I were dreaming. "So you approve?"

"You're an adult, dear," Grace said as she refilled our cups. "What you decide to do is not subject to our approval."

Okay, now I knew I was dreaming.

"Remember how reluctant you were to accept Marco's first dinner invitation after your breakup?" Lottie asked. "Well, you wouldn't be standing here with that smile on your face if you hadn't taken our advice and gone out with him."

"I know," I said, "and I thank you both for encouraging me to take a risk."

"In the words of J. C. Macaulay," Grace said, " 'Keep your heart right, even when it is sorely wounded.' "

Two quotes in five minutes. Grace had set a new personal record.

"Please keep our trip a secret. Nikki is the only other person who knows. You can imagine what would happen if my parents found out. They'd want to know what it meant, whether we were planning to get married or move in together or what." I shuddered, imagining the phone calls, the quizzing, the gossiping between my sisters-in-law, and I didn't even want to consider what my cousin Jillian would do with the news of our little getaway. Put it on her MySpace page? Hire a pilot to fly a banner over New Chapel that says ABBY AND MARCO WENT TO KEY WEST — WHY?

"Sweetie, I'm not gonna pretend I wouldn't like to see an engagement ring pop up on your finger," Lottie said, "but I understand that you don't need more pressure right now."

"Remember how Mrs. Salvare took over Marco's sister's baby shower?" I asked. "I don't even want to think what she'd do if she thought there were wedding plans in the air. And thanks for understanding, both of you. After I rushed into an engagement with Pryce, I vowed never to make that mistake again. 'Slow and easy' is my new motto."

"As William Congreve pointed out," Grace said, " 'Marry in haste, repent at leisure.' "

"And as my granny used to say," Lottie added, " 'You have to summer and winter with a man before you know you're compatible.' "

"So does that mean you're okay with keeping my secret?"

"We shan't breathe a word," Grace said.

"I have to tell you, this was a tough decision for me," I said, "but three weeks ago, Marco and I had a long talk about our going away together and came to an understanding. So I wasn't actually throwing caution to the wind. Would you pass the sugar bowl, Grace?"

"You had a talk?" Lottie asked. "That's all you're gonna say about it?"

"A *long* talk," I reminded her, dropping two sugar cubes into my cup.

"Now, looky here, sweetie," Lottie said, shaking her index finger at me. "I know it wasn't easy for you and Marco to get to this point, so I ain't buyin' that one little talk was all it took to cinch the deal."

"*Long* talk," I corrected again. Thinking about the conversation Marco and I had had brought a smile to my lips. "It *was* kind of romantic the way it happened."

Lottie folded her arms and sat back. "Then stop grinning like Mona Lisa and start telling."

CHAPTER THREE

Saturday, January 8

"Hi, Chris," I called to the head bartender at Down the Hatch as I made my way to the last booth in the back, past thirsty customers standing at the long mahogany bar. Chris touched his hand to his forehead, then went back to serving up drinks.

The bar and grill dated back to the 1950s — and looked it, with walls covered in dark wood paneling, orange vinyl booths, and a corny fisherman theme, complete with a fake blue carp on the wall over the line of booths, and a huge net hanging from the ceiling over the bar. Marco had bought Down the Hatch over six months ago, but had yet to remodel it, fearing an uprising from its longtime patrons, none of whom were big fans of change.

Before I could slide into the booth where I was to join Marco for dinner, Gert, the gravelly-voiced waitress who had worked there since before I was born, said, "The boss wants you to meet him in his office."

I walked up the short hallway and rapped on the door marked PRIVATE, then entered the sleek, ultramodern office done in silver, gray, and black. Marco rose from his desk to greet me, a vision of masculinity in his brown leather boots, snug blue jeans, and black T-shirt with the Down the Hatch name and logo on the front. His dark hair had that wavy casualness that begged to be tousled, and his chocolate brown eyes snapped with intelligence and vitality.

Seeing him always caused my heart to twang, but it was the tiny grin tugging on the right corner of his mouth that really intrigued me. "What's up? I thought we were going to have something to eat."

"We will." He sauntered toward me. "I want to show you something first. Close your eyes."

With a shiver of anticipation, I scrunched them shut. "Okay."

I felt the air move around me and got a tantalizing whiff of Marco's aftershave. He was very near when he said, "Now open them."

I found myself staring at the front of a shiny pamphlet. "Key West?"

"Have you ever been there?"

"No."

Marco opened the brochure and pointed to some of the inset photos. "Snorkeling, parasailing, scuba diving, Jet Ski adventures, sunsets at the famous Mallory Square, and a very cool shop called 7 Artists that I probably shouldn't even be mentioning because once you see it, I doubt whether I'll be able to pry you out of it.

"But wait. The best part of the trip? Right now it's seventy-four degrees there. I just checked. That's fifty degrees higher than it is here. So, what do you think? Want to go?"

"With you?"

"No, with my mother." He pulled me into his arms. "Yes, Sunshine, of course with me. I thought I'd make reservations at a cozy bed-and-breakfast inn for a long weekend. We can fly down early on a Friday morning, be there by one thirty or so, and take a red-eye flight home Sunday night. You'll only have to miss one day of work. How does that grab you?"

Gazing up into his handsome face, I melted inside. How many times had I fantasized about Marco whisking me away to a romantic spot? If only I didn't have to turn him down now.

"It's a grabber, all right," I answered with forced cheerfulness, slipping out of Marco's embrace. "I'll have to get back to you on that. I've got some weddings coming up that are going to keep me really busy for a while, and I sure wouldn't want to blow those moneymaking opportunities. Gotta pay those bills. Gotta put food on the table —"

"Abby, if you don't want to go, just say so."

I glanced at Marco and my heart ached with regret. Here he was, the man of my dreams, asking me to spend a romantic weekend with him, and I was making up excuses not to go. But after the debacle of having my identity stolen, and then Marco not believing me, although he'd apologized, I still found myself holding back, not completely trusting him. "It's just that you kind of sprang it on me."

"Not a problem. Think about it for a while. Let's go eat."

He tossed the brochure onto his desk and escorted me up the hallway to our booth. We ordered our usual sandwiches and beers, and I entertained him by describing some of the unusual customers I'd had that day. Yet I felt an underlying tension between us that kept me from enjoying his company.

After dinner, Marco walked me to my car in the public lot on the next street. The sky was black and the weather was lousy, with frigid temperatures and a bitter wind that whipped snow in our faces. Even with my knit scarf covering my neck and half of my face, and my thickest gloves on, I couldn't stop shivering — or thinking about those seventy-degree temps in Key West.

For the entire walk, I warred with myself, part of me wanting passionately to say yes to Key West and the other part hiding in a corner, shaking like a leaf at the thought of putting my trust in him and having it broken all over again.

What a coward you are, my conscience chided.

"Want me to drop you back at the bar?" I asked Marco.

"Sounds good. The wind has picked up since I was out earlier."

He got in on the passenger side as I started the engine. It took a moment for the old Corvette to kick to life; then I let it idle while the engine warmed up. To fill the awkward silence I began to chat about the weather. "I hope we don't get that snowstorm they're predicting. All we need is more snow. How many feet have we had so far this winter?"

"Abby?"

At his serious tone, I turned to look at him. His face was visible only by the glow

45

of streetlights, making his eyes seem darker, more intense, giving me a nervous flutter inside. "Yes?"

"Are you afraid to go with me to Key West?"

"Afraid?" I made a scoffing sound. "No way."

"Then what's holding you back?"

"Like I said, I've got some big jobs coming up . . ." I shrugged, knowing it sounded lame.

"We can work around your jobs."

I let out a long breath. "I suppose."

"What is it then?"

"I don't know. . . . Maybe because Key West is so far away." I was doing a terrible job of explaining my feelings, mostly because I wasn't quite understanding them myself.

"How does distance matter?"

I stared at him, trying to come up with a reason.

"It's only a weekend getaway," he said.

Marco made it sound so uncomplicated, and that angered me. "Only a weekend getaway. Easy for you to say. You don't have parents who are going to have expectations. I can hear my mom now. 'You're taking a trip together? What does that mean, Abigail?' "

"So it's your parents' expectations that are holding you back? That's never stopped you before."

Marco was right. It usually had the opposite effect.

"Just so you know," he said, "asking you to go away this weekend wasn't an easy decision."

"Why not?" I asked, slightly miffed that there was any doubt at all on his end.

"I've never asked a woman to go with me anywhere."

"Seriously?"

"I'd considered it a few times, but" — he paused, as though trying to find the right words — "it never felt right."

"Did it feel somehow like a commitment? Like you would be giving up your independence, or your privacy, or, I don't know . . . control?"

Marco studied me for a long moment. "Do you feel like you're giving those things up?"

"Maybe. I mean, after the whole law school disaster, and my near miss with Pryce, and trying to make Bloomers profitable, I feel like I'm just now regaining some control over my life."

"Sunshine, it's only a weekend away."

I could sense Marco's frustration, but I

felt I was getting closer to some important truth. "Then why didn't it feel right to you with other women?"

He took a long time to answer, then said very softly, "Because they weren't you." Then he took my hand in his and, with his other hand, slipped off my glove. Letting it drop onto his lap, he raised my fingers to his lips and kissed each one in turn. Then he turned my hand over and traced circles around the inside of my palm as he talked quietly.

"I feel safe with you, Abby. It doesn't seem like I'm giving up anything by going away with you. It's more like gaining something I've never had before."

My throat was so dry I couldn't speak. I watched, transfixed, as he bent his dark head over my palm and pressed his mouth against the fleshy center. My senses reeled. My hand felt as though it were liquefying. Tingles of desire pulsed up my arm, then tunneled down deep inside me. I lost awareness of everything outside our intimate circle. It was undoubtedly the most sensual experience of my life — and it was all coming from my hand.

Still, I couldn't shut out that cold, persistent voice of reason. *Do you believe him? Can you trust him?*

I studied Marco with as much objectivity as I could muster, given that he was nuzzling my palm. But there was such purity in his gaze, such earnestness, that I knew he was speaking from his heart. This was Marco, after all, a man I knew to be brave and sincere, who had always watched my back, and who had saved me on numerous occasions — and *he* felt safe with *me.*

With my hand still in his grasp, I drew him toward me. "I want to go with you, Marco. . . ."

He looked up expectantly.

"But I'm" — I paused, searching for the right word — "*concerned.* I don't know what I'd do if it ever came up again that you didn't believe in me."

"I never stopped believing *in* you, Abby. You'd put me in an impossible position. I can say I'm sorry a hundred times, but until you trust that our relationship can weather a few storms, it won't make a difference. I don't know about your parents, but mine never agreed on everything, and it wasn't that they didn't believe in each other. They simply had different views."

I paused to consider my parents' relationship, remembering some rocky times that I feared would end in their divorce, and realized that Marco was right: Disagreements didn't have to mean the end of a relationship.

"Come to Key West with me. It'll be just us, away from work and family and friends and all the stresses in our lives. Just you and me." He kissed my palm again, then gazed at me with eyes so sincere my heart expanded twice over. Maybe a getaway would be the perfect remedy for us, a time to sort things out and heal our wounds.

"I think the last weekend in January is open," I told him.

Marco smiled, his eyes glittering in the glow of the streetlights. "Done."

"I have only one request," I said. "We can't tell anyone we're going."

"You got it, baby."

We kept our trip a secret for over a week, going about business as usual with no one the wiser. But then Nikki's boyfriend, Scott, broke up with her unexpectedly, causing Nikki, as well as our clandestine plan, to unravel.

The more Nikki pined for Scott, the more depressed she got and the more ice cream she ate, until I feared she'd make herself ill. I urged her to get back into the dating scene, but she was afraid of being rejected again, so she stayed home, feeling sorry for herself. And because I felt sorry for her, I tried to include her in our activities, but that didn't go over well with Marco, especially coming at a time when we were trying to fix things between us.

Then, late on a Sunday night, a mere five days before we were to leave for Key West, everything came to a head.

"Your building super should be more on top of things," Marco grumbled, scowling at a burned-out lightbulb overhead, as I rummaged through my purse for my key.

"I know. I told Mr. Bodenhammer about it three days ago."

Marco ran his hands over my shoulders and down my arms, pressing his lips against my neck as he murmured, "We could go back to my apartment."

"It's after one o'clock in the morning, and we're already here."

"Are you sure Nikki will be asleep?"

"She's depressed and dateless. Trust me, she'll be asleep. She sleeps a lot."

I found the key at last and opened the door. It had barely closed behind us when Marco braced his arms on either side of my body and leaned in for a deep, hot kiss. I dropped my purse on the floor and kissed him back, until our passions took over and we began fumbling at each other's clothing.

"Bedroom," I managed between kisses.

We stumbled past the kitchen and into the tiny living room, where the sound of sniffling caused us to freeze.

I felt for the wall switch — and there sat Nikki on the sofa, wrapped in a blanket, her big doe eyes red and watery, and her mouth in a rippling line that signaled sobs on the horizon. Simon lay beside her, paws twitching as he dreamed, oblivious to her misery.

"Nikki, what happened?"

"Nothing." *Sniffle.*

"Why are you about to cry?"

"What makes you think I'm about to cry? Just because everyone in the world is out on a date tonight? Because only losers sit on the sofa watching other people make out?"

With a muffled sob, she threw off the blanket and ran out of the room, followed by Simon, who clearly thought she had woken him to play tag. Down the hallway, I heard her bedroom door slam. A moment later, the door opened and I heard a thud. The door shut again and at once Simon came trotting toward Marco, the only male he'd ever bonded with. Obviously Nikki wasn't up for feline company, either.

Marco crouched down to rub Simon's head, causing him to purr loudly and butt his head against Marco's knee. "You'd better go talk to Nikki."

"It's pointless, Marco. I've talked to her until I'm blue in the face, and blue doesn't come easy with these freckles. Trust me — nothing I say seems to help."

Loud sobs could be heard coming from Nikki's bedroom.

"Would you like a glass of wine?" I asked, pretending not to hear her.

Marco raised his head to gaze at me in disbelief.

"Okay," I said with a sigh. "I'll go talk to her — again."

Giving Simon a final scratch behind the ear, Marco rose and came toward me. "I'll see you tomorrow."

"Wouldn't you like to wait while I talk to her?" I entwined my hands behind his neck and leaned into him. "Our weekend doesn't have to end right now, Salvare."

"I think it already ended." He cast a pointed look toward Nikki's room.

"I'm truly sorry about that."

He pulled me into his arms and gazed down at me with those sexy brown eyes. "That's okay, Sunshine. We'll have next weekend in Key West all to ourselves. Imagine us snuggled into that cozy little bed-and-breakfast just blocks away from Mallory Square. We'll watch the sunset from the pier, then hit the town for a few hours, maybe listen to a band at Sloppy Joe's or Schooner Wharf, then go back to the inn and . . ." He lifted an eyebrow.

Oh, baby. "I can't wait."

"Me either."

After a long, dreamy kiss, Marco left. As I locked the door behind him, I thought, *Key West, here we come!* I just hoped I could get Nikki out of her funk before we went so I could leave with a clear conscience.

I poured two glasses of cabernet and carried them to Nikki's room. "Hey, open up. I've got full glasses in my hands."

Nikki opened the door, then went to sit on her bed, long legs folded beneath her, back pressed against the headboard, a purple stuffed bear hugged against her chest. I put her wine on the bedside table, then sat on the edge of her bed. "Talk to me."

"About what? Being a big loser?"

"Will you stop throwing yourself a pity party? It's getting old."

"Well, I *am* a loser. I mean, look at me, twenty-six years old and all alone again. And there you two are — kissing, cuddling, holding hands, showing off your coupleness."

"Coupleness? Is that even a word?"

"Shut up. You know what I mean. You

flaunt being together."

I blinked at her in surprise. "No, I don't."

"Oh, please. Every other word out of your mouth is *Marco.* I get it, Abby. You're happy with him."

"Well, excuse me for being happy." Scowling, I took a sip of wine, but didn't enjoy it.

Nikki sighed miserably. "I didn't mean it the way it sounded. I'm glad you're back together. I just wish you wouldn't be so . . . I don't know . . . smug about it."

"Okay, now you're pissing me off. I am not being smug, or trying to flaunt my relationship. In fact, we've bent over backward to include you in our plans."

"Well, thanks for the favor." She tossed the bear aside and got up. "Nothing like trying to make me feel worse."

Time for some tough love. "Poor Nikki Ann Hiduke," I said, grabbing both glasses and following her to the kitchen, "can't find a decent date. Well, *here's* an idea. Get off your duff and go look for a guy, instead of whining in my ear every day about not *having* a guy."

She pulled a carton of ice cream out of the freezer, slammed the door, and whirled to glare at me. "Get off my *duff?* Who says *duff?*"

"I was trying to be nice. But you know

what? I'm sick of having this conversation with you. For the last time, stop being such a coward and get back out in the dating scene."

Nikki shoved the carton back into the freezer, then marched toward the living room in indignation. But by the time she reached the sofa, she was crying again. "You're right," she bawled into her hands. "I *am* a coward. I'm afraid of being dumped again. It hurts so much, Abby. I love Scott!"

I put down our glasses and went to hug her. "I'm sorry, Nik. I know you've been deeply hurt. It's totally understandable. I've been there, remember?"

"I thought we were going to get engaged at Christmas," she sobbed.

"Yeah, well, I was two months away from walking down the aisle when Pryce pulled that petal-strewn rug right out from under me. Try explaining that to your family and friends."

"I'll wind up an old maid," she wailed. "I'll take in stray cats and grow out my fingernails until they curl and everyone will call me the crazy cat lady of New Chapel."

Back to the pity party. "Okay, stop that. You're going to find someone."

"I don't know where to look!"

"Well . . . how about the hospital?"

She wiped tears off her face with the backs of her hands. "Yeah, right. The doctors are engaged, gay, or married and wanting to fool around. Great selection there."

"How about the single guys at Marco's bar?"

"College students and lawyers, all of whom drink too much. No, thanks."

"You could try an online dating service."

"Are you serious? I'd probably choose a too-good-to-be-true, 'loves holding hands and walking on the beach at night' guy who turns out to be an ax murderer."

"You're being ridiculous. It's not that hard to meet someone. If I tried, I'll bet I could find a really nice guy for you in one week."

She lifted her head and gazed at me with watery eyes. "You'll do that for me?"

"What? No, wait, I said *if* I tried, not —"

"Thank you, Abby," she cried, and wrapped her arms around me, squeezing so hard my eyeballs bulged. Then she picked up her glass of wine and held it to mine. "To my best friend, the one person in the entire world I can count on."

Hear, hear?

CHAPTER FOUR

At noon on Monday, instead of grabbing a bite to eat from the deli on the square, I rushed home to share some exciting news with Nikki. She was standing at the kitchen counter making herself a tuna-salad-and-cream-cheese sandwich on white bread, with a side of ice cream, something the old Nikki never would have eaten.

"Hey, Nik, you'll never guess what I saw in the *New Chapel News* this morning."

"Oh, I don't know — news?"

"Ha. Funny. Try an ad for a speed-dating event." I held the newspaper ad in front of her. "See? Listen to this: 'Meet your dream date and you'll be on cloud nine. Register today for the Cloud Nine Date Night event. Nine dates, nine minutes. If you don't meet at least one person you'd like to see again, come to the next event for free.' "

"It's being held in Maraville," she said with a scoff.

"So? That's a mere forty minutes away. Come on, Nik. It's a win-win situation."

She ran her index finger down the flat side of the knife, then licked the cream cheese off her fingertip. "No way."

"Why not?"

"Because I'm horrible at picking out guys. Look at my track record. Five guys in two years. How can I trust my instincts?"

"Nikki, listen to me. You'll have nine guys to choose from. Nine!"

"How do I know the one I pick won't be a loser?"

"You *don't* know. But at least give it a try."

She thought about it for a moment, then shook her head. I watched in dismay as she took her plate into the living room and turned on the TV.

Great. Now what?

"Come on, Nikki. How can I find someone for you if you won't work with me?"

"No speed dating."

I sat beside her on the sofa, thinking hard. No bar, no online dating service, no doctors, no speed dating . . . and only four days left before my romantic weekend in Key West. Out of desperation I said, "How about if we both go?"

She turned to stare at me. With her mouth full of bread she said, "Seriously?"

"I'll arrange it so we can meet the same nine guys, and then we can compare notes afterward and make a choice."

She swallowed her food. "What are you going to tell Marco? He's not going to be thrilled about your meeting nine single guys."

"Once I explain everything, he'll be fine with it. He wants you to find someone to be happy with, too, Nikki." She had no idea how much.

"You know," she said, perking up, "it just might work."

"So you'll go?"

Nikki smiled, her dimples deepening. "Yes."

Before she had time to rethink her decision, I ran for the phone and dialed the number in the ad. "Hi, I'd like to register two people for your speed-dating event this Thursday."

I wrote down the info, registered the two of us, and hung up. "Okay, here's the scoop. According to the event organizer, Carmen Gold, there won't be a problem getting into the same group. All we have to do is show up at the restaurant at seven o'clock Thursday night with our credit cards in hand."

"*All* we have to do? Are you kidding me? I have to find something to wear." Nikki rubbed her hands together, her eyes sparkling with excitement for the first time in weeks. "This could be fun. Great idea, Abby!"

I hoped Marco saw it that way.

"You're going to a speed-dating event?" Marco swung his feet off his desk and sat forward. "Why?"

I'd stopped by Down the Hatch on my way back to Bloomers to tell him what I'd signed up for, and found him in his office, his nose buried in the sports section of the newspaper. I went around behind his chair to massage the muscles in his shoulders. That always mellowed him. "I'm going along to screen the guys. Nikki begged me, Marco. How could I refuse?"

He leaned back to gaze at me speculatively. "She *begged* you?"

"Well, she didn't get down on her knees, if that's what you mean." That was a little diversionary tactic I called fudging.

"How will the guys know you're there only to screen for Nikki?"

"I'll tell them up front."

"What about the safety issue? Is every client given a background check?"

"I doubt it, but I did look at the Cloud Nine Web site, and their policy is to prohibit any personal information from being exchanged during the event. Besides, I didn't check your background before I went out with you. Did you check mine?"

"Sure."

"What?"

"Kidding."

I gave his shoulder a playful push. "You checked me out, didn't you?"

"We're talking about you and Nikki subjecting yourselves to the scrutiny of nine strangers, not what I may or may not have done in the past."

Changing the subject was apparently Marco's diversionary tactic.

"Think about it, Marco. Is meeting someone at this event any different from hooking up in a bar? No. And with nine guys to choose from, Nikki can't miss. Plus there'll be a mixer afterward where she can meet even more guys."

"What will you be doing during this mixer?"

"Checking out every guy she talks to. That's my role."

"Want some advice? Let Nikki meet guys herself. You don't need to hold her hand. If she's not brave enough to go alone, then maybe it's not meant to be. Don't force her."

"I didn't force her. I merely suggested she attend; then she leaped on the idea of me going along." I leaned down to murmur in his ear, "Besides, I'm doing this for us as much as for Nikki. You don't want me to be all worried about her when we're down in Key West, do you?"

Marco pulled me around to sit on his lap. "No, I don't want you to be worried, but I'm still not sold on the idea. How soon is this event?"

"Thursday evening."

He leaned his head toward me to kiss me, then stopped. "Wait. We're leaving early Friday morning. That's cutting it close, isn't it?"

"I'll have my bags all packed and ready to go Thursday afternoon."

"*Bag,* Abby. Not *bags.* We're traveling light, remember? Carry-ons only? No waiting at the airport carousel? No lost luggage? Besides, it'll be hot down in Key West, so you won't need much, just a bikini, some sunscreen. . . ." He paused to think. "Yep, that should do it."

"Silly. I can't wear a bikini all the time."

He lifted one dark eyebrow. "I know."

Oh, baby. This was going to be quite a weekend. "Just think," I said, winding my arms around his neck. "Five days from today we'll be sunning and funning down in Key West, Nikki will have found a new guy, and everyone will be happy."

"How happy?"

I leaned forward to kiss him and his desk phone rang. Marco put the receiver to his ear and practically growled, "Salvare."

At once he straightened, nearly spilling me onto the floor. "No, my throat isn't sore. I'm fine. No, I haven't been ignoring you, *Mama.* I've been very busy. Listen, I'll call you right back. I know I said that last time, but . . ."

Mama Salvare. With a sigh of regret, I got up and headed for the door, wiggling my fingers at him. "Bye."

Marco shrugged, his way of apologizing. Having been in that situation many times with my own mom, I forgave him.

Between Nikki having second thoughts about going to the speed-dating event, and Marco voicing his misgivings about *my* going to the event, I thought Thursday would never arrive. Fortunately for me, Mom and Dad were planning to spend the weekend in Chicago, taking in a play and the new exhibit at the Field Museum of Natural History. That would wipe them out until the following Tuesday. Perfect timing.

But that was next week. This week I was more concerned about Nikki backing out, especially after we pulled into the parking lot of the just-opened Wild Boar Steak House.

"It's a barn, Abby. A giant red barn."

"So? You've eaten breakfast in a building shaped like a giant glazed doughnut."

"Doughnuts and breakfast go together. Barns and future husbands? Scary."

"Barns and cowboys. Duh." I opened my car door. "Come on, Nik. There's nothing scary about a barn. Who knows? You might meet a guy in there who'll change your life."

The decor inside carried out the barn theme, down to the straw on the wooden floor; a hay loft for extra seating; waiters and waitresses in cowboy hats and shirts with fringe; and booths covered in black-and-white faux cowhide. The hostess pointed us toward a wide doorway at the far end of the Western-style bar, beyond a group of guys standing around trying to act cool.

Nikki poked me in the back as we threaded through them. "Is it too late to cancel?"

"You have to give this a chance, Nikki. And P.S., you look really great tonight."

She poked me again. "What do you mean

by *tonight?*"

We entered a cozy, private dining area with warm maple wainscoting below butter-colored walls, and red candles on red-and-white-checked tablecloths. The round tables had been arranged along opposite sides of the room in double lines, with a wide aisle in between. At the back was a smaller bar where all the women attendees were now gathered.

"Excuse me," said a snippy voice from behind. "Your names, please?"

I turned toward the speaker, a woman in her late thirties who sported a tag that read CARMEN GOLD, EVENT ORGANIZER. Ironically, Carmen Gold was dressed almost entirely in silver — a silver shrug covering her black satin halter top, a silver whistle on a black silk cord around her neck, silver bangles on her wrists, a dove gray satin pencil skirt, and glimmering silver high heels. She had long platinum hair, diamond cuff earrings, and soft pink lipstick with silver sparkles in it. Even her PDA was silver.

Carmen had a heart-shaped face with hazel eyes accented by wing-shaped eyebrows, an upturned nose, double-wide mouth, and a long, sharp chin punctuated at the jawline by a large brown mole with two coarse black hairs growing out of it. Trying not to focus on her mole, I lowered my voice — heeding Lottie's warning — to say, "Abby Knight and Nikki Hiduke."

Carmen pressed keys on her PDA, then pointed a daggerlike pink fingernail toward a young black woman with wavy black hair, coffee-colored skin, and almond-shaped eyes, seated behind a table nearby. "My assistant will run your credit cards."

"Carmen isn't too friendly, is she?" I whispered.

"She redefines the word *aloof*," Nikki whispered back. "And please, she couldn't pluck those mole hairs?"

After we paid, Carmen's assistant gave us name tags, our lists of guys, and our table assignments. Nikki and I quickly compared lists, relieved to see that they contained the same names.

"Remember," Carmen said to our group, "you are to stop talking when the buzzer sounds, you are to have no body contact with anyone, and you are *never* to give out any personal information during this event. That includes last names, home addresses, work addresses, e-mail addresses, and phone numbers. This is for your protection. We've had some incidents in the past, so it's very important you understand and follow the rules. Questions, ladies?"

"You've had incidents?" Nikki asked, looking ready to make a break for the door.

Sensing that she might have to refund some money, Carmen snapped her fingers and a waitress rushed over to hand Nikki a glass of white wine. "It's nothing to worry about," Carmen told Nikki. "Just follow the rules and you'll be fine. All right, ladies. Be seated please. The guys will be right in."

Too late to back out now.

I took a seat at my assigned table, third in the line, with Nikki at the table behind me. After accepting a glass of wine from the waitress, I turned and gave Nikki a smile. "Ready?"

Nikki looked pale. "Maybe I should rethink this."

"Coward," I whispered. I didn't tell her I was having a few last-minute misgivings myself. What if all nine guys were duds? Even worse, what if we found Nikki the perfect guy but he didn't like her?

Carmen waited for a straggler to find her table, a hunched, odd-looking woman who didn't seem to know what to do. She wore a gray wool jumper over a white turtleneck sweater with black hose and flats, and had a head that was too large for her body, shoulders that rolled forward, giving her a hunchbacked look, with skinny legs and impossibly small feet. With her limp brown hair, tiny eyes, and hollow-cheeked face devoid of color except for two poorly placed circles of pink blush, she struck me as the type least likely to attend a speed-dating event. I almost expected her to apologize for stumbling into the wrong room.

"Iris," Carmen called impatiently, pointing to the left side of the room. "You're seven."

"Don't I wish," she cracked, sidling toward her table. "Life was so much simpler then."

Everyone laughed as Iris made a show of slinking into her seat. Carmen merely rolled her eyes at her assistant. Then Carmen blew her whistle and the guys swaggered in from the other room.

"Okay, everyone, please remember to follow the rules," Carmen called. "Violators will be asked to leave, and no money will be refunded. At the buzzer, move quickly to your first assigned table and to each table thereafter. We'll take a short break in the middle so you can refill your drinks, and at the end we'll have an hour for a mixer. Ready?"

Carmen glanced at her assistant, who then pressed a buzzer, setting the men in motion. The assistant gave Carmen a nod, then left the room just as a mousy, slightly built man with thinning pale blond hair approached my table. According to my list, his name was D.I.

I watched D.I. check the table number twice, then pull out a chair across from me and dust off the seat with a white cotton handkerchief before settling onto it.

Don't judge him yet, Abby. He's merely being neat. Neat can be good.

D.I. placed his hands on the table, laced his fingers, then smiled at me. "Hello, Abby."

"Hi, D.I."

"Call me Del. It's short for Delroy, an old English name meaning 'dweller in the dell.' Ms. Gold thought D.I. sounded better, although I can't see why."

"Dweller in the dell. That reminds me of a song I used to sing in kindergarten — 'Farmer in the Dell.' "

At his blank look, I said, "You know, 'Hi-ho, the derry-o'?"

"The dweller guards the jeweler's cape," he said with a straight face.

"I'm sorry? Did you say you guard the jewel escape?"

"Jeweler's *cape*." Del put a hand to one side of his mouth and said secretively, "It's encrusted with precious gems and must be

70

protected."

My turn for the blank look. Was there a way to end a speed date early? Shouldn't Carmen have given us whistles or flares or something?

"I take it you're not into science-fiction fantasy games?" Del asked. "I belong to an Internet sci-fan club that meets every Monday evening. We created a kingdom called Diamondo, and the jeweler is the leader. He wears a magic cape. As the dweller, it's my duty to protect the cape."

I picked up my pen and wrote in tiny letters beside Delroy's name: *Weirdo.* "But if the cape is magic, shouldn't it protect the jeweler?"

"Only inside Diamondo."

I reached for my glass of wine. Delroy might work for the jeweler but he was no gem.

Is that what this man has reduced you to? the little voice in my head exclaimed. *Making bad puns?*

"I'm scaring you, aren't I?" Del asked. "Maybe I should tell you that in real life I'm an architectural draftsman. I work in Chicago and live in a condo overlooking Lake Michigan."

I perked up. Now, that was more like it. Nikki would love a lake view. "Did you grow

71

up in Chicago?"

"Minnesota, Saint Paul area. So what do you do, Abby?"

Lottie's warning to not give out any information ran through my head. "I, um, work with flowers."

"Do you own a greenhouse?"

"Actually, I'm not here for myself. I'm interviewing for a friend of mine."

"What a shame." Del leaned toward me. "You know, with your wild red hair, you'd make a perfect Ruby Royale. She's the dweller's concubine, also known as the Red Vixen. Let me give you our Web site so you can check us out."

Del took a slim leather case from his blazer pocket and opened it, revealing business cards inside. He was about to hand me a card when a loud whistle blast made me jump three inches off my chair.

"Stop!" Carmen cried, storming toward us. Del instantly crumpled the card, looking like he wanted to crawl under the table.

Carmen snatched up the card and tore it into pieces. "No personal information! If it happens again, D.I., you'll be asked to leave." Huffing, she clicked away in her silver spikes.

Del looked at me apologetically. "I'm sorry. How about if we meet in the parking lot afterward and exchange e-mail addys then?"

Someone shoot me now.

As soon as the buzzer sounded, I glanced back at Nikki and mouthed, *How did it go?*

With a scowl, she gave me a discreet thumbs-down. Not a good start.

"Hey, there, chili pepper."

I turned just as a short, thick-bodied man with coal black hair and a Fu Manchu mustache took a seat adjacent to, rather than across from, me, which made me instantly uncomfortable. I glanced at his name tag. Strike one against José.

"Hey, there, José," I said, scooting my chair a few inches away. *"¿Que pasa?"*

"Not much until now." He smiled, revealing a handsome set of choppers. Okay, good oral hygiene. A point in his favor. He wore a Cuban-style flat-bottomed shirt and casual slacks, with black boots that sported quite a heel, making me wonder how tall he really was.

"You like to ride cycles?" he asked, leaning back with his arms crossed over his chest.

"Depends on who's driving."

He laughed, a nice warm laugh. Another point for him. "Listen, José, I should tell you I'm not here for myself. I'm interviewing dates for a friend of mine."

"Sure you are."

"No, really, I am."

"Okay, whatever. Does that mean you're not available?"

"I have a boyfriend."

"We can work around that."

I pretended not to hear him and discreetly glanced at my watch. Ye gods, seven minutes to go. "What do you do for a living, José?"

"I own a tattoo parlor. Want to see an example of my work?"

Before I could reply, he unbuttoned his shirt to reveal a chest covered with black ink swirls. "How about that?" he asked proudly.

"What's your theme?" Not that I cared.

"My *theme*? It's art, *chiquita*. Wait till you see the rest."

Fearing he was about to drop his drawers, I slapped a hand over my eyes, then separated two fingers to peer through them. *Dear God.* José had removed his hair! Make that a toupee. He leaned forward to show me a bald head covered with more swirls. As I stared at them, they appeared to undulate hypnotically, making me feel dizzy.

While José replaced his toupee, I took a few deep breaths followed by a healthy swallow of wine. "Why do you keep it covered?"

"For shock value." With a leer, José put a hand on my knee. "So how do you like your eggs in the morning, chili pepper?"

I pushed his hand away. "Unfertilized."

Beside his name I wrote: *No way, José.*

My third date, a man by the name of Aidan, was sneezing so hard he could barely find the chair. He was a tall, nicely built yet nerdy guy around thirty years old. He wore narrow black glasses, a tan blazer, a blue denim shirt, and a red-striped tie that coordinated well with his red-rimmed, watery eyes.

"Sorry about the sneezing," he said, tugging his jacket lapel over his shirtfront.

Not as sorry as I was. Three dates into the event and so far it was a bust. The only thing this evening seemed likely to produce was a viral infection in everyone seated in the vicinity, including me.

"I'm Aidan," he said, then turned his head and sneezed into his arm.

I pulled a pack of pocket tissues from my purse and slid them across the table. "Here you go." Then I reached for my pen, ready to cross him off the list.

"I'm really sorry to be wasting your time. I shouldn't have come tonight."

"If I were you, Aidan, I'd go home and

take care of that cold."

"It's not a cold. It's allergies." He turned away to blow into the tissue.

Sure it was.

"On my way over here, I stopped to help a woman fix a flat tire" — he lifted one side of his blazer to show me a big smear of grease on his denim shirt — "and stained my shirt in the process. Then the woman's dog got out, so I helped her capture it and carry it back . . . and I'm allergic to dog dander."

My opinion of Aidan was changing. "That was very kind of you to help her."

"I kept imagining my mother being stuck on a road at night, with no one to help her." Aidan shrugged. "It seemed the right thing to do. Anyway, I appreciate your patience." He stood up and was about to leave.

"Wait, Aidan. According to my watch, we still have six minutes left."

He gave me a hesitant smile. "Are you sure?"

"I have a confession to make, too."

He sat down, looking a little more cheerful, so I went into my spiel about helping Nikki and got a favorable reaction. "So, tell me, Aidan, are you allergic to cat dander, too?"

"Just to dogs, thank goodness, because I

like cats."

Score another for Aidan. However, the next question would be important because of Simon. "Do you have any cats?"

"Had one, but recently lost him — a tabby I'd had for twelve years."

"I'm sorry. My roommate has a white cat I've practically adopted as my own. I'd miss the little furball if something happened to him. So what do you do for a living, Aidan?"

"I'm an endodontist."

"Endo . . . ?"

"A dentist who specializes in pulp and tissue treatment — you know, like root canals . . ."

A specialist. Oh, man, Nikki's mother would sing for joy. "Are you from around here?"

"I moved to New Chapel two months ago. I'm out at the new dental clinic on Route Forty-nine."

This guy was racking up points faster than I could calculate them. "How would you feel about dating an X-ray technician?"

CHAPTER FIVE

When the buzzer sounded a few minutes later, I turned to give Nikki a quick thumbs-up.

She pretended to clap; then her gaze widened at the sight of someone behind me.

I glanced around and my jaw dropped. My next date was the most perfectly constructed man I'd ever seen, and looked like a cross between Brad Pitt, Johnny Depp, and Leo DiCaprio. He had dark blond hair, brilliant blue eyes, and a dimple in his chin. He appeared to be in his midthirties, a little older than I'd hoped for, but still in the acceptable range, especially with all that perfection going on: perfect hair, perfect features, perfect body, perfect clothes. Perfect.

"This is for you," he said, handing me a white carnation from the wrapped bouquet in his other hand.

Perfect voice, too, although the carnation

was a bit over-the-top. As soon as he was seated, I held out my hand. "I'm Abby."

As an earsplitting whistle shattered the air, I realized my mistake and quickly pulled my hand back. Carmen marched over to scold me anyway.

Pointing her index finger at me, she said, "You'd better watch yourself. That's the second time I've had to come over here."

Knowing my face was bright red and that every eye in the room was staring, I murmured an apology, then couldn't help adding, "The last time wasn't really my fault, though."

Her eyes flattened into slits of hostility and her mole quivered with ire. "I *know* that." Casting a venomous look at the gorgeous guy at my table, she marched away.

"I won't make that mistake again," I told my date.

"Ignore her. She's a bitch." He gave me a brilliant smile. "I'm Jonas, by the way."

He started our date by calling the EO a bitch? Way to kill a great first impression.

I watched Jonas pull back his French-cuffed sleeve to check his watch, a diamond-encrusted Rolex. "Okay, let me tell you a little bit about myself so we can get that part over with. I'm a University of Chicago grad, MBA from Harvard. I started out in real estate, then switched to land development, a smart move considering the growth in this part of the state. I work the entire tricounty area, turning unused acreage into viable public space."

Viable public space? Was that developer talk for parking lots?

"I've never been married, but I'd sure like to be. I've got my career well established and can support a wife and children in a luxurious lifestyle . . . two cars and a four-bedroom house on forty acres. I love to travel, first-class, of course. And I love strong, independent women."

I gazed at him in awe. Handsome, wealthy, educated — and hunting for a spouse. Could he be any more perfect? Glancing at his white carnation, I thought, *Make that too perfect,* and held off on revealing my reason for being there. "You certainly have great credentials."

"What can I say?" He gave a large shrug, a weak attempt at modesty.

"You can say why you need to come to a speed-dating event to meet women."

His smile never faltered. "If I didn't, how would I meet fascinating women like you?"

Smooth.

Jonas gazed at me as if I were the most engaging creature he'd ever laid eyes on.

"I'm betting you're a nature lover."

I was betting that was part of a pickup line. "What gave me away?"

"You're like a breath of fresh air on a spring morning."

Yep, a pickup line. I had the perfect comeback, too. "Being a breath of fresh air on a spring morning was my major in college."

"No kidding," he said, trying to look impressed but clearly not paying attention. "So, do you like Ferraris?"

"Love them. I'm something of a car nut. I own a 1960 Corvette convert—"

"You'll have to see my Ferrari. It's parked outside. A fully loaded F430 coupe in racing red with camel leather interior. Top-of-the-line in every respect" — he dropped his voice — "and priced at a cool two hundred thou and some change."

Two hundred thousand dollars for a car? Imagine that. Was I impressed? Jonas sure hoped so. Awed? Nope. Bored? *Yawn.*

He held out one arm so I could examine the sleeve of his stylish dark gray suit. "It's a Brioni. Also top-of-the-line. I won't settle for less — in my life *or* my women. It's got to be top-of-the-line all the way."

I was starting to wish he was on the *end* of a line so I could use him as shark bait.

81

■ ■ ■ ■

After Jonas, I met a young ad executive with green-stained teeth who told me he was a gourmand, loved to help out in the kitchen, and suggested I'd look wonderful wearing nothing but a frilly lace apron and my freckles. His ideal woman, it seemed, was a nude freckled chef. I barely made it through all nine minutes without calling for a wine refill.

I also met a forty-year-old bank teller named Kipp who lived with his mother, had never been married, and said Mom would approve of my wholesome looks. He suggested a perfect date would be at home, with his mother cooking dinner, after which the three of us could play Scrabble. Next to Kipp's name I wrote: *Missing a game piece.*

The last three guys were pleasant, well mannered, but not right for Nikki. My bets were on Aidan. I couldn't wait to compare notes with Nikki.

"I found the perfect guy for you," I said to Nikki when we met in the ladies' room to freshen up before the mixer.

"I did, too! I'll bet it's the same guy, but you go first."

"Okay. It's Aidan."

"Aidan?" She gazed at me as though I'd just stepped off a bus from Jupiter. "He was okay."

"Come on, Nikki, he was way better than okay. He was a nine and a half out of ten. Did he tell you what happened to him on the way here?"

She pulled out her lip gloss and leaned toward the mirror over the sink to apply it. "No."

"Did he explain why he was sneezing?"

"No."

"Then what did you talk about?"

"He mostly asked me questions. He was very interested in my job at the hospital."

"Probably because he's in the medical profession, too, not to mention that he liked you! Nikki, you need to talk to him during the mixer. Aidan is perfect for you."

"But I found one even better, Ab. Actually, I'm surprised you didn't choose him for me."

"Who?"

"Jonas."

"Jonas! With the French cuffs and the Ferrari?"

"Wasn't he to die for? I mean, could he have been more drop-dead gorgeous, not to mention rich and successful *and* looking for a wife?"

"He made sure to point all that out to you, didn't he?"

"Look what he gave me." She showed me the white carnation she'd tucked in her bag.

"Big deal. He gave one to all his dates."

Nikki scowled at me in the mirror as she dropped her lip gloss in her clutch bag. "I thought he was cool. In fact, I rated him an eleven out of ten."

"Come on, Nikki. Jonas was so full of himself, I'm surprised he had room inside for a drink. He treated my nine minutes like kindergarten show-and-tell, flashing his Rolex and his Brioni suit. Trust me, Nik, this is not the guy for you. Avoid him like the plague."

"I liked him," she said firmly.

"Think about it, Nikki. This guy has it all — looks, a fancy car, his own business — yet he needs a speed-dating event to meet women."

"What are you implying? That only losers come to speed-dating events?"

"No! It just seems like Jonas should have women falling all over him."

"Maybe they do fall all over him," she said as we left the ladies' room, "but maybe he hasn't found the right one yet. Personally, I thought he was gentlemanly, good-natured,

84

and most important, very interested in me. In fact, he said I was like a breath of fresh air —"

"— on a spring morning. Don't flatter yourself. He said that to me, too."

"There he is," she whispered excitedly.

"Look, there's Aidan at the end of the bar," I said, steering her in the opposite direction. "You really need to give him a chance."

Nikki resisted, pushing me off to one side to say quietly, "I know why you don't want me to go out with Jonas, and it's not because you don't think he's right for me. It's because you don't think he's right for you!"

"That makes no sense, Nikki. I've got a guy, remember?"

"It makes perfect sense. Answer this for me. Who does Jonas remind you of, and I don't mean Johnny Depp or Brad Pitt."

"Leo DiCaprio?"

Nikki scowled at me. "No."

I glanced over my shoulder at the man in question. Perfectly groomed hair, smoothly shaved face, immaculately dressed down to the shine on his shoes . . . *Dear God.* He was Pryce all over again, my ex-fiancé who had dumped me when I flunked out of law school because his parents didn't feel I lived up to the Osborne family standards.

I shuddered at the memory. "Okay, yes, I agree that on the surface he reminds me of Pryce, but this goes deeper than that, Nikki. I have a sixth sense about people, and that sense is saying Jonas is an accident waiting to happen. Please, Nikki, stay away from him."

At that moment, a smooth male voice said, "Hello, again." I turned to find the giant ego in question standing behind us with a fluted glass in each hand. "I thought you ladies might like a fresh drink. Champagne okay?"

"Thanks," Nikki gushed, gazing dreamily at him. "That's so sweet."

"Happy to oblige." He gave her a movie-star smile. I half expected to see his teeth twinkle.

Handing me the other glass, Jonas slid neatly between us, singling Nikki out. Finding myself suddenly facing his back, I moved away, debating whether I should butt back in or just trust that Nikki would eventually get sick of his smarmy charm and give him the brush-off.

Suddenly, I spotted Carmen Gold standing at the end of the bar, staring at Jonas with a look of pure contempt. She saw me and left the room.

What was that about?

"My lady Ruby Royale," Del said, giving me a sweeping bow. "How dost thou fare?"

"Fare thee well," I sang, and turned squarely into Iris. She was holding a glass of red wine, and as it sloshed onto her jumper she glanced at me, her misshapen mouth agape.

"I'm so *sorry,*" I cried, grabbing a stack of cocktail napkins off the bar and handing them to her. "I didn't see you there. Oh, look at your jumper. Listen, I'll pay to have it cleaned."

"That's okay," she said, sopping up the wine. "I own a dry cleaner's. Usually I'm the one getting people to spill on themselves. It's a great way to drum up business." She waited a beat, then went, "Badum-bum. That was supposed to be a joke."

"Oh, sorry."

Iris rolled her eyes. "Not as sorry as I am."

To cover the awkward moment I asked, "So is your dry cleaner's here in Maraville?"

"New Chapel."

"No kidding. I'm from New Chapel."

"I know. I've seen your picture in the newspaper. You're the underground florist."

I stared at her. "Underground?"

"Under. Ground. You know, like flowers grow in soil? Like you use your flower shop as a cover to solve crimes?"

"Ah. I get it."

"Tough crowd," she muttered, pretending to tug on an imaginary necktie.

"What's the name of your dry cleaner's?"

"Frey's. It was my father's business until he died; then it passed to Mother and me."

"Did you go to New Chapel High?"

"Private school. My parents wanted to make sure a better class of kids were making fun of me."

What could I say to that? At least I knew why I hadn't recognized her.

"It's okay to laugh," Iris said. "I'm a stand-up comic."

"Are you serious?"

"I hope not. A serious comic? Now, there's an oxymoron for you. I perform at the Three Cs Club — that's short for Calumet Comedy Club — on Wednesday nights."

Judging by the jokes I heard, I could understand why they put her on a slow night. I glanced around and saw Delroy waiting for an opportunity to approach me again, so I decided to hang on to Iris a while longer. "First time here?" I asked her.

"And the last, if Miss Silver-and-Gold has her way."

"Did Carmen say something to you?"

"Are you kidding? Even her mole shudders when I come close. And would someone please buy her a lawn mower for that turf on her chin?" Iris waited for my laugh, then tapped on her thumb and said, "Is my microphone on?"

Not that a mic would help her any. "Have you met anyone interesting tonight?"

She used her glass to point to someone behind me. "Have you met *him* yet?"

She was pointing at Jonas. He was still talking to Nikki, who appeared to be in some kind of hypnotic trance — or maybe she'd fallen asleep with her eyes open. "Oh, yeah, I met him, all right — for nine very long minutes."

"What about her?" Iris asked, pointing toward Nikki. "Who is she?"

"My roommate, Nikki."

"Lucky girl."

"Yeah, right," I said with a laugh. Then I noticed the envy in Iris's tiny eyes and realized she was being serious. She studied Nikki for a moment, then, without so much as a good-bye, set her glass on a tray, dropped the wine-soaked napkins beside it, and walked toward the door.

Was it something I said?

"Hey, chili pepper."

With a silent groan I turned, and there was José, grinning broadly. "Want to go for a ride on my hog?"

Thank goodness I knew that he was referring to his Harley; otherwise I might have had to deck him. "No, thanks. And by the way, I'm not a food."

I turned to walk away, saw Delroy's face light up — as if he had a chance! — and hurried in the opposite direction. I spotted Aidan picking out cheese bites from the appetizer table and headed his way, figuring he'd be a safe person to talk to.

Suddenly, there was a loud crash outside the restaurant, as though two cars had collided. Everyone stopped talking, but because the back room was windowless, there was no way to know what had happened. A moment later, the restaurant hostess stuck her head into the room and called, "Anyone here own a red Ferrari?"

"Oh, shit," Jonas said, and started jogging toward her. When Nikki followed, I put down my glass and dashed after her.

By the time I reached the parking lot, a number of restaurant patrons had already gathered there. I managed to squeeze through the crowd to catch up with Nikki, who was watching in dismay as Jonas circled his new Ferrari, sizing up the damage. The sleek red coupe had been rammed from the rear, crumpling the back end and pushing the front into a cement light pole hard enough to smash the headlights and dent the hood. I glanced around for the vehicle that had hit it, knowing it would be pretty banged-up, too, but I didn't see a likely candidate.

"Poor Jonas," Nikki said, watching him struggle to get the door open.

"An accident waiting to happen," I reminded her. I just hadn't thought it would be so soon.

"The police should be here in a few minutes," the restaurant manager called, weaving through the people to reach the scene.

Jonas tugged on the handle, then hit his fist against the roof like a spoiled child on the verge of a temper tantrum. He turned toward the gawkers, "Did anyone see who hit my car?"

No one spoke. As a police car arrived at the scene, I caught sight of Carmen Gold standing on the other side of the crowd, watching Jonas with a look of smug satisfaction. Obviously she was enjoying his suffering. Remembering the glares she'd given him earlier, I wondered what was behind her animosity.

"We might as well get our coats and go home," Nikki said, shivering in the cold night air.

"You haven't found a date yet. Don't you want to go back inside and talk to Aidan?"

Nikki pointed across the parking lot. "*That* Aidan?"

I followed her index finger and saw Aidan getting into a Camry. Great. There went my last hope for finding Nikki a date before I left for Key West.

"I was really hoping you'd find someone tonight, Nik."

"I know," she said, not sounding terribly disappointed.

"At least you'll be able to attend a second event free. That's Cloud Nine's policy. But I still feel terrible about leaving you all alone this weekend."

"You're going somewhere this weekend?"

Good job, Abby. Sheepishly, I said, "Marco and I are taking a little trip to Key West."

"Oh? Did you just plan it?"

"Well, actually, we made plans before you and Scott broke up; otherwise I would have delayed it for a while."

Nikki looked hurt. "You kept the trip a secret from *me?* I thought we didn't keep secrets from each other."

"I don't usually, Nikki, but I asked Marco not to tell anyone, so I felt obligated to stick to the same rule. And it was only to keep my parents and his family from finding out.

I'm sorry if I hurt your feelings."

"I'll survive. And don't worry about leaving me alone. I've got my guys Ben and Jerry to keep me company. Besides, once you and Marco are down in the Keys, you won't even remember I exist."

"That's not true!"

Okay, so once in a while I was wrong.

CHAPTER SIX

Monday, January 31

"Nikki was right," I told Lottie and Grace. "Once we stepped off the plane at the Key West airport, I forgot all about her dating problem. Sunshine, perfect weather, a cozy B and B . . . it was wonderful. Then we came home and all hell broke loose."

I finished my story with an account of the cops showing up at our door to take Nikki away for questioning, and their later return for her clothing and shoes, and how I felt responsible for her predicament because I'd insisted she go.

"Don't feel bad, sweetie," Lottie said. "As you said, if Nikki had taken your advice, she wouldn't be in this pickle. You didn't arrange that date with Jonas. She did."

"If I thought about it," I said, "I could get really pissed off with Nikki about that."

"Yet, as you also pointed out, dear," Grace said, "it's water under the bridge now, isn't it? What's important is that Nikki be cleared right away and brought home. Shall I call Dave's secretary for a status report?"

We trooped to the workroom and waited while Grace made the call from my desk. After a full minute of saying, "I see," she hung up and turned to face us. "It appears the police have released Nikki for now."

"For now? They might have to bring her back?" I asked in alarm.

"All Helen would say is that Nikki is supposed to meet with Dave at his office at eleven thirty this morning."

Lottie glanced at her wristwatch and gasped. "Lordy, it's nine o'clock. I'd better run up front and unlock the door."

"I don't have a good feeling about Nikki, Grace," I said. "The police should have released her unconditionally."

"Don't be hasty," Grace said, rising. She cleared her throat. "As Helen Keller, that inspiring woman, once said —"

Lottie stuck her head through the curtain. "Six customers are headed for the parlor."

Grace gave her a nod and continued, " 'Keep your face to the sunshine and you cannot see the shadow.' And now I must go."

Hastily, too, I noticed.

I called home to see how Nikki was faring

but got our answering machine. After leaving a message for her, I tried her cell phone, only to be sent straight to her voice mail. Why wasn't she answering? Was she so distraught that she'd shut off her phone?

Trying to keep my mind occupied so my worry motor didn't kick into overdrive, I sorted the orders on the spindle, then started on one that was to be delivered to the courthouse at noon, a birthday bouquet a group of secretaries had ordered for one of the judges. While I put together an arrangement of callas and roses, I heard the bell over the door chime repeatedly as customers came and went. It was music to my ears.

Then I heard, "Where's my fave little cuz?" and the music became crashing cymbals as the curtains parted and Jillian glided in.

"Abs!" she cried, as though we hadn't seen each other in years.

Jillian Knight Osborne was my only female cousin. She was a year younger, pounds lighter, and tons prettier. I used to say that she was much luckier, too, but that was until she married Claymore Osborne, my ex-fiancé's younger brother, in a ceremony that remained legendary in New Chapel's history for the murder that took place during it.

Always the fashionista, today my cousin sported a white faux-fur swing coat, black faux-fur earmuffs, red mittens, black boots, and a red leather purse trimmed in black. Before I could duck, she wrapped her arms around me and squeezed. Since she was also a head taller, my face got mashed against the front of her coat, which set me off on a sneezing fit.

"*Ew.* You're sick," She backed away as though I had cooties.

I brushed fine strands away from my nose and mouth, then picked more out of my lip gloss. "I'm not sick. It's your fur coat."

"It's *faux* fur, Abby. How can you be allergic to faux?" Jillian tossed her mittens onto the worktable, scattering a pile of loose rose petals, then swept off her earmuffs and shook free her long, copper-colored hair, her pride and joy. She pulled out a tall wooden stool and perched on it. "So what's this I hear about you attending a speed-dating event? Don't tell me you and Marco are splitsville again."

"Splitsville? Have you been watching sitcoms from the sixties? Of course we're not. I merely went with Nikki to a speed-dating event to help her screen guys. Who told you about it?"

"I have my sources. So poor Nikki has lost her mojo, huh? Did you find anyone for her?"

"Is that why you're here, Jill? To get fodder for gossip?"

"Abby, I'm hurt. Can't I stop by to see how you are?"

That would be a first. "What do you need, Jillian?"

"A floral arrangement for a dinner party, but not just any floral arrangement. I want something spectacular. Something so awesome that mouths will drop open."

"And you need this awesome arrangement when?"

"Tonight."

"Are you serious? I can't pull an idea like that out of thin air. I'll have to study my books and floral magazines, ask Lottie's advice. . . ."

"And I want to help you put it together."

"Forget it."

"Abby, I'm desperate! Claymore is bringing over his bosses and their wives, and those women are so clever and accomplished that there's no way I can compete. But if I can say that I had a hand in creating a jaw-dropping floral arrangement, at least I have something to offer."

"You don't have to compete, Jill. It's

not a race."

"But I do need to make a good impression. Claymore is up for a very big promotion. He's counting on me to dazzle them."

"By saying you made a floral arrangement? That's ridiculous. Besides, you have a lot to offer on your own."

"Like what?"

I searched for something positive to say, trying to keep my face toward the sunshine, as Grace had suggested. "Well, you're fashionable. I mean, who knows clothing better than you? And then there's your business as a wardrobe consultant."

"All that makes me is a shopper, Abby. A *shopper!*" She dropped her head into her hands, her hair cascading forward like a waterfall, her shoulders shaking in silent sobs.

Add *drama queen* to that list. "Jill. Here's a thought. Why don't you create a spectacular, jaw-dropping, gourmet meal for them?"

She lifted her head to give me the evil eye. "That's the caterer's job."

Silly me. I forgot. Jillian knew how to make only one thing: Jell-O.

She put her head down again, moaning in agony.

Hearing groans, Lottie came through the curtain in a rush, saw Jillian's bent head, then tried to back through the curtain before my cousin noticed her.

"Lottie," Jillian exclaimed, jumping up, "you'll help me, won't you?"

"Well, I don't know," Lottie replied warily. "Depends what you need."

Jillian quickly filled Lottie in, while Lottie's eyes darted between my cousin and me, as though trying to gauge my reaction. "I suppose we can do that," she said at the end.

"Oh, thank you!" Jillian gushed, and tried to wrap her arms around Lottie, but it was a stretch. "What time should I be here to work on the arrangement?"

"Closing time," I muttered.

"No, seriously," Jillian said, pulling on her gloves.

"Five minutes before closing time."

"Be here at four thirty," Lottie said.

"Thank you so, so, so much!" Jillian blew kisses at us, then swept out of the room.

"Sorry, sweetie," Lottie said. "It was the only way I knew to get her out of your hair. But don't worry. I'll figure out something she can help us with that'll knock the socks off her guests." She started away, then stopped to mutter, "Did I just say that?"

I kept my eye on the clock as I worked on orders, watching the hands inch toward eleven thirty. Then, with the Monday-morning coffee rush winding down, I grabbed my coat off the back of the chair and slipped it on.

"Would you mind if I dashed down to Dave's office?" I asked Lottie and Grace. "Nikki is supposed to meet with him, and I'd like to be there."

"We'll cover, sweetie," Lottie said.

"Keep your face to the sunshine," Grace called.

Thick gray clouds blanketed the sky as I took a shortcut across the courthouse lawn. The grass was crunchy and brown, the ground frozen, and the temperature cold enough to make me reach for the knit gloves wadded in my coat pockets. As I waited to cross the street, I pulled out my cell phone and hit speed dial number two. Marco answered in one ring.

"What's the news?"

"All I know is that the police released Nikki for now, and she has a meeting with Dave in five minutes. I'm on my way to his office to get more information."

"Dave isn't going to let you butt into their meeting, Sunshine."

"I won't be butting in. I just want to know what's going on."

"That's butting in. And you're forgetting about lawyer-client confidentiality, not to mention that Nikki might not even want you there."

"Why wouldn't she want me there? Besides, it's a little late for me not to be involved, don't you think, considering that I got her into this predicament?" I stopped in front of Dave's door. "I'll call you afterward and let you know what happened."

Tucking the phone in my coat pocket, I pushed open the door and trotted up the stairs to Dave's second-floor suite in the early 1900s building. "Hi," I said to Helen, as I entered the small reception area. "Has Nikki arrived yet?"

"Yes," she said, her fingers flying over the keyboard.

"Good. I'll just slip quietly inside the office —"

She threw out an arm to stop me. "No, you won't, not without Dave's okay." Then she picked up her phone and buzzed Dave. "Abby is here." She listened a moment, then hung up. "Dave says to have a seat in the waiting area." She pointed to the row of chairs against the wall.

Why was he keeping me out of the meeting? Surely Nikki would want me at her side.

A few minutes later, Dave's office door

opened and he motioned for me to come in. I sprang out of the chair and hurried in to find Nikki seated in one of the chairs facing Dave's desk. She had changed her outfit and styled her hair, so obviously she'd been home to clean up. Upon seeing me, she stood to give me a hug.

"Are you all right?" I asked, leaning back to study her face for signs of stress. "Did the cops try to rattle you? Did they mistreat you in any way?"

"I'm okay, just jittery."

"What's this nonsense about them releasing you *for now?*"

"Abby," Dave said, "Nikki's had a rough morning. Sit down and I'll fill you in — with Nikki's permission, of course."

At Nikki's nod, I sat down and clasped my hands tightly in my lap. "Okay. Shoot."

"Here it is," Dave said, "and please hold your questions until I finish. The cops received an anonymous tip alleging that Nikki was at the crime scene with the victim. They were also able to match her boot prints to prints found at the scene. Now they're analyzing clay samples from the soles to see if they're a match, too."

"Wait a minute," I said, massaging my temples. "Nikki went out to dinner with Jonas — the victim — so I'm sure a lot of people saw them together. That's no big secret. And I don't understand about the clay on her boots. Where was Jonas killed?"

"At the site of his latest development," Dave said. "A subdivision called Chateaux en Carnations. His body was discovered in his sales office inside a model home. He'd been stabbed in the neck several times and apparently bled out there."

"Back up a minute," I said. "The murder happened at his development? Then how did they find Nikki's boot prints there?"

Dave cleared his throat, casting a glance at Nikki as though waiting for her to speak up, but she seemed preoccupied with chipping dark purple polish off her thumbnail. It was a nervous habit she'd carried over from childhood. As I remembered, it meant she was hiding something. Was she more involved than she was letting on?

CHAPTER SEVEN

"Nikki?" I asked with growing suspicion, watching her working furiously on her thumbnail. "What am I missing? How did the clay get on your boots? Did you go to the development with Jonas?"

She hesitated a moment, then nodded, confirming my fear. At least now I understood why the police hadn't released her.

Practically holding my breath, I asked, "Did you go inside the model home?"

She lifted her head, gazing at me with wounded eyes. "Are you asking if I killed him?"

"Of course not. But why didn't you tell me this earlier?"

She shrugged again, glancing away, probably to avoid seeing my disappointment.

"Abby," Dave said, "you can talk to her about that later. We have more important matters to discuss right now." Turning to Nikki he said, "Were you able to come up with any witnesses?"

Nikki shook her head, chewing on her thumbnail now. "It was after midnight when Jonas dropped me off at our apartment building. I didn't see a soul around."

Dave frowned in thought, tapping his pen on the yellow pad. "If the detectives are able to prove you were at the murder scene, it's imperative that we establish a solid alibi for you during the time the murder took place" — he paused to check his notes — "which, by the coroner's estimate, was between one and two o'clock Monday morning."

While I was flying home from Key West. I glanced at Nikki in concern. "I can't vouch for you."

"I know," Nikki said, her big doe eyes starting to tear up.

"Are you sure none of our neighbors were around?" I asked her. "What about the Samples across the hall? Sometimes they take Peewee out for a walk late at night."

Nikki shook her head. "No one was around, Abby."

"What about Jillian?" I asked, since my cousin also lived in our apartment building. "She and Claymore come in late sometimes."

Nikki shook her head again, a lone tear

running down her face. "I'm screwed, aren't I?"

I grabbed her hand and gave it a reassuring squeeze. "Don't think that way. There has to be someone who saw you."

"Which is why I'm going to suggest hiring a private investigator to canvass your apartment building," Dave said, "and the neighborhood, if need be, to find witnesses to corroborate your alibi. Abby, stop waving at me. Don't even think about volunteering for the job. This needs more time than you've got to give. You have a flower shop to run, remember?"

I lowered my hand.

"What if we can't find anyone?" Nikki asked, wiping off the wet trail down her cheek.

Dave leaned back in his chair. "Then I wouldn't be able to use an alibi defense. There'd be no way to support it."

"What would that leave?" Nikki asked him.

"If it came to that — and I trust it won't — we'd have to decide whether to take our chances with a jury or investigate ourselves to try to point the detectives toward the real culprit."

Take our chances with a jury? No way was I about to leave Nikki's fate to chance. But we were far from reaching that point. "Let's back up a moment," I said. "Have the police ruled out the possibility that Jonas was killed by a robber? Couldn't someone have broken in, not realizing Jonas was there?"

"There's no mention of it in the police report," Dave said, "which would indicate that there was also no evidence of it — no signs of a break-in or of anything ransacked or stolen. It would also indicate that Jonas let the killer in."

"Have they done a fingerprint check?" I asked.

"Too soon to have a report on that."

"If Jonas let someone in," I said, "then was killed by that person, doesn't it make sense that the killer had it in for him? That's a reasonable conclusion, isn't it?"

"I'd say so," Dave replied.

"That should automatically rule Nikki out because she just met the guy. What would her motive be?"

"Abby, think back to what you learned in your law classes," Dave said. "A motive isn't needed to indict someone. All it takes are means and opportunity. The prosecutor would propose his own motive."

Since thinking back to my law classes usually brought on a migraine, I moved on to my next argument. "But look at the flimsy evidence they have, Dave. A boot print? A lot of women wear the same brand. There's nothing unique about that. It's circumstantial. And as for the clay, half the land in town has a clay base."

Dave clasped his fingers behind his head and leaned back. "This isn't the kind of clay found in our soil. It's a distinctive blue-gray clay dredged from the bottom of a retention pond up north, near Lake Michigan. Jonas bought it on the cheap and trucked it in to use in the landscaping. He got as far as laying it around the model home; then the Indiana Department of Environmental Management got wind of it and pulled his permits, fearing any runoff would destroy the wetlands. The clay is so dense that water can't get through and plants die. Naturally, the scrapings from Nikki's boot will have to be analyzed before they can be presented as evidence, but together with the boot prints and the anonymous tip, the police have got enough to peg Nikki as a suspect."

The bad news just kept on coming. "Did they find the murder weapon?"

"Not as far as I know. The report lists it as a wide-bladed knife."

"What about the anonymous tipster?" I asked. "Why would the cops trust the word of someone who won't even give a name?"

"If that were all they had, it probably wouldn't be enough, but as I said, put it together with the print and the clay . . ."

I didn't say anything to Dave or Nikki, but I suddenly had the unwelcome thought that Nikki's being the target of this investigation might be partly my fault, too. How many of the detectives had I ticked off by stepping in and helping solve their cases? That only added to the guilt I already felt for insisting Nikki attend the speed-dating event.

"If our investigator isn't able to establish your alibi," Dave said to Nikki, "then we'll have him come up with a list of possible suspects and narrow it down to the most likely, so we can point the detectives in the right direction. So my suggestion is to hire Marco for the job. He's proven his worth many times over. But it's your call."

"I want Marco," Nikki said.

I smiled at her. Naturally she'd want me to work on the case *with* Marco.

"Abby?" Dave said.

"Yes, sir?"

"I want you to keep out of it and let Marco do his job."

Damn. "Yes, sir."

"You're too close to Nikki to be objective."

"Yes, sir."

"You're crossing your fingers behind your back, aren't you?"

"Yes, sir." Sheepishly, I uncrossed my fingers and put my hand in my lap.

Dave picked up his pen and jotted a note on his yellow pad. "Consider yourself banned from this case."

He wasn't serious, was he?

"I mean that," he added, as though reading my mind. He turned to Nikki. "I'll contact Marco right away so we can get started. In the meantime, don't talk to any reporters or cops without checking with me first, okay? Good. Then I think that covers things for now. Do you have any questions for me?"

Nikki said shyly, "What will your fee be?"

"At this point, I'll be charging my standard hourly rate, plus the cost of the investigator. However — and I have to be candid with you — if we're not successful in establishing your alibi or in finding a viable suspect, and you're indicted for murder, then the fee would be quite substantial and a large retainer would have to be paid."

Nikki swallowed hard. "I understand."

"It won't come to that," I assured her.

"I'll give you a call as soon as I know more," Dave told her, "and I'm always available by cell phone. If anything comes up or you have more questions, don't hesitate to call."

As Nikki and I stepped onto the sidewalk outside Dave's building, the bell in the church tower on the next block began to toll the noon hour. "Do you want to grab some lunch at the deli?" I asked her.

"No, thanks. I don't have much of an appetite."

"Then you can have a cup of tea and keep me company," I said, threading my arm through hers, "because we need to talk."

"Why?"

"You don't really have to ask that, do you?"

Nikki was quiet until after we'd settled at a little corner bistro table. I'd ordered a turkey sandwich on homemade rosemary bread and a cup of hot coffee for me, and mint tea for her. I gave her half my sandwich and urged her to eat something, but she shook her head.

"I just want to go home and kick back for a while before my shift starts at the hospital."

"Are you sure you want to go to work today? You know everyone at the hospital will be talking about the murder. Nothing escapes attention in this town. You have sick days saved up. Use one today. No one is going to say anything."

"What am I going to do at the apartment except sit around and worry? I might as well go in. It'll keep my mind occupied."

I chewed a bite of my sandwich, studying Nikki as she stirred honey into her tea. "Why didn't you tell me the whole story this morning?"

"The cops were waiting. There wasn't time."

"How long would it have taken to tell me you went with Jonas to his development?"

Nikki put down the straw, a troubled expression on her face. "I was dazed, Abby. Those cops really scared me. I'm sorry if I hurt your feelings."

I had to concede her point. Given the way the cops acted, I would have been rattled, too. "So when did Jonas ask you out to dinner?"

"He phoned me around six o'clock Sunday afternoon."

"Wow. Short notice, wasn't it?"

"Yeah, and I usually say no when a guy pulls that, but this was Jonas. I was too excited to care." She shook her head. "Boy, was I an idiot."

"You said Jonas hinted Thursday evening

113

about asking you out. Is that when you gave him your phone number?"

"Yes, but I was still surprised when he called. I figured he was just flirting with me."

"Tell me what happened."

With a weary sigh, Nikki began to recite her story. "Jonas picked me up at eight and took me to a restaurant not far from the Wild Boar Steak House. We were there for about two hours; then on the way home, he had this great idea to show me his new development. He said it wouldn't be that much out of the way, but it was after eleven o'clock when we finally got there."

"I don't get why you even agreed to go. What could you see in the dark?"

"I know it sounds ridiculous now, but Jonas was very convincing. And to be fair, he had really rolled out the red carpet for me: champagne, caviar, lobster tails, chocolate soufflés. . . . He even brought me a bouquet of white carnations. So I thought I should at least go see his new development. Honestly, the way he'd bragged about it, I thought it would be an exclusive, gated community with million-dollar homes, but it was just another muddy subdivision under construction with a fancy name over a fancy stone entrance.

114

"Anyway, he parked the car in front of a model home and asked if I wanted to go inside for a nightcap. I told him it was late and asked him to take me home."

"And he did?"

She nodded, then took a sip of tea.

"Then how did you get clay on your boots?"

"Oh, I forgot. Jonas showed me a little footbridge that spans a creek beside the home. The lawn hasn't been put in yet and the ground was all muddy from melting snow."

"You forgot?" I leaned closer to say in a hushed voice, "It seems like something you'd remember, considering your boots are now evidence."

Her lips pursing angrily, Nikki tore a hunk of bread crust off her half of the sandwich and began to shred it. "I'm sorry if you don't believe me, but I *did* forget."

"I didn't say I didn't believe you."

"You implied it. And FYI, I didn't forget to tell the *cops* about getting out of the car, if that's your next question. Forgive me if I forget a detail. I've told this story so many times I can hardly remember my name anymore."

"I'm sorry, Nikki. That was totally insensitive of me. I remember what it's like to be questioned by the cops. It's not pleasant. Let's just wipe out the last few minutes, okay? All I want is to help you."

Her eyes filled with tears and she immediately dug in her purse for a tissue. "I hate feeling like a criminal. All I did was go on a date with the guy. I didn't do anything wrong."

"I know you didn't, Nikki."

"You were so right about Jonas. He seemed so gentlemanly at first, with the bouquet of flowers and champagne and all. But it was just to make himself look good. Every word out of his mouth was about him. How I wish I'd taken your advice."

That made two of us. But at least she allayed my concern that she was hiding something more from me.

"Do you really think Marco can find witnesses to back up my alibi?" she asked.

"With both of us working on it, we should be able to find someone who saw you."

"But Dave said you weren't supposed to get involved."

"Dave always says that. You don't mind if I help Marco, do you?"

"Are you serious? I need you in my corner."

"Then don't fret your pointy head about it. And if you need any assistance with

116

Dave's fees — a loan or anything — just ask, okay? We'll find a way to pay him."

"Thanks, but I've got some savings, and my parents will help — if I need it."

That was a relief. The total sum of my personal savings was in an old piggy bank in my bedroom. "Have you told your parents what happened?"

She nodded. "I didn't want them to hear it from someone else. Even though they live in Chicago now, Mom still talks to friends here."

"How did they take the news?"

"Dad wasn't too freaked out, but Mom got kind of hysterical. You know how she can be."

I knew all too well. I'd spent enough time at her house to know not to mention anything that might give rise to alarm. Mrs. Hiduke made my mother look like the Sea of Tranquility.

I glanced at my watch. "I've got to get back to Bloomers."

Nikki wrapped up her uneaten food and disposed of it, while I hurriedly finished mine. Before heading our separate ways, I said, "Good luck at the hospital."

"Thanks." Impulsively, Nikki gave me a hug. "I don't know what I'd do without you."

On my way back to Bloomers I phoned Marco to give him an update. By the noise in the background, I knew he was working behind the bar. "Did Dave reach you?"

"Yep."

"So you know all about Nikki's boot prints and the clay and everything?"

"Yep."

"So we should start canvassing my neighbors. Can you get away after supper tonight?"

"Whoa, there, Sunshine. You're not working this case."

"Why not? They're *my* neighbors."

He began to talk softly, his voice sounding as though he were cupping the receiver so as not to be overheard. "I appreciate that, but you have to understand that Dave hired me to do a job, and I have a professional obligation to —"

"Yada, yada. I know the drill. And you know there's no way I can sit around twiddling my thumbs when my best friend's life is at stake."

"Okay, hold it right there. It's way too soon to be making that kind of remark —"

The rest of his sentence was lost in loud

cheers from customers at his bar. Obviously, the TV was tuned to a sports channel.

"Listen, I'm kind of busy at the moment. Why don't you come down here at five o'clock for dinner? We can talk more then."

"It's a date, Salvare." He didn't realize it yet, but that date included some canvassing.

Back at Bloomers, Grace had a full house in the coffee-and-tea parlor, and Lottie had a customer at the counter, so I hung up my coat, stowed my purse, and hurried in to refill people's coffee cups and pour freshly brewed tea. As soon as the rush was over, we took a break at one of the white ice-cream tables in the parlor, with cups of vanilla-flavored coffee and a plate of Grace's homemade scones in front of us.

"Tell us the news about Nikki," Grace said, handing me the clotted cream.

"I'll give you the bad news first," I told them, spreading cream on a scone. "As it turns out, Nikki *was* at the murder scene, and her boots might be the evidence that proves it."

I offered Lottie the cream, but she shook her head. I noticed she bypassed the scones, too, and just stuck with her coffee. "What's the good news?" she asked.

"Marco is on the case," I said. "Dave hired

him to canvass the neighbors so we can back up Nikki's alibi."

"Won't you be helping?" Grace asked.

"Dave doesn't think I'll be objective. . . . Lottie, are you ill? You look pale all of a sudden."

Lottie used a napkin to mop sweat from her forehead. "I'm just feeling a little overheated. I might be coming down with a stomach bug. I haven't had much of an appetite today."

"Shall I turn down the heat, do you think?" Grace asked her.

"I'll be okay. Go back to what you were telling us, Abby. Where was Jonas killed?"

"In a model home in a development called Chateaux en Carnations."

"Rather an odd name," Grace commented, while Lottie shifted as though she were in pain.

"Jonas seemed to have a thing for carnations," I said. "According to Dave, someone stabbed Jonas inside his model home and left him there to die."

"How did Nikki happen to be there?" Grace asked. "I thought she'd only gone to dinner."

"That's what she said this morning, but over lunch just now, Nikki admitted that she was so rattled by the cops, she forgot to tell me the rest, which is understandable."

The women exchanged glances; then Lottie said, "You asked her point-blank this morning what happened, right? And she told you she went out to dinner and that was it."

"Right. But she wasn't thinking clearly."

"She was thinking clearly enough to omit part of her story," Lottie said.

"So what are you saying?" I asked.

"You've heard the term 'a lie by omission,' haven't you, dear?" Grace asked.

"Nikki didn't lie," I said, growing perturbed.

"Everyone lies," Lottie replied, "either to protect themselves or to protect someone else's feelings. Herman lies to me every time I ask him if my pants make my butt look big. Truth is, my butt *is* big, no matter what's covering it."

I pondered that observation while I sipped my coffee. "Say you're right about Nikki. Then here's what must have happened. She knew I was upset that she'd gone out with Jonas, so she didn't want to admit to anything more, figuring the whole thing would pass. But then it didn't."

Neither one said anything for a moment; then Grace, being tactful, said, "You know her better than we do, love."

Hmm. I'd always thought so, anyway.

"Good heavens, look at the time," Grace exclaimed. "The Monday-afternoon Ladies' Poetry Society will be here in an hour."

"And let's not forget Jillian will be here at four thirty," I reminded her.

"Don't worry about Jillian," Lottie said. "I've already come up with an idea —" With a gasp of pain, she clutched her abdomen.

"What is it, Lottie, dear?" Grace asked, rising in alarm.

"Sharp . . . pain." Lottie gasped, pressing a hand to her rib cage. "Can't . . . breathe."

Grace quickly felt the back of Lottie's neck. "You have a fever. Abby, run to get our thermometer. Now, tell me exactly where you feel this pain, love."

"Below . . . my ribs," Lottie managed. "Probably indigestion. Breakfast didn't . . . sit well."

I dashed to get the thermometer from our first-aid kit in the kitchen, trusting that Lottie was in capable hands. In one of Grace's previous careers, she'd been a surgical nurse.

When I hurried back, Grace was on the phone calling for an ambulance, and Lottie was nearly bent in two and looking worse by the second. I ran to the coffee counter to get a cool washcloth, then knelt on the floor beside Lottie's chair and put the cloth on her forehead.

"What's wrong with her, Grace?"

"I'd venture to say it's either her gallbladder or a case of gastritis," Grace said.

I prayed she was right, that it wasn't a heart attack. I didn't even want to think about the possibility of losing Lottie.

Five minutes later, the paramedics arrived, and after a brief check, they put Lottie on a gurney to take her to the hospital. As they pulled away with siren blaring and lights flashing, I saw Marco coming up the sidewalk toward Bloomers, concern etched on his masculine features. He stepped into the store, spotted me standing at the bay window, and visibly sighed in relief.

"I was afraid something happened to you."

"Lottie's ill," I said. "Grace thinks it's her stomach or gallbladder."

"I'll call Herman," Grace said, and headed off to phone Lottie's husband.

"I hope it's not a heart attack," I said.

Marco put his arms around me. "I hope not, too, but in any case, we've got excellent trauma care at the hospital. Lottie will be in good hands."

The bell over the door chimed as one of the poetesses came into the shop. "Where is everyone?" she asked, glancing into the empty parlor. "Am I early?"

"I'll let you get back to work," Marco said. "If there's any news, let me know."

Fifteen minutes later, twelve sprightly senior citizens showed up for their weekly poetry session. Grace served tea and scones to the group, answered the phone, and waited on customers, while I worked on my orders, some of which had to be delivered by the end of the day.

At four o'clock, Herman Dombowski called from the hospital to say that Lottie had gastritis and was receiving an antibiotic. Her doctor felt she'd be home within a day or two. I was so relieved, my eyes filled with tears. Grace's did, too, but she claimed it was her allergies and left the room.

Then, half an hour before closing time, Jillian breezed in. Tossing her coat over a stool, she drew back her long hair with a tortoiseshell comb, pushed up her sleeves, and said, "Okay, I'm ready to roll. Where's Lottie?"

Chapter Eight

"Sorry to disappoint you," I said, pushing strands of hair from my face, "but Lottie was rushed to the hospital this afternoon with gastritis."

Jillian stopped modeling her caramel-colored suede slacks and cashmere sweater in front of one of the shiny stainless-steel walk-in coolers. "How awful! Do they have to operate?"

"Apparently all she needs is an antibiotic and rest."

"I'll have to send her a get-well card tomorrow." With a last backward glance at her reflection, she walked around to see what I was doing. "So what are we making?"

"A funeral wreath."

"I mean for my party."

"See those slips of paper on that spindle on my desk? Half of them are orders that have to be delivered to the Happy Dreams

Funeral Home before seven o'clock tonight. The rest have to be ready to go out in the morning."

"Looks like someone has a long evening ahead of her. So what are we making for my party?"

Jillian wasn't good at taking hints. "I can't help you. All those orders are ahead of yours."

"Here's an idea. Let's get mine done and then you can work on the others."

"Here's a better idea. Be creative. Find something else to use as a centerpiece."

"Abby, you know I'm not creative." She flipped back her long hair. "I got the looks, remember? You got the creative gene."

I put down my clippers before I was tempted to use them on her hair, slid off the stool, opened one of the coolers, and scanned the buckets of flowers on the floor. "Jillian?"

As soon as my thickheaded cousin stepped in behind me, I handed her a small bucket filled with floral solution. "Choose the flowers you want in your arrangement and put them in here. Pick two dozen of whichever ones you like. And greenery for filler."

I left her humming happily inside the cooler and returned to the funeral wreath. In ten minutes, Jillian was back with a bucketful of blossoms of various types, all in white. She put the bucket on the work-table and stepped back to admire them. "What do you think?"

"*Lilium,* stephanotis, Madonna Lily, daisy, camellia, spider mums . . . Very nice. I like your choice of greenery, too. Now choose a container." I pointed to the back wall, covered with three long shelves stocked with pots, containers, and vases of all shapes, colors, and sizes.

"How am I supposed to choose from all those?"

"Easy. Find something to fit your color scheme that will look nice in the middle of your dining room table. You don't want a tall container or your guests won't be able to see over your arrangement. Something low-profile, maybe oval, would be nice."

While Jillian perused the shelves, I finished the wreath, stored it in the other walk-in cooler, and pulled the next order from the spindle.

"I like this one," Jillian said, placing an opalescent white oval bowl beside her flow-ers.

"Great choice. Next comes the green foam." I cut a hunk of wet foam to fit Jillian's bowl, another for my container, then showed her how to fasten it securely to the bottom. Then, using a floral knife, I demonstrated how to trim the lower leaves from the stems, cut the stem to the desired length underwater, then insert the cut end into the foam.

"The tricky part," I said as I worked on my own project, "is deciding on an overall shape for your design, such as triangular, round, low, Oriental, et cetera, and then figuring out where you want each flower to go. For instance, a spider mum is frilly and full, so to balance it out, you'd want to pair it with something sleek and elegant, such as a calla. See? Like this." I paused to demonstrate with the arrangement in front of me. "Don't worry if you have to redo them. Floral arranging takes a creative eye and a lot of experience."

We both worked intensely for a while; then Jillian said, "How's this?"

I glanced over at her arrangement and my mouth fell open. She had created a beautifully balanced, all-white centerpiece that was worthy of a photo in a florist's magazine.

"It's gorgeous. How did you do it?"

"I just imagined the oil painting of flowers hanging in my dining room."

"You imagined it?"

"I stare at it every evening during dinner.

Claymore isn't the sparkling conversationalist he appears to be, you know."

I nearly laughed out loud. Claymore appeared to be many things — nerdy, wimpy, and shy among them — but never a conversationalist, sparkling or otherwise.

"What's the next step?" Jillian asked.

"You're done. You just need to wrap it so you can carry it home."

"How much do I owe you?"

That was a first. Jillian never paid for anything. "Don't worry about it."

She got her wallet from her purse and pulled out a hundred-dollar bill. "That should cover the cost of the flowers."

I was stunned. "That's way too much. I can't accept that."

"Then it's for the floral lesson, too. Now, how do I wrap this? I've got to get home before the caterer arrives."

Wow! Maybe there was hope for Jillian after all.

She picked up her arrangement and headed for the curtain, pausing to leave me with one last thought. "I never realized I had such a knack for flower arranging. I just might have to open my own flower shop."

Grace waited until the coast was clear, then poked her head through the curtain. "It's five o'clock, love. How are we doing?"

I glanced at the stack of orders. "I've got a long way to go."

"If you have any funeral arrangements ready, I'll take them over to Happy Dreams."

I helped Grace load our leased minivan, then came back inside to hear my cell phone ringing. "Hey," Marco said. "Any word on Lottie?"

I updated him on Lottie's condition, then began to vent about Jillian, until he said, "It's almost five thirty. Why don't you come down for dinner and tell me all about it?"

"I'm not going to be able to make it, Marco. I'm still working on orders that have to be at Happy Dreams by seven tonight, and there's more that have to go out in the morning."

"Then I'll bring dinner to you. See you in a few minutes."

Fifteen minutes later, Marco and I were sitting at the tiny counter in the kitchen discussing Nikki's case while downing pulled-pork sandwiches and sweet-potato fries, a new addition to Down the Hatch's menu.

"I'm going to start canvassing people in your apartment complex as soon as I finish here," Marco said, polishing off his fries. "Chris is working a double shift to cover for me so I can get going on this. It could take a few days to catch everyone at home."

"When I get these orders finished, I'll join you. And by the way, this sandwich is great."

Marco raised an eyebrow. "As good as the pulled-pork sandwiches in Key West?"

"Is there any way I can answer that and not hurt your feelings?"

One corner of his mouth curved mischievously. "I can think of a way. Tell you what. You finish up here, I'll do the canvassing, and we'll meet up at your apartment later."

"We can get the canvassing done a lot quicker if I help."

"Abby, I know you're in a hurry to clear Nikki, but you've got to respect Dave's wishes. He told you not to get involved for a good reason — objectivity."

I rolled my eyes. "I helped find the murderer when you were a suspect, didn't I? So why is it so important that I be objective now?"

"Because otherwise you're going into it with as much of an agenda as the cops have. They want to prove their suspect is guilty, so they'll ignore any evidence to the contrary, while you'll ignore any evidence that points to her guilt. See what I'm saying? An investigator's mind-set has to be totally focused on seeking the truth no matter what the outcome."

"I can do that, Marco."

He folded his arms and leaned back. "Let me ask you a question: Is there any way Nikki could have killed Jonas, even accidentally?"

"No. She's not a killer."

"And there it is. You're not being objective."

"What I'm doing is weighing what I know to be true about Nikki against what the cops want to believe about her. Kind of a checks-and-balances system."

"Considering how much Nikki kept from you, what *do* you know to be true about her?"

At once, Grace's words came back to me — *You've heard the term "a lie by omission," haven't you, dear?* — and a sliver of doubt began to creep in. What if I didn't know my best friend as well as I thought I did?

The phone rang, saving me from further argument, at least for the time being. I glanced at the screen and saw *Mom* on the caller ID. "It's my mom," I told Marco as I reached for the phone.

He balled up the paper from his sandwich, tossed it in the waste can, and rose. "Give her my best, okay?"

"You don't have to leave," I whispered.

"I need to start canvassing." He gave me a kiss on the forehead, then headed for the back door. "See you later."

"Hi, Mom! How was your weekend in Chicago?"

"Fun! We got back only an hour ago — but we can talk about that some other time. What's this about Nikki being a suspect in a murder investigation?"

I groaned inwardly. I'd have to tell her just enough to satisfy her curiosity; otherwise I'd be on the phone for an hour explaining what happened, Mom would be up all night worrying, and everyone would suffer . . . except I was about to do what Nikki had done — lie by omission. Disturbingly, it came easier than I thought.

"Okay, here's the story. Nikki went on a date with a guy she met last week, and, unfortunately, he was murdered later that night. So naturally the cops have to check her out. It's routine stuff. Ask Dad if you don't believe me."

"I don't want to involve your dad unless I have to. You know how he worries."

There was the pot calling the kettle black.

"Poor Nikki. Such a little lamb. I can only imagine how this is affecting her."

Little lamb? Nikki was a gazelle. "She's doing okay, Mom. She even went to work today. And speaking of work, I really have to get back to mine. I have orders to get over to Happy Dreams and more orders to go out tomorrow, so if I hear anything more, I'll let you know."

"Abigail, are you keeping something from me? Is there something else going on?"

Oh, no! Had she heard about my trip with Marco? "Why would you think that?"

"You sound different, like when you were little and had a secret. A mother knows these things. Is there something you're afraid to share with me?"

Divert, Abby, divert!

"Well . . . I don't want to alarm you, Mom, but Lottie is in the hospital."

Ten minutes later, I was off the hook, but only after assuring Mom I would send Lottie a get-well basket from her and my dad first thing in the morning. I finished the remaining funeral arrangements and took them over to Happy Dreams, then completed the orders for morning delivery, cleaned up the workroom, and wrote out a list of supplies to replenish.

When I finally dragged myself in the apartment door at nine o'clock that evening,

134

Simon was waiting to greet me. To express his delight at having me home, he wound between my legs, becoming a moving obstacle course as I stumbled to the kitchen to fix his supper. Then, as he gulped down salmon, my cell phone began to chirp. I glanced at the screen and saw Marco's name.

"I'm done canvassing for the night. Want me to come up?"

Like he needed to ask. I buzzed him in, then waited by the door, hoping for some good news. Marco stepped inside, gave me a kiss, then scratched Simon behind the ears.

"Want a beer, glass of wine, cup of coffee?" I asked.

"Water, thanks."

"Did you have any trouble getting people in the building to talk to you?" I asked as Marco took off his leather coat and hung it over a chair back.

"Nope, and only a few people weren't home, so I lucked out."

"Did you find any witnesses to verify Nikki's alibi?" I called from the kitchen.

"Yep, a couple on the first floor who saw her enter the apartment building at two o'clock in the morning."

"Two o'clock? That can't be right. Nikki

was home around midnight."

"They were certain about the time, Abby."

I handed him the glass of water. "Then they mistook her for someone else."

"They identified her from a photo."

"That's impossible . . . unless Nikki was wrong about the time she got home."

"Or lied."

She couldn't have lied. Not about that, too. I rubbed my forehead, trying to come up with a logical explanation. "Maybe Nikki came home at midnight, then went back outside later to . . . I don't know . . . maybe get something out of her car — like her cell phone."

"Go back outside in the middle of a cold January night two hours after she supposedly got home? Come on, Sunshine, you know that doesn't make sense."

I couldn't think of an explanation that did make sense. It made me wonder if Nikki was hiding anything else. "Have you told Dave about the witnesses?"

"Right before I got here. He was trying to reach Nikki to set up a meeting tomorrow."

"She'll have her phone turned off until her shift ends. Hospital policy." I glanced at the clock. "She'll be home in a couple of hours. I can't wait to hear her explanation."

"I'd be glad to stay and wait, but I need

to make arrangements with my bar staff tonight so I can take time off to investigate. I'm going to meet with Dave at eleven o'clock tomorrow morning to lay out a plan."

"I understand."

Marco put his arms around me and rested his chin on top of my head. "I know this is tough on you, baby, but you need some shut-eye. Talk to Nikki in the morning."

"I won't even be able to close my eyes until I get some answers, Marco. I don't know whether I'm more worried about Nikki or angry with her. She's always seemed like a sister to me, but now she's this person I don't understand."

Marco didn't say anything, just held me.

"Did I ever tell you how I met Nikki?"

"Didn't she fall off her Rollerblades in front of your house?"

"The summer before third grade. We'd just moved into our house, and I hadn't met any of the kids on the block yet. One afternoon, I was sulking on the porch, bemoaning my lack of a social life, when this skinny, gawky blond girl skated past, secretly checking me out. On her fourth pass, she hit a crack in the sidewalk, took a bad spill, and tore up her knees. My mom and I got her bandaged up, I helped her limp home, and we've been best friends ever since." I sighed sadly. "I wish I could slap a bandage on this and make it go away."

"Anything I can do to make you feel better?"

Without a moment's hesitation I said, "Let me help you investigate."

Marco sighed. "Abby, we've already discussed this. Remember Dave telling you he didn't want you to get involved?"

"With the *canvassing*, Marco. He didn't say anything about a suspect search."

"You're splitting hairs."

I pushed away from him. "If you know me at all, then you understand I have to be a part of the hunt for the killer."

"Don't put me into another impossible situation, Abby. I won't go behind Dave's back. That could cost me my private investigator's license as well as any future cases from him, not to mention the strain it would put on us. I just got you back, Sunshine. Let's not tempt fate, okay?"

What could I say to that? It wasn't right to ask Marco to do something unethical. I didn't want to be unreasonable, but at the same time, it wasn't my nature to give up. "What if you were to take on an intern? Would he object to that?"

"A PI intern?"

I wrapped my arms around his ribs. "Your very own private intern. I'm sure there are still a few things you could teach me." I pressed my lips against his, giving him a long, intense kiss that nearly made me forget what we'd been talking about.

Then Marco nuzzled my earlobe and murmured, "You're not trying to bribe me with a kiss, are you?"

"Would I stoop to bribery? Besides, it wouldn't work on you . . . would it?"

"No." Marco wound his fingers through my hair, his kisses growing more passionate. I could feel his heart thudding against mine as our bodies locked together. "Abby," he murmured after a few moments, his lips hot on my throat, "if we keep this up, I won't get back to the bar to do my work before closing time."

"Would that be such a bad thing?"

"This doesn't mean I'm agreeing to the internship."

"Consider it my audition then."

"An audition?" Marco's mouth curved up at one corner in a roguish smile. "I like the sound of that." He dipped his head down for another steamy kiss that left both of us breathless; then he turned off the lamp beside the sofa and led me toward my bedroom.

It appeared Marco's work would wait after all.

CHAPTER NINE

When Nikki walked in the door after midnight, Simon jumped off the sofa and ran to greet her. I played it cool, lounging on the sofa in my pj's, flipping through a floral magazine.

"How did it go at work?" I called, as she hung up her coat in the front closet.

"Not bad. Everyone was very kind and supportive. I can't tell you what a relief that was."

I heard Nikki open the refrigerator; then she called, "I'm surprised you're still up. Want some Chubby Hubby ice cream?"

"No, thanks. I'm about to hit the sack." I followed her to the kitchen, watching as she scooped two mounds of chocolate ice cream into her bowl.

She glanced at me. "Sure you don't want some?"

"Positive."

She put the carton in the freezer, rinsed

out the scoop, then carried her bowl of ice cream to the living room to turn on the TV as though it were just another normal night. Trying to maintain my cool, I perched on the arm of the sofa. "I was thinking about lunch today. I felt bad that I had to cut you off so I could get back to work."

"You didn't cut me off."

"Don't you remember? You didn't finish telling me what happened on your date."

"Yes, I did."

"Oh, wait, that's right. You said Jonas took you home around midnight."

Nikki took a big mouthful of ice cream, then started flipping through the TV channels.

Trying not to be too obvious, I said, "You must have been exhausted after putting up with his bragging all evening. I'll bet you came home and went straight to bed."

She found a home-decorating show on HGTV and put down the remote. I couldn't tell whether she was avoiding the question or felt there was no need to answer.

"So, did you?" I asked, trying to sound casually interested.

"Did I go straight to bed? What kind of question is that?" she asked, digging her spoon into the mound of creamy delight.

A weird one. But I couldn't think of a way

to get the information without sounding like I was interrogating her, so I sat there swinging my feet, feeling stupid.

She gave me a quick glance. "What's wrong? I thought you were going to bed."

"Okay, look, I'll just be blunt. Did you go back out again after you got home that night?"

"Why are you quizzing me? I already told you what happened." She flipped to the DIY Network. "Besides, what makes you think I went out again?"

"Because Marco found witnesses in our building who saw you come in at two o'clock in the morning."

Nikki went completely still. "Is that why Dave wants to see me tomorrow?"

"I'd bet on it."

She shut off the TV, put her bowl aside, then stared at the blank screen until her eyes filled with tears. Her hands came up to cover her face as she sobbed, "Yes, I went back out."

"For God's sake, Nikki, why didn't you tell me?"

"I didn't want you to know."

"You didn't want Dave to know either? Your attorney? The man who's looking out for your well-being? Are you crazy?"

She shook her head, sobbing harder. "I

can't believe this is happening."

She couldn't believe it? I was totally floored. Nikki had withheld *more* information. What else hadn't she revealed? With a sick feeling in the pit of my stomach, I asked, "What were you doing until two o'clock in the morning?"

She looked at me, aghast. "You say that like you think I murdered Jonas. Is that what you think, Abby?" She jumped up and ran to her room, crying, "You are unbelievable."

With more calmness than I thought I had in me, I collected her bowl and spoon and took them to the kitchen. Nikki had lied three times and was still dodging my questions. Did I even want to know more?

I found her on her bed, facedown on her comforter, weeping her heart out, with a startled Simon pressed up against the headboard, ready to run.

"I don't think you killed Jonas, Nikki, but would you give me some kind of explanation for where you were?"

Sniffling back tears, she sat up and reached for a tissue from the box on her nightstand. "Jonas dropped me off at midnight, Abby. I *swear* it. Then I got in my car and drove around."

"For two hours?"

"Yes!" Then she looked at the tissue in

her hand. "No."

My stomach tightened. "What else did you do?"

She blew her nose, got up to throw the tissue away, and came back, sinking onto the bed with a big sigh. "Went over to Scott's house."

"You went to your ex-boyfriend's house? The guy who dumped you? Why?"

"To see if we could work things out and maybe get back together." She glanced sheepishly at me. "I know that was a stupid thing to do, but after spending the evening with Jonas, I started appreciating what a really great guy Scott was."

"So great that he dumped you."

"It wasn't exactly like that. He *broke up* with me because I was acting like an idiot. I thought he was seeing someone else, and I kept bugging him about it. He finally said that if I couldn't trust him, then we shouldn't be together. So I stormed out and that was the end of it."

"You couldn't have confided in me?"

"You couldn't have told me about going to Key West with Marco?" she shot back.

"This is a little more serious than a weekend getaway."

Her chin began to quiver. "You have no idea how humiliating this has been, Abby."

"Don't even talk about humiliation until you've been kicked out of law school and very publicly dropped by your fiancé. Besides, nothing could be worse than letting people think you killed Jonas. At least you have an alibi witness now. Scott can verify that you were at his house."

She reached for another tissue. "Scott didn't see me."

"What?"

"After I got there I chickened out, so I sat in my car trying to talk myself into it. Then, when I finally gathered up enough courage to go to the door, I caught a glimpse of him through the blinds" — her chin quivered faster — "with another woman. I was too embarrassed to tell anyone." She flopped over onto the bed, sobbing.

I was so angry with her for not confiding in me, I wanted to walk out and close the door on her *and* our friendship. Then I reminded myself that Nikki had been there for me in many crises. I couldn't desert her because she'd hurt my feelings. And, in fact, I *had* kept my trip with Marco from her, which I knew hurt her feelings.

Taking a steadying breath, I said, "I'm sorry, Nikki. That must have hurt to see Scott with another woman."

"That wasn't the worst part. I waited in

my car for over an hour, hoping the woman would leave so I could beg Scott to take me back. How pathetic is that?"

So pathetic I didn't know where to begin. When had my best friend turned into such a wuss? "Did the woman finally leave?"

She shrugged. "I gave up and went home."

"Didn't it occur to you the detectives would eventually discover that you went back out? Nikki, do you have any idea how much trouble you're in? You can't keep this kind of information a secret. That's suicide. You need to explain everything to Dave tomorrow so he can figure out how to repair the damage — *if* he can repair it."

She gazed at me tearfully. "You believe I didn't kill Jonas, don't you?"

"No doubt about it. I just wish you'd been straight with me. What am I supposed to think when I keep finding out that you're holding back? It makes me feel like you don't trust me."

"God, Abby, I'm so sorry. You know I'd trust you with my life."

"Then you've got to be up-front with Dave and me from now on, no matter what, okay? Will you promise?"

She sighed wearily. "I'd better tell you the rest then."

There was more? Could her situation possibly get any worse?

"I went into the model home with Jonas."

Oh, yeah, that was worse. "Why?"

"He cut his hand on the wooden railing over the footbridge, so we went inside to wash off the blood. I helped him remove a big splinter and clean out the wound; then he took me home. I swear on the Bible that's *all* that happened."

"Nikki, if you were inside the model home, your DNA and fingerprints will be there."

"All I touched was a bathroom faucet."

"That's enough to leave fingerprints!" I wanted to throw up. With what the cops already had, that was more than enough evidence to make her look as guilty as hell. "What time is your meeting with Dave tomorrow?"

"Ten thirty." She gazed at me through red-rimmed eyes. "Are you worried?"

"Yes."

"Me too." She curled up on her bed in a fetal position, reminding me of the little girl who'd fallen in front of my house. "How I wish I'd never met Jonas Treat," she whispered.

How *I* wished I'd never seen the ad for Cloud Nine. I lay down beside her and put my arm around her. "It'll be okay, Nikki.

148

You've got Dave, Marco, and me on your side. And tomorrow, Marco and I are going to start looking for the real killer in earnest."

I meant it, too. Nikki wasn't a murderer, and I'd stake my flower shop on it. I only hoped it didn't come to that.

When I walked into Bloomers at eight o'clock the next morning, I smelled the welcoming aroma of Grace's coffee but didn't hear the familiar sound of Lottie's humming to her country music on the radio. I missed that.

"Morning, Grace," I called, shedding my scarf and coat.

"Good morning, love. How are we today?"

"Tired," I called from the workroom. "Late night."

Grace breezed through the curtain moments later with a cup and saucer in hand. "This should perk you up. I've taken the liberty of adding your half-and-half. I hope that's all right."

I tasted the coffee and smiled. "It's perfection. Thanks, Grace."

"Now tell me what has you so down in the mouth."

Grace clicked her tongue as I gave her a rundown on Nikki's current situation. Then she said, "I was afraid Nikki wasn't being truthful. Given her circumstances, it defies belief that she could be so imprudent. As Albert Schweitzer said, 'Truth has not special time of its own. Its hour is now — always and indeed then most truly when it seems unsuitable to actual circumstances.' "

"That's what I told her last night." Only not nearly as eloquently.

"Has she finally revealed everything that happened, do you think?"

A week ago I wouldn't have hesitated to say yes. Now, I just wasn't sure. "For her sake, I hope so, Grace."

"For your sake, too, love." She handed me a message, then, in usual Grace style, spared me the effort of reading it. "Your mother will be in after school today. She promised you'd be bowled over by her visit."

"Sounds like Mom wants to drop off a new art project."

"I'm afraid I must agree, love."

My mother, Maureen "Mad Mo" Knight, taught kindergarten during the week and created art on the weekends. Her medium changed constantly — neon-colored clay, giant wooden beads, small mirrored tiles, and rainbow-colored feathers, to name a few. Usually, Mom showed up at Bloomers on Mondays to surprise us with her latest endeavors — she was a big fan of surprises

— but due to her trip to Chicago, she was off schedule this week.

Unfortunately, Mom expected us to sell her so-called works of art, thinking she was helping us boost sales. We usually displayed her piece until someone with a sense of humor bought it or, if it was really ugly, until Lottie could sneak it down to the basement.

"Is she making bowls now, do you think?" Grace called, returning to the parlor.

I massaged my temples, trying to stop a headache from coming on. "Let's hope that's all it is."

While Grace prepared the parlor for our usual morning customers, I started the get-well basket for Lottie from my parents. I was putting off calling Marco to tell him the rest of Nikki's story because I'd slept very little and wasn't in the mood to debate the issue of helping him hunt for the killer. In my mind, the decision was made. If he wouldn't let me work with him as his intern, I'd find a way to work without him.

I filled a short, square glass vase with white narcissuses, pink tulips, and blue grape hyacinths, pink and blue being Lottie's favorite colors. The vase was small enough to fit into a gift basket, and short enough that it shouldn't get knocked off a bedside table. I left the bulbs attached to the flower stems so Lottie could replant them in her garden in the spring; then I tucked the arrangement inside a generous wicker basket along with wrapped scones, herbal teas, a Dove chocolate bar, and the latest edition of *Florists' Review* magazine.

Arranging flowers always gave me a fresh perspective, so as I worked, I started a mental list of who I needed to talk to about Jonas Treat. First on my list was Robin Lennox, the jilted ex-fiancée, followed by Carmen Gold, the Cloud Nine event organizer. Maybe her hostile glances had meant nothing more than that Jonas had been rude to her, but I needed to know. If nothing else, Carmen might share with me the names of the other women Jonas met at the event.

As I was trimming ribbon to tie around the basket handle, Grace came into the workroom to announce that it was time to open the shop. Seeing the basket she said, "Is that for Lottie?"

"Yes. My mom ordered it."

"A paperback mystery would be a lovely addition, wouldn't it? You know how Lottie loves them. Perhaps you can stop at the hospital gift shop. . . ." She paused, hearing furious rapping on the front door, then went to peer through the curtain. "Good heavens, it's your cousin."

Jillian? At nine in the morning? I put down my scissors and followed Grace into the shop. "Something bad must have happened to get her out of bed so early."

Strangely, Jillian didn't appear to be in any distress. In fact, she was smiling and waving through the beveled-glass pane in the door, then pointing to her watch and wagging her finger. "It's two minutes after nine," she chided, as I stepped back to let her sail past me. "You're late."

She made straight for the workroom, where she draped her coat over the back of my desk chair, removed her beret, shook out her shimmering coppery locks, and pushed up the sleeves of her emerald green silk sweater. "What should I do first?"

"What are you talking about?"

"You said yesterday that you're short-handed, so I'm here to help."

The curtain trembled behind her. Grace was eavesdropping again.

"I appreciate the offer, Jillian, but I don't have time to train you today."

"Train me? I know how to run a business, Abby. And by the way, my all-white arrangement was the hit of the dinner party. So tell me what you need done."

This was so unlike my self-centered cousin

that I couldn't help but suspect she had an ulterior motive. "Why are you doing this?"

"Because I wuv my wittle cuz," she said, and came at me as if to hug me. Luckily, the bell over the door chimed, causing her to change direction. "Customers," Jillian sang out, and headed for the curtain. Her hormones had to be out of whack.

The bell jingled twice more as I hurried after her. Seeing the new arrivals head toward the parlor for their morning caffeine fix, Jillian stationed herself behind the cash register in the shop. "Grace has the parlor, so I'll manage this room. You go do your thing in the workroom."

"You don't know how to work our cash register, Jillian. It's an antique and takes some getting used to."

"Abby, I'm a Harvard grad. How hard can it be? Now would you be an angel and bring me a cup of coffee? No, make it a latte. A soy latte. With cinnamon. No, nutmeg. Wait. Make that chocolate . . . a soy mocha latte."

I took a deep breath and marched into the parlor, where Grace was waiting on customers. At the coffee counter, I prepared my cousin's latte just as Grace came back to refill her pot.

"Sorry," I whispered. "I had no idea Jillian was coming today."

"As long as she's here, you may as well make the best of it," Grace whispered back. "We could use a delivery-person."

Grace was a genius. That would keep Jillian out of my way.

"Here you go, Jill." I put her coffee on the check-out counter. "When you're finished, I'd like you to make some deliveries."

She sucked in her breath.

"What?" I asked.

"Deliveries?"

"Yes, deliveries. That's one of the best parts of the floral business. You get to hand people their flowers and watch their faces light up."

"But then I'd have to drive that bugly leased delivery van."

"It's not . . . Wait. Did you just say *bugly?*"

"I'm not about to say *butt-ugly.* It's too . . . bugly. So I shortened it."

"The van isn't *bugly,* Jill; it's serviceable. And it's not actually a van; it's a minivan."

"Frog or toad, Abby. They're both bugly. I wouldn't be caught dead kissing either one."

"Fine. I'll make the deliveries, but that means you'll have to wait on customers."

"Not a problem. I wait on my clients all the time."

"I don't mean waiting on them as in while

155

they try on clothing in a dressing room. I mean help them make choices, take their orders —"

"Will you stop treating me like I'm five years old? Just go do your deliveries and leave everything to me." At my hesitation, she motioned me away. "Go! Bloomers is in good hands with Jillian on the job."

I felt Grace's shudder from a room away.

CHAPTER TEN

After making my deliveries, I stopped at the hospital to give Lottie her basket. She looked much better than the last time I'd seen her, and wouldn't let me leave until I'd filled her in on everything she'd missed. I kept my report light, figuring she didn't need any depressing news, and returned to Bloomers just as one of my steady customers exited the shop without her usual bouquet of flowers, which she liked to select herself from the glass-fronted display case.

"Good morning, Mrs. Tanner," I called.

She was about to cross the street, but came back toward me. "It was a good morning until I came *here*. Abby, you really should screen your help before you hire them. Your new clerk refused to sell me the flowers I wanted."

"I'm so sorry. The young woman is my . . . um" — did I really want to admit sharing a gene pool with Jillian? — "my temp. She'll be gone tomorrow. Why don't you come inside and have a cup of coffee or tea on the house? Then you can select flowers for your bouquet afterward. I'm offering a one-day-only special, half off any order." Made up on the spot just for her.

Mrs. Tanner gave it a moment's thought, then accompanied me inside. Jillian was on the phone behind the counter and started to wave at me. Then she saw Mrs. Tanner and her eyes narrowed.

I ushered Mrs. Tanner into the parlor and turned her over to Grace, who would know just how to placate the woman. Then I headed straight for Jill, who was still on the phone.

"Is that all you want to spend?" she said to the person on the other end of the line. "Didn't you just say this was for your mother? Would it kill you to throw in some roses?"

I grabbed the phone from her hand. "Hello, this is Abby Knight. I apologize for my rude employee, who I assure you won't be working here after today. How can I help you?"

"Abby? What happened to my wife? What's going on?"

Yikes. It was Claymore, Jillian's husband. Brother of my ex-fiancé.

158

With a sigh of regret, I handed the phone back to my cousin and went straight into the workroom to bury myself in flowers.

"That was rude," Jillian said, sailing through the curtain moments later.

"*That* was rude? How about the way you treated Mrs. Tanner? Why wouldn't you let her pick out her own flowers?"

"She has abominable taste. She wanted to mix freesia with baby's breath."

As if Jillian had suddenly become a flower expert. "It's Mrs. Tanner's choice, Jill. She's paying for them. Do you understand? The customer is *always* right. Memorize that!"

Jillian flipped her hair away from her face and started toward the curtain. "You'd never make it as a personal shopper."

If Jillian wasn't careful, she wouldn't make it to noon.

At eleven thirty, Marco stopped in to tell me about his meeting with Dave. I led him into the parlor, which was empty at the moment and, more important, away from Jillian's alert ears.

"Why is your cousin here?" Marco asked quietly as I brought over our coffees.

"I made the mistake of telling her about Lottie's gastritis. For some as-yet-unknown reason, Jillian decided that she should help me out." I paused to stir half-and-half into my cup, then glanced over my shoulder to be sure my cousin couldn't hear me.

"She's a disaster, Marco. She's rude to the customers and won't make deliveries because the minivan is ugly. I spent fifteen minutes trying to teach her how to answer the phone with, 'Bloomers Flower Shop, how can I help you?' instead of, 'Jillian Knight Osborne, personal shopper and florist extraordinaire. Talk to me.' "

"Fire her."

"How do I fire a volunteer? And if I order her to leave . . . well, I don't even want to think about the repercussions within our family. The truth is, we *are* shorthanded. I don't know how I'm going to get away to —" I caught myself before I made the mistake of finishing that sentence, since I hadn't talked Marco into letting me help him, and instead ended with — "make deliveries." I took a break for a sip of coffee to give my mind time to regroup. "How did your meeting go?"

"Dave filled me in on the latest development with Nikki. I suppose she told you last night what she did between midnight and two o'clock Monday morning."

"Yes. Now I'm really scared. Her finger-

160

prints are bound to be inside that model home."

"They are. The cops lifted them yesterday. Dave said he wouldn't be surprised if they indicted Nikki for murder before the week is out."

A week? How would Marco clear Nikki in such a short time? And how was I going to squeeze in a few hours to assist him? With one employee out sick, and a self-indulgent cousin to monitor, my hands were tied.

Marco pulled a notebook out of his coat pocket. "Do you want to help?"

I immediately perked up. "Sure, but I don't know when I'll be able to get away."

"Not that kind of help." He opened his notebook so I could see it. "Here are the names Dave and I came up with. Take a look at them, see if you can think of anyone else."

It wasn't what I was hoping for, but it was something. " 'Number one,' " I read. " 'Anyone who filed a recent complaint or lawsuit against Jonas Treat or his development company.' "

I thought about it for a moment and decided it would be a good time for me to mention my internship again. "That's going to take some time to investigate."

"I know, but it's going to the bottom of

my list, so I'm not concerned at this point. I've got a greater chance of finding viable suspects by talking to the others on the list first."

Crap. That hadn't turned out the way I'd hoped. I took a sip of coffee and continued. " 'Number two, Jonas's last partner, Duke Kessler, of Kessler Realty.' "

I glanced up at Marco. "The Duke of New Chapel? Marco, do you remember those crazy television ads he did where he wore a long purple velvet robe and gold crown, and sat on a throne? Duke Kessler was quite a showman. But didn't he leave town?"

"Not according to Dave. After Kessler and Jonas split their partnership, Kessler closed his realty office and opened up a fitness club called Put Up Your Dukes Boxing Gym."

"From real estate to a fitness club? That's quite a career switch."

"Especially considering that Kessler had built up a little fiefdom in the real estate world. Dave said the business community was shocked when he suddenly called it quits. I don't know how Jonas fits into that picture, but since Kessler's switch came after their split, it's worth investigating."

From out in the shop I heard Jillian give a yelp, then cry, "I hate this cash register!"

I continued down the list. " 'Number

three, former girlfriends.' That reminds me — Lottie mentioned that one of the employees at Tom's Green Thumb Nursery and Greenhouse was engaged to Jonas. Damn. I can't remember her name. It'll come to me, though. . . .

" 'Number four,' " I continued, " 'the construction crew'?"

"The crew Jonas hired to build homes in Chat-too whatever Carnations," Marco said.

"It's pronounced *shattose ahn carnah-syion*," Jillian said from the other side of the doorway. "I took French in college." The phone rang just then, sending her clicking away on her spike-heeled boots.

Marco lowered his voice to say, "I'm not pronouncing it that way."

I patted his hand. "You don't have to. So what's your reason for interviewing the construction crew?"

"Developers often have reputations for getting in financial binds and not paying their workers. You know, disgruntled employee kills boss?"

From the other room I heard, "Jillian Knight Osborne, personal shopp— I mean, Bloomers. Talk to me."

I glanced at Marco. "How about disgruntled boss chokes employee?"

"Fire her."

"If only that were an option. But going back to the construction crew, there must be dozens of them working on houses out there. It'll take time to interview them." I was still angling for that internship.

"But only one crew was working for Jonas," Marco explained.

"Still, I'll bet there's a dozen guys you'll have to talk to."

"If it comes to that, I may have to get the okay from Dave to hire additional investigators."

"Nikki can't afford that, Marco."

"She can't afford not to, Sunshine."

"But *you* can afford a free intern." I gave him a big smile.

"I think you have enough to handle here." He nodded toward the doorway, where Jillian was probably lurking.

Damn it, I *had* to find a way to help somehow. " 'Number five, Jonas's family members.' "

"Cross that one off. Jonas doesn't have any family in New Chapel. He has only one sister, and she just arrived from Phoenix, Arizona, this morning to take care of funeral matters. Jonas's father also lives in Phoenix, but he's in a nursing home and is too sick to travel."

I borrowed Marco's pen and drew a line

through five. "Number six, the women on Jonas's list at the speed-dating event." I pushed the notebook toward Marco. "Put down Carmen Gold, the Cloud Nine event organizer. I saw her give Jonas some surprisingly angry glances during the evening. Later, after we learned his Ferrari had been pushed into a cement post by a hit-and-run driver, she seemed very satisfied about it."

"Carmen Gold," Marco said, writing down her name. "Do you know anything about her?"

"I think someone at the event mentioned that Carmen is from Chicago. She's probably in her late thirties, very stylish, with a real passion for anything silver — clothes, jewelry, even a platinum dye on her hair."

"Okay, anyone else from that event? Women Jonas made passes at? Guys he ticked off?"

"Not that I saw. There was this odd woman who wanted to know if I'd had the pleasure of meeting Jonas. I thought she was being sarcastic; then she pointed to Jonas talking to Nikki and wanted to know who Nikki was, almost as though she was jealous of Nikki. After I told her, she walked out of the room. Come to think of it, Jonas's car was hit shortly after."

Marco wrote it down. "I'll have to see

what I can find out about the hit-and-run investigation. Was this woman still around when the Ferrari was hit?"

"I don't know. I wasn't looking for her."

"Did you get her name?"

"I'm trying to remember. . . . Her family owns a dry-cleaning business. Frey's. That's it. Iris Frey, because I remember thinking that she looked nothing like her floral counterpart."

Marco added her name. "Anyone else I should write down?"

"Is there a way to find out the name of the anonymous tipster? I'd sure like to know who alerted the cops that Nikki went out with Jonas. It sounds to me like a spiteful act."

"That's why I put ex-girlfriends on the list. Could be a vengeful ex who's been tailing Jonas or having him tailed. I've worked on a few cases like that."

"How would the ex know Nikki's name to call in a tip?"

"Follow Jonas, get addresses of people he visits, do a Web search. That's how I'd find out."

"Or perhaps the tipster recognized Nikki from the speed-dating event, or even the hospital, for that matter. Did Dave have any more information on the knife used in the murder?"

Marco checked his notes. "From the stab wounds, they know the blade is at least two inches wide and four inches long, very sharp, which means it was either brand-new or someone had recently sharpened it. The cops are dredging the stream by the model home."

He stuck the notebook back inside his coat pocket and got up. "I'm heading to Nikki's ex-boyfriend's neighborhood now to see if I can find any alibi witnesses there; then I'll pay a visit to Duke Kessler at his gym." Marco feigned a punch at an imaginary opponent. "I'm a little rusty. It's been a long time since I've boxed. Maybe he'll have some tips for me."

"You were a boxer?"

"In the army." One corner of his mouth curved up as he pulled me against him. "Want me to show you some of my moves?"

"If they're anything like the moves you showed me in Key West, Salvare, I'm in for quite a workout."

"I think I've created a monster," he murmured, then dipped his head for a steamy kiss.

From the other room I heard Grace say, "What are you listening to, Jillian?"

At once, quiet footsteps moved away from

the doorway.

"Thanks for the java," Marco said, cutting our kiss short. "I'll call you later."

I walked him to the front door, then stood at the bay window to watch him stride down the block. If only I had time to help him.

"You two sure have become disturvable," Jillian remarked from behind the counter.

"What does that mean?" I asked, in no mood for Jillian's nonsense.

"Ooey-gooey. You know, like, *ew,* with goo attached."

"Why do you make up words? It's really annoying. And we're not ooey-gooey."

"I don't make them up. It's a fusion process. 'Disturbingly lovable' sounds so" — she waved her hand in the air — "duller-less. But *disturvable* has panache."

"Marco and I are close, Jill; that's all."

"Just close? With that kind of kiss? Right. When's the wedding?"

"We just got back together, for God's sake. As you well know, I've never had a relationship that lasted more than a year, so I'm not about to rush this one."

Jillian made a sad face. "You're right, poor thing. You weren't exactly the most popular girl in high school, were you?"

I gave my cousin a scowl. "I had dates."

"With gerds," she said, snickering.

168

"Gerds?"

"You know, geeky nerds."

"I just hadn't blossomed yet. I was very popular in college. In fact, I was, well, wild."

She howled with laughter. "Yeah, right. Wild Abby."

"Don't you dare call me Wabby." Tired of her snickers, I marched toward the curtain.

"Hold it," she said. "I just remembered something. I called you Saturday to see if you wanted to go to a trunk show, but Nikki said you were busy and would get back to me — which you didn't. You weren't home on Sunday either. Did you sneak off somewhere with Marco?"

I froze. What excuse could I give her?

"And what's up with Nikki? My mom said she was questioned for hours before the cops let her go, and just now I heard you talking about a tipster and fingerprints and — Ouch! Abby, this stupid cash register closed on my fingernail again. Why do you keep this thing anyway? Computers work so much better. Wait! Where are you going? Come back! I could really use some fresh coffee. And when is lunch?"

Oh, how I wished I were going with Marco.

When it came time to make deliveries later

169

that afternoon, I tried once again to recruit Jillian, but she adamantly refused to step foot in the van. "You make the deliveries," she said. "I'll work on orders, and Grace can wait on customers."

"You can't work on orders. You're not a trained florist. All you did was copy a flower arrangement from a painting."

"I *imagined* them," she corrected.

I snatched a slip of paper from the spindle. "See this? A customer wants a funeral arrangement. Do you have any idea how to make a funeral arrangement?"

"Well, duh. I've been to funerals." She pressed her fingertips to her temples and closed her eyes, as though meditating. Then she opened them and said, "Okay. All set."

"Forget it."

"Come on, Abs. I promise I'll do a great job for you. *And* it'll ease your workload so you can spend more time with Marco. Pretty please?"

I studied her skeptically. If she really could make floral arrangements by imagining them, it certainly would ease my load. On the other hand, what if my cousin had a natural talent for flower arranging that surpassed anything I could do?

What was I thinking? Jillian had a career she loved — shopping with other people's money. Why would she give it up? Plus, she had the attention span of a gnat. Even if she could make arrangements by imagining them, after doing a few she'd be bored out of her mind.

"Just let me show you what I can do," Jillian coaxed. "Test me."

A test? *Hmm.* Maybe she'd hit on the right solution. I sorted through the orders and found three fairly simple arrangements for her to try. If she screwed them up, it wouldn't take me long to redo them, and the waste would be minimal.

"Okay, Jill, you work on these three orders, under Grace's supervision, and I'll make the deliveries. Is that okay with you, Grace?"

Grace, being a good sport, put on a brave smile and gave a nod, so I handed Jillian the first order. "A mixed funeral arrangement using lilies, mums, and roses. Can you imagine it?"

Jillian closed her eyes for a moment, then said, "Got it. Okay, first step, pull the flowers. Or wait. Maybe I should pick out a container first. No, flowers."

I left her meditating on it.

After making my first delivery to an elderly woman who insisted on making me a cup of cocoa and showing me her collection of muffin recipes, I called Nikki to see how she was doing.

"I'm okay, I guess," she said in a listless voice.

"Was Dave angry with you?"

"Yes," she said, sighing. "He told me I should have been up-front at the beginning, when he could have taken steps to ameliorate the damage, because now" — her voice began to sound tight — "it looks like I'm going to be charged with murder." Nikki started to cry. "Abby, what am I going to do?"

"Don't give up hope, Nikki. Dave said he would have Marco look for someone in Scott's neighborhood who might have seen you parked near Scott's house."

"The way my luck is going, I don't hold out much hope for that."

"Give Marco a chance to do his job, Nikki. As some famous person said, you have to keep your face aimed toward the sunshine."

"What are you talking about?"

"You have to stay positive."

She blew her nose. "Easy for you to say. You aren't the one being accused of murder."

"Not this time, anyway. Remember what happened when one of my law school professors was found dead right after I delivered a flower arrangement to the law school?"

When Nikki merely sighed, I said, "Are you going into work today?"

"I called in sick. I'm still in bed. I don't have the energy to get up."

"You need to get moving, Nik. Go take a shower and grab a bite to eat; then go to the mall. Look for a new pair of shoes."

"What good are shoes going to do me in prison? I'll be wearing green booties." She started to weep again.

"Nikki, stop that. You're not going to prison."

"I'm tired, Abby. I'll talk to you later, okay?"

After I hung up, I sat in the minivan trying to think of something that would cheer her up. Obviously being cleared by the cops would do it. What else? When Nikki was blue, she usually shopped for new shoes, but since she had nixed that idea, what did that leave? A new guy?

Wait a minute. Why not? What was to stop Nikki from going out on a date? She hadn't been charged with anything . . . yet. But then I was back to the problem of finding her a nice guy.

Hold it right there, my conscience ordered. *You've got way too much on your plate to worry about finding her a guy. Besides, that's how you got Nikki into this mess, remember? If she wants to find a guy, let her go out and look.*

It wasn't easy ignoring the voice of one's conscience, but for the well-being of my best friend, I had to. What a shame I hadn't gotten Aidan's last name. He'd seemed perfect for Nikki.

Hmm. Carmen Gold would know how to contact Aidan. And while I was at it, maybe I could persuade Carmen to reveal what had caused those hostile looks she'd aimed at Jonas.

I phoned Bloomers to ask Grace to look up Carmen's work number, but, oddly, the machine picked up. Obviously Grace and Jillian were busy. I'd have to wait until I got back to the shop and do it myself. And of course there was the problem of finding time to visit Carmen.

I crossed my fingers and hoped that Jillian was as good at arranging as she was at imagining. That would give me the extra time I desperately needed.

My last delivery was to a neighborhood on the southern edge of New Chapel on the other side of a busy county highway. As I waited for the light to change at the intersection, I glanced to the left and spotted the big green-and-white sign that read: TOM'S GREEN THUMB NURSERY AND GREEN-HOUSE.

It reminded me that I hadn't given Marco the name of the girl Jonas jilted. Lottie had mentioned it only in passing. But what was it? Roberta? Ramona? Rhonda? I couldn't remember! There was one sure way to find out — stop at Tom's and ask . . . and maybe sneak in a little sleuthing, too.

When the light changed, I turned left, then pulled into the gravel lot in front of the greenhouse. I sat for a moment remembering the last time I'd been there, when I'd had a nasty run-in with the former owner, Tom Harding, while investigating my first murder case. Thank heavens Tom was no longer there. I had no use for bullies.

I walked up the flagstone path that, in the summer, was flanked by rows of potted perennials, large containers of blooming annuals, and dozens of rosebushes. Now it was just frozen ground. Automatic glass doors whooshed open to let me into the building, where I stood for a moment taking in the view and breathing in moist air, a welcome relief from the cold, dry air outside.

The greenhouse had a high glass ceiling and wide aisles that led through rows of tables that were mostly bare now, except for some early landscaping plants and indoor tree specimens. Off to the right I saw a young woman about my age working at a computer in an office with glass windows. Since no one else was around to help me, I walked toward the window, waving to catch her attention.

She saw me and came to the doorway. "Can I help you?"

"I hope so. I'm Abby Knight. I own Bloomers Flower Shop."

"Robin Lennox." She shook my hand. "I'm the assistant manager."

Robin! That was it.

She was half a head taller than me and had a heart-shaped face, brown eyes, a short nose, a small, full mouth, and a narrow chin. Her shoulder-length medium-brown hair was parted down the middle and tucked behind her ears. She wore a gray sweatshirt with Tom's Green Thumb on it and a pair of blue jeans with yellow work boots.

"Robin, would you have time to answer a few questions?"

"Certainly. Are you looking for plants for your flower shop or are you interested in starting a garden at home?"

"Neither. This is about Jonas Treat. I'm sure you've heard he was murdered."

"So?"

"I know you have a history with Jonas. I was hoping you could fill in some details about his life."

Robin instantly stiffened. "Pardon me, but you're a florist. Why are you so interested in Jonas's life?"

I debated whether to make up a story or be honest with her, and honesty won out. "My best friend went out to dinner with Jonas a few hours before he was killed. It was only their first date, but since she was allegedly the last person to see him alive, she's become a person of interest to the police. I know she didn't kill him and I'm trying to help her clear her name."

"Look, I feel sorry for your friend, but it's her problem, not mine."

"I totally understand, but just quickly, can you think of anyone in Jonas's life who might have had a strong grudge against him?"

"I haven't seen Jonas in years. I don't know who's in his life now, and I don't know anything about his death other than what I read in the newspaper. If you'll excuse me, I have things to do."

"You dated Jonas, didn't you?"

She tucked a stray lock of hair behind her ear. "A few times but, like I said, years ago."

That wasn't the way Lottie told it. Either she got the story wrong or Robin was lying. I decided to find out which. "Where did you meet Jonas?"

She sighed impatiently. "At a frat party back in college."

"When was that?"

"Four years ago."

"So you've known him for quite a while."

"No, I *met* him quite a while ago. Now, if you don't mind?" She indicated the door.

"Just one more question? Please? Why did you stop seeing him?"

"I really don't like talking about it."

No help there. I'd have to be sneakier. "Would you say Jonas was well liked?"

"Well liked?" Robin laughed sarcastically. "Tell me something: What was your friend's opinion of him after her date?"

"A handsome jerk."

"Most people would agree with you. Actually, I think you'd have a tough time finding anyone who had a good word to say about Jonas. Anyone who wasn't insane, that is. Now, please, I've answered your questions. I need to get back to work. You'll see yourself out?"

Not quite yet. "You must have liked something about Jonas," I said as she walked away. "You were going to marry him."

CHAPTER ELEVEN

Robin stopped and came back, her face bright red, though I wasn't sure whether it was from anger or embarrassment. "I was engaged *briefly* to Jonas. Luckily, I found out what kind of man he was before I made the biggest mistake of my life."

"What kind of man was that?"

"A lying, cheating, self-centered son of a bitch who I never wanted to see again. Believe me, after I broke off our engagement, I couldn't even stand to drive past his signboard on the highway."

"When you say cheating, do you mean he cheated on you?"

She pushed up her sleeves. "Oh, yeah. Many times."

"How did you find out?"

"*Jonas* told me, the jackass. Said before we went any further with our wedding plans, he had a confession to make, like he wanted me to give him absolution. I'm so glad I didn't spend any money on that wedding or I'd really be pissed."

"Do you know the names of the women Jonas was seeing?"

Robin shook her head. "I didn't want to know. Can you believe that jerk actually admitted he used our engagement as an excuse to keep other women from getting too involved with him? I knew he'd do the same thing while we were married, so I canceled the wedding and said good riddance to Jonas."

"How did he take it?"

"It really didn't seem to bother him."

"How long ago was this?"

She shrugged. "I've lost track."

"You mentioned his signboard, so it wasn't four years ago."

She scowled at me. "Several months ago, okay? But I swear I have not laid eyes on that man since."

"So you have an alibi for Sunday night?"

"I didn't kill Jonas, if that's what you're implying. If you want someone with a motive, talk to Duke Kessler."

Remarkable how quickly Robin supplied Duke's name when I asked for her alibi. "Why should I talk to Duke?"

"You're aware that he closed his real estate office, right? Do you know why?"

"Because of something Jonas did?"

Robin walked to the doorway of her office, then paused to say, "I think you need to get that answer from Duke."

On my way to the minivan, I dug out my cell phone and called Marco to see what he'd found out. Which, as it turned out, was nothing.

"No one in Nikki's ex-boyfriend's neighborhood saw her or her car there," Marco said.

"Damn! Nikki was afraid that would happen. There goes her alibi."

"Why was she afraid that would happen?"

"Because of the way her luck has been running."

"Abby, are you absolutely certain you believe Nikki's latest version of events?"

"I'd give anything to be able to say yes. Did you get out to the boxing gym?"

"Kessler wasn't there. His gym manager, a guy called Borax, said Kessler would be back first thing in the morning. I tried to get a little background info on Kessler, but Borax clammed up, so I'll stop by there again tomorrow morning."

"The guy's name is Borax? Is that his professional boxing name?"

"Could be a nickname — the dude looked

like Mr. Clean."

"Remember that name I was supposed to come up with, the woman Jonas was set to marry? It's Robin Lennox. She works at Tom's Green Thumb, and since I was out making deliveries this afternoon and happened to pass right by Tom's, I stopped to talk to Robin."

"You *happened* to pass by?"

"Within a hundred feet . . . I mean, the greenhouse was right there, Marco. How could I not stop? Anyway, Robin's responses to my questions were very interesting."

"I'm listening."

"First of all, she claimed she hadn't seen Jonas in years, until I called her on it and then she changed it to several months. She admitted to being engaged to him, but said she canceled the wedding when he confessed to cheating on her. She also said she didn't spend any money on the wedding, which I find hard to believe. She would've had to order a wedding gown, reserve a banquet room, order invitations — something. Finally, she suggested I talk to Duke Kessler, hinting that Jonas had had a hand in closing his real estate business. I'm not sure whether she really knows something about Duke or just wanted to divert the attention away from herself."

"After I go out to Jonas's subdivision, I'll pay Robin a visit, see if I can get more info from her. I'm hoping to get back to the bar before six o'clock. Think you'll be able to join me for dinner?"

"It'll depend on what Jillian gets done. With Lottie being gone, I've got my hands full. I'll be so glad when she gets back. Oops. I've got another call. I'll let you know about dinner."

I saw *Bloomers* on caller ID and clicked over to the other line. "Hello?"

"Abby, dear, are you about finished with deliveries?" Grace asked. "Your mother is here with something to show you."

"Her new art project?"

"Yes, that's right." By the way Grace had answered, I knew my mom was nearby.

Just what I needed to end my workday. "I'm about ten minutes away, Grace. Would you do me a favor? Do an Internet search for Cloud Nine and get a phone number where I can reach Carmen Gold?"

"Of course, dear."

"And one more thing, Grace. Can you tell me if Mom's new project is really bad? I want to prepare myself."

"It will bowl you over, love."

It was bad.

"Oh, and Abby, I should probably men-

184

tion that we've had quite a number of customers in the coffee-and-tea parlor this afternoon, which is good for the cash register but rather limited my ability to oversee the workroom."

I did a rapid translation in my head: Grace was tied up with customers, so Jillian had free reign with my flowers. Double bad. "Prepare me, Grace."

"Let's just say that your cousin's output will bowl you over, too. And one more bit of news: Lottie called. She's feeling better, but the soonest she'll be back to work is next Monday."

A trifecta of badness.

I walked into Bloomers at four thirty to find Grace behind the counter taking payment from a customer, and my mom standing near the parlor doorway making a sales pitch to three women she'd managed to corner.

"You'll never lose a hat again," Mom was telling them. "It's a bold accent piece for an entranceway. I call it *The Bowler,* and I promise your guests will indeed be bowled over by it."

They all laughed at her joke. Since they were standing in a semicircle in front of her creation, I still hadn't caught a glimpse of it, but from Mom's comment, I was betting it was a hat rack rather than a bowl.

"Does *The Bowler* come with a bowler?" one of the women asked, and again they all laughed.

"Yes, it certainly does," Mom said. "And it has a stand for umbrellas, too."

A bowler with a bowler? As Mom lifted her work of art onto its stand, I peered between two of the women for a look, then clapped a hand over my mouth to stifle my horrified gasp. It was a ginormous, grinning bowling pin.

The five-foot-tall wooden pin was painted in sections, each one in a different bright crayon color, with various patterns applied to each section. One had bull's-eye red circles on a black background; one had pink hearts on a green background; another had yellow polka dots on an orange background, all the way to the bottom.

Mom took an old-fashioned bowler hat out of a bag and placed it on top of the pin. The hat, with its characteristic rolled brim, was uncharacteristically covered with colorful glass beads. A smiley face on one side of the bowling pin peered out from under the hat, clearly "*The Bowler* wearing a bowler."

Through the neck of the bowling pin, Mom had inserted pegs, also painted in bright colors, apparently designed to hold more hats. The entire creation sat on a brightly painted, two-foot-tall stand that had metal rings attached on each side, no doubt to hold umbrellas.

Dear God. It was a totem pole on drugs.

"It's quite an, er, eye-catching piece," one of the women said, "but it wouldn't work in my house. It's much too, ah, modern."

"Same here," her friend said immediately. The third woman nodded frantically.

I inched backward, hoping Mom hadn't spotted me.

"Abigail! Here you are at last!" To her captive audience, Mom said, "This is my daughter, Abigail. She owns Bloomers. Honey, what do you think of my new art?"

All four women gazed at me expectantly.

"Well, would you look at that," I said, walking around the bowling pin. "What a unique hat rack. Mom, you continually manage to outdo yourself."

"Surprised?"

"Oh, yes."

"Abigail loves surprises," she told her audience. Then she beamed at me. I smiled back. She lifted her eyebrows. The women looked at one another, then at me. None of us knew what to say next.

Then my brilliant assistant glided up to

our confused little assembly and said, "Dreadfully sorry to interrupt, ladies, but Abby is needed in the workroom."

Grace to the rescue. I wanted to hug her, but that would have been a little too obvious. Making a hasty departure, I followed her to the back of the shop, where I whispered, "No amount of money could ever compensate you for saving me."

Just before she pulled back the curtain she said, "Hold on to that thought."

Taking a deep breath, I stepped into the workroom and in a cheerful voice asked, "How's it going, Jillian?" Grace did not follow me in.

"Oh, hi, Abs. Just one last touch and . . . voilà!" My cousin moved aside so I could see the arrangement on the table.

My mouth fell open. "It's all white."

"I know. Isn't it pretty?"

"It's not supposed to be white. I remember the order, and it definitely did not call for all-white flowers." I circled the table for a closer look. "Jillian, it's just like the one you did yesterday."

She stood back to study it. "Do you think so?"

"Yes, I think so! You were supposed to make a funeral arrangement. You can't take *that* to a funeral. It's for a dinner party —

or a wedding." I ignored her protruding lower lip and glanced around. "Did you do the other two orders?"

"They're in the cooler," she said, pouting.

"Please tell me they're not all white, too."

She didn't say a word. With a sinking feeling I pulled open the insulated door, and surprise! There sat two more all-white arrangements, clones of her original.

I pulled them out, plunked them on the worktable, and began to yank flowers from their foam bases. I hated surprises. One more just might tip me over the edge. "You told me you could imagine funeral arrangements, Jill."

"I did imagine them, but somehow they kept turning out just like the one I did yesterday."

I opened the other cooler and pulled more appropriate stems, then put them on the table beside the two nearly bare containers.

"Want the floral knife?" Jillian asked.

I held up my palm, warning her to keep away. In my frame of mind, I didn't want a weapon in my hand while she was in the room. "I think you should go home now."

"But it's not five o'clock yet."

"Go home. Now."

"I was only trying to help," she said in a little girl's voice. When I didn't reply, she picked up her coat, hat, and purse and slipped through the curtain.

I breathed a sigh of relief, believing that was the end of it, but ten minutes later she returned to gather up the remaining white arrangement.

"Where are you going with that?" I called.

"I just sold it — sight unseen," she said proudly. "The customer said it was just what she was looking for." Then the curtain fell behind her.

Muttering under my breath, I redid the other two arrangements and stowed them in the cooler. Just as I started on the next order, my mom breezed in.

"I'm going home now, honey. Your dad will be getting hungry." She gave me a hug. "I'm so glad you like my new artwork."

"It's bold and sassy, Mom, just like you." If only it were leaving, just like her.

"Your cousin liked it, too. And by the way, wasn't that sweet of Jillian to help you out today?"

Jillian, Jillian, Jillian. I was really sick of hearing that name. But just as I was about to fill my mother in on all the trouble my cousin had caused, Mom added, "She bought it, you know."

"Bought what?"

"*The Bowler.* Jillian is giving it to her

mother for her birthday tomorrow."

I had to cough to cover my laugh. Jillian was going to present Aunt Corrine with a huge psychedelic bowling pin? The same Aunt Corrine who'd hired an expensive interior designer to decorate her house in Far Eastern style, using pricey Oriental antiques? My aunt would throttle her.

Sweet.

Grace came into the workroom at five o'clock to give me a slip of paper with Carmen Gold's business number on it and to announce that she had closed shop for the day. "How much longer will you be, love?"

I stuck the piece of paper in my purse, then glanced at the orders still to be completed. "Probably another two hours. I'm hoping to stop for a dinner break at six o'clock."

"I think we should call a temp agency tomorrow to see about getting professional assistance, at least for our deliveries, until Lottie returns."

"You're right, Grace. I hate to spend additional money, but Jillian isn't working out, and I need to have time to get my work done here and help with Nikki's case."

"Will your cousin be in tomorrow, do you think?"

191

"No, thank goodness. I made it perfectly clear that I was not pleased with her work."

"Jillian isn't one to take hints, though, is she? Well, let's think good thoughts about it, then." Grace paused to watch me put finishing touches on a spray. "Shall I deliver the funeral arrangements to Happy Dreams for you?"

"That would be a big help. Thanks."

"Are there any errands I can run while I'm out? I have to drop off a dress at the dry cleaner's on my way home. It wouldn't be a bother if you needed anything."

The dry cleaner's? That gave me an idea. "You don't happen to use Frey's, do you?"

"Actually, I do. Why? Do I detect an ulterior motive? Never mind. I know the answer. My dress is in the coat closet."

Who said I couldn't find time to investigate?

Bundled in my wool coat, gloves, and scarf, and with a garment bag hanging over my shoulder, I trotted across the courthouse lawn to reach Lincoln Avenue, then hurried up the next three blocks to Frey's Dry Cleaner. The family-owned business occupied the first floor of a World War I–era two-story white frame house, with living quarters on the second floor. A driveway ran past the dropoff window on the side of the building and exited onto the alley in back, where a small parking lot had been carved out of the yard.

I dodged a lumber truck backing up the driveway, carrying a load of drywall, and headed toward the deep porch on the front of the house. As soon as I stepped inside the house, I was enveloped in damp air laden with chemical solvents. I gazed around with interest at what had most likely been a parlor at one time. The walls were covered in sepia-toned wallpaper with sprays of pink roses on it, and had elegant crown molding at the top. But there the old charm ended. The floor was covered with industrial-grade carpeting, and a gray laminate counter ran along the back where five women and a man waited in line.

Iris Frey was standing behind the counter, looking *dullerless* in a beige smock over a white blouse. She was totally devoid of color except for the bright spots of pink above her hollow cheekbones and her stringy brown hair had curly wisps sticking up all over, no doubt due to the humidity. Behind her was a doorway through which I could see clothes in clear plastic bags hanging from an oval track on the ceiling, and hear hisses of steam, such as clothespresses might make. Overhead, I heard the sounds of electric drills and nail guns.

As I got in line, I noticed the women were listening to a conversation between Iris and the man, who appeared to be trying to renegotiate the price of his dry cleaning.

"It's a dollar increase," Iris told the guy with a shrug. "Everything costs more these days."

"It's a rip-off," he snarled, throwing several bills on the counter. "I shouldn't have to take out a second mortgage to pay for five shirts to be washed and ironed. Next time I'll take my business to a reputable establishment."

The women sucked in their breaths as Iris's small eyes narrowed and her face turned a blotchy red. Then, as the man stormed toward the door, she called, "Here's an idea to save you a few bucks. Instead of spending your money to have your shirts dry-cleaned, donate them to the Salvation Army. They'll clean them and put them on hangers, and the next morning you can buy them back for seventy-five cents apiece."

"Up yours," he called, letting the door slam behind him.

Iris opened and closed her fists, as though willing herself to be calm, then turned to her customers with a shrug. "Men! What can I say? They're a lot like dry cleaners. They work fast and leave no ring." She waited for a laugh, and when it didn't come, she pretended to hold a microphone and said, "Is this thing on?"

The customers chuckled politely as Iris rang up the next ticket at her cash register. She stepped into the back room, switched on the oval track, waited for it to come around, then plucked a dress off the track. "Here you go, Hildy. See you next week, right? I'll have a great new joke ready for you. And don't forget to take a free newspaper."

I waited my turn and when I finally laid Grace's dress on the counter, I said, "Free newspapers — that's a nice touch."

Iris glanced at me. "Hey, I remember you from last Thursday. You're the underground florist from . . . Wait, I know this one . . . Bloomers, right?"

"Good memory, Iris," I called over a sudden loud drilling from above.

"Sorry about the noise," she called back, just as the drilling stopped. "We're having some rooms upstairs renovated."

To put her in a genial mood before launching into serious questioning, I said, "So, as one businesswoman to another, is it cost-effective to hand out free newspapers?"

"Are you kidding? Nothing dirties clothes more than newsprint. Hey, here's a question for you. When a man comes into your flower shop and it's not Valentine's Day, do you ask him, 'What did you do?' "

I blinked. Was I supposed to answer that, or was it a joke?

"Get it?" she prompted. "What did he *do?*"

"That's a good one, Iris. I'll have to remember it." If I ever used that joke, I'd have to ask Grace to kill me. "What did you think of the speed-dating event?"

"Complete waste of time. Would you fill out the top half of this ticket for me?"

"Sure." I took the pen and filled in my name. "So you didn't meet any likely prospects?"

"Go out with anyone from that bunch of apes? Not if you paid me." She turned to place Grace's dress on a pile of laundry in a low, canvas-sided pushcart. "How about you?"

"I wasn't interested in anyone either. Wasn't that shocking news about Jonas Treat being killed?"

She glanced over her shoulder, then covered one side of her mouth, as though there were someone else in the room to overhear

196

us. In a confidential tone she said, "He had his share of enemies."

"Really? For instance?"

She wagged her index finger at me, grinning. "Hey, you're investigating this, aren't you? Sure you are. You can't fool a fool. Look, all I know is what I pick up from rumors — people are always gossiping in here — but have you ever heard of Hank Miller? He owned the farmland on the west side of town where Chateaux en Carnations is now."

I cringed at Iris's *cha-tux*. Jillian would slap her silly. "I've heard of him."

"Well, Miller's name has come up more than a few times, let me tell you. There was bad blood between him and Jonas. And that Lennox woman was going around town bad-mouthing Jonas, too, not that I ever met her, but you know, you hear things."

"Robin Lennox, his former girlfriend?"

Iris's upper lip curled in distaste. "That's her, the witch."

A strong opinion for someone who'd never met Robin. "What did she say about Jonas?"

"Oh, you know, what an a-hole he was, how he led her on, how she'd like to kill him." Iris glanced at me, as though expecting a reaction. "Personally," she continued, "I thought Jonas was a complete gentleman.

He always treated me like a lady."

"Was he one of your customers?"

"Indeed he was. He brought his dry cleaning here every Wednesday evening at five."

That was a connection I hadn't expected.

"He had the most gorgeous suits, I'll tell you that. Italian silk, cashmere, wool, always the best." She heaved a sad sigh and for a moment was lost in thought. Casting me a quick glance she added sheepishly, "I was just thinking about how I'll miss those suits. You don't find that kind of quality much in New Chapel."

Iris was going to miss his *suits?* I had a feeling she meant Jonas but was too embarrassed to say so. And why the vitriol against Robin when Iris had never met her?

At that moment, an older version of Iris trudged out of the back room to retrieve the cart of clothes. She had the same overly large head and hollow-cheeked face, small eyes, and beige smock, and walked hunched over, as though the weight of the world rested on her shoulders. She had to be Mrs. Frey.

Iris glanced around with a start. "Excuse me," she said to me, then turned to say quietly, "What are you doing here, Mama? I thought you left an hour ago."

"What am I gonna do when that stupid

girl calls me and says she can't come in?" the older lady muttered. "You wanna tell the customers they can't have their laundry on time?"

Iris whispered something in her ear, then came back to the counter with an apologetic grin. "Sorry. What were you saying?"

"I was about to ask how you heard about the Cloud Nine event."

The older woman paused to cast Iris a wrathful look before pushing the cart away. Iris's face flushed red under her scrutiny. She tore off the lower half of my ticket and pushed it across the counter, waiting until her mother moved away to mutter, "A friend mentioned it."

I wanted to ask if that friend was Jonas, but from the signals I was getting, her patience for my personal questions was growing thin. I tried something safer instead. "Was that your first time at a speed-dating event?"

Mrs. Frey paused at the doorway to glance back at me, her eyes angry slits and her upper lip drawn into a snarl, as though I had no business asking Iris questions.

"First and last time," Iris said tersely. She walked to the front door, flipped the sign to CLOSED, then held the door open for me. "Don't forget your free newspaper."

CHAPTER TWELVE

When I walked into Down the Hatch, Marco was behind the bar, mixing a drink for a customer who was yammering on about a football game. Marco had on a royal blue T-shirt with the bar's logo on the front, setting off his dark hair and eyes. His mouth curved up at one corner when he saw me. He pointed to the last booth, then went back to the drink.

Not that I'd ever admit it to Jillian, but he was definitely *disturvable* tonight.

As I made my way past the bar, several of the regulars, whom I had dubbed Moe, Larry, and Curly, began to tease me.

"Hey, Abby, go anywhere interesting last weekend?"

"Got any tan lines, Abby?"

"So, Abby, did you see any interesting sights *outside* your room?"

These were followed by guffaws. Obviously, they'd found out about the trip to

Key West. At the risk of sounding like Iris, I stopped to drape my arms across their shoulders and asked, "Know what you guys remind me of?"

"Why don't you tell us?" Moe said, lifting a beer bottle to his lips.

"Slinkies."

"Slinkies?" Larry asked, glancing at the other two in puzzlement.

"Yeah, you know those springy toys? They're not really good for anything, but I still laugh when they tumble down the stairs."

Being Stooges, they didn't get it, but everyone around them did. With a satisfied smile, I sashayed over to the last booth and slid in.

"What'll it be, doll?" Gert asked in her gravelly voice.

"How about two cold beers?" Marco asked, and slid into the booth on the other side. He set two icy mugs down and pushed one toward me.

We gave Gert our dinner orders, then clinked our mugs together. "Who told the Stooges about Key West?" I asked, licking foam off my lips.

"I think Gert let it slip."

"Gert knows?" I leaned forward to whisper, "How did she find out?"

"I think Chris told her."

"Your head bartender knows? Does everyone in the bar know?"

"Would you be upset if they did?"

Did I care that people knew we went away together? That we were romantically involved? Marco certainly didn't. "No, but if my parents find out, it'll get awkward. They'll read all kinds of things into it. But, hey, I'm twenty-seven years old. I own a flower shop. I bought my own car. I pay my own bills. I should be able to make my own decisions. Right?"

"Was that a dry run for your parents?"

"How did it sound?"

"Take off the question at the end. It's more forceful."

"Duly noted."

Marco lifted an eyebrow. "Want to go back to Key West next month?"

Just thinking about another weekend with Marco made my spirits soar. Then reality set in and my spirits took a dive. "That depends on what happens with Nikki, I guess."

Gert brought our food, so I paused to take a bite of juicy turkey burger. "Remember my telling you about Iris Frey, from Frey's Dry Cleaner — how she was watching Jonas at the speed-dating event and walked out after I told her who Nikki was?"

"Yeah."

"Well, guess what? Jonas was one of her regular customers, and by the way she talked about him, I think she had a little crush on him."

"When did you talk to Iris?"

"Just now, when I dropped off some dry cleaning for Grace."

Marco regarded me skeptically, but let me continue while he ate his sandwich. So I told him how Iris had gushed over Jonas's suits and gentlemanly behavior, how her mother had reacted when I asked Iris about the speed-dating event, then how Iris rushed me out the door when I started asking more personal questions.

"What I'd like to know is how Iris and Jonas happened to attend that event on the same night. It seems too coincidental, doesn't it? I'll bet Carmen Gold might be able to shed some light on that."

"How about letting me take care of Iris and Carmen," he said, "and you attend to your shop? Do you have a phone number for Carmen?"

I dug Grace's note out of my purse. "I wouldn't neglect my shop, Marco — you know I can't afford to make that mistake — but we'll get a lot farther on this case with a team effort. I'm not asking for much, just a reciprocal sharing of information that might help us catch a killer."

Marco leaned forward, gazing intently into my eyes. "Don't you trust me to do the job?"

"Yes, but as I tried to explain before, I can't sit on the sidelines and hope it works out."

He put his hand over mine. "Listen to me, Sunshine. I don't mind sharing information with you, but you're not a trained investigator, and this case is too important to screw up."

I pulled my hand away. "You think I'll screw it up?"

"Do you think I will?" he retorted.

It was a stalemate, a no-win situation, but for the sake of our relationship — and for Nikki's sake, as well — I had to step around my ego and face facts. I very well could screw it up. I'd nearly done that on several other occasions, but fortunately luck — and Marco — had been on my side.

This time I reached for *his* hand. "I know I'm not a trained PI, Marco, and I'm well aware of the importance of the investigation, so I'll try not to interfere. But if an opportunity arises, shouldn't I make the most of it?"

"If the opportunity arises, of course you

should make the most of it. And I didn't mean to imply that you would screw up. Just be very careful. Don't make anyone nervous. Someone killed Jonas in cold blood and may not hesitate to kill again." Marco brought my hand to his lips. "Above all else, I don't want you to be the next victim."

I gazed into those soulful eyes and smiled all the way down to my toes. "Thanks."

"You're welcome."

Feeling as though we'd crossed a major obstacle, I told Marco about my meeting with Iris. "Her hostility toward Robin Lennox stunned me. She actually referred to Robin as a witch, which seemed way too personal for someone who claimed to not know her. That and the way Iris gushed over Jonas's gentlemanly behavior are the reasons I suspect she had a crush on him. But the only thing she said about Hank Miller was that there was bad blood between him and Jonas. Did you learn anything helpful from Jonas's construction crew?"

"Not really. I spent the whole afternoon talking to various employees, which is why I didn't make it out to see Robin, but none of them had any major complaints or insights about who might have killed him."

"You're kidding."

"Jonas may have been a jerk on the social

scale, but when it came to business, he understood that getting things done meant keeping his workers happy. The proof is in the subdivision. It went up in record time. But here's something interesting, and maybe this is why Iris heard there was bad blood between them. Hank Miller paid Jonas a visit at the sales office on the Wednesday before Jonas was killed, and the two almost came to blows. I haven't found out what the dispute was about, but I got a phone number for Miller. I'll give him a call this evening and see what he says about it."

Marco stopped for a sip of beer. "Tomorrow morning I'll call Carmen Gold, pay a visit to Robin Lennox, and hit the boxing gym to talk to Kessler. We've got to get this case moving."

The boxing gym? *Hmm.* That gave me an idea. "Could you go to the gym around one o'clock?"

"Probably. Why?"

"That's usually a slow time at Bloomers, and I'd like to tag along with you to check out the men —"

That was the moment Gert chose to stop at the table to see if we needed anything. It was also the moment when Marco lifted his mug to take another drink of beer. Both of them froze.

"— for Nikki," I quickly finished. "I'd like to find her a date."

Gert let out a wheezy sigh as she distributed the plates, clearly relieved I wasn't scouting for myself.

Marco leaned toward me. "Abby, Nikki is a suspect in a murder investigation."

As if that had slipped my mind. "That's exactly why she needs a date, Marco. Nikki is as low as I've ever seen her. She's always been upbeat and fun, and now she can barely drag herself out of bed. It breaks my heart to see her like that. What harm would it do to have a nice guy take her out to dinner? Think how it would raise her spirits. Besides, she hasn't been charged with anything. She's attractive, smart — why shouldn't someone want to take her out?"

He gave me an incredulous look. "You're joking, right?"

"No one has to know she's a suspect."

At his scowl, I gave up. I wasn't too keen on keeping something like that from a potential date anyway. "Fine. I'll tell them, if it comes up."

"I don't know why you won't let Nikki find her own date. Her happiness isn't your responsibility. Keeping Bloomers from going under *is*."

Instead of arguing, I stuck a french fry in

the mound of ketchup on my plate. Marco just didn't get it. I couldn't live in the same apartment and pretend like I didn't see how Nikki was hurting. If Marco didn't want me to go to the gym with him, I'd go alone. In fact, he wouldn't even have to know I'd been there.

When I finally wrapped up my work at Bloomers around eight thirty that evening, my back and neck were stiff from bending over the worktable. I hadn't been able to squeeze in my morning walk at the track in quite a while, and I was starting to feel it. What I needed was a good workout . . . hmm . . . like on a treadmill at a gym, especially since I wanted to look good in my bathing suit when we returned to Key West.

I left Bloomers and headed for Put Up Your Dukes Boxing Gym, located at one end of a strip mall on the north side of town. The brightly lit gym was visible through the huge plate-glass windows along the front and side walls, where I saw all kinds of exercise equipment, free weights, boxing bags, a boxing ring, and, most important, guys.

As I walked toward the door I took the precaution of shutting off my cell phone, in case Marco decided to call while I was working the room. Inside, I was assailed by heat and the strong odor of sweaty bodies and dirty socks, though the building itself appeared clean and modern.

In the center of the vast room was their small boxing ring, where two guys in leather headgear and boxing gloves were sparring. Beyond the ring, a group of mommies-to-be was engaged in a yoga session. Through a wide doorway in the center of the opposite wall, I saw a kickboxing class in progress. To my right was a reception counter, with a door behind it labeled OFFICE.

A well-built guy in a sleeveless T-shirt, standing behind the reception counter, said, "Need some help?" He sported a good head of hair, so clearly he wasn't the bald Borax Marco had met. I eyed his left hand as I walked toward him. No ring. Clean fingernails. He was going on the date list. "I'd like some information, please."

Smiling, he put his hands on the glass countertop and leaned into them, flexing his biceps for me. Then he said in a husky voice, "Tell me what kind of info you need, sweetcakes, and I'll do my best to get it for you. Name is Link, by the way, as in, 'Wanna link up with me?' And you are . . . ?"

Definitely not a sweetcakes. It looked like Link wasn't going on the date list after all. "I'm Abby, and I was thinking about joining your gym, so I stopped by to check out your equipment." I blushed hotly. "Well, not *your* equipment . . ."

He leered at me. "It's okay by me, sweetcakes."

"I really don't like that nickname, Link. Could you call me Abby, please?"

He raised his eyebrow. "Spicy. I like that."

Link walked me over to the other side of the gym, where three guys were running on treadmills facing the windows. Because it was dark outside, all they could see was their own reflection, but they didn't seem to have a problem with that. I walked around with Link as he explained the benefits of being a member; then I asked if I could have a guest pass for the evening. He was happy to oblige, and I was happy he stopped calling me sweetcakes.

Since I hadn't brought my workout clothes, I had to make do with my tan khakis and lime green long-sleeved T-shirt with the Bloomers logo on the back. Luckily, I had an old pair of running shoes in the trunk of my car. I locked up my boots, coat, and purse in the women's locker room, then headed straight for the treadmills, where only two guys were now working out. Since both were nice-looking and weren't wearing wedding bands, maybe two was enough.

I stepped onto one of the machines, figured out how to start it up, then, walking at a pace that allowed me to converse, I introduced myself to the guy on my right, who said his name was Ted. After making small talk for a few minutes I said, "So, Ted, I noticed you're not wearing a ring. Are you seeing anyone special? Because I have a gorgeous roommate who —"

"Sorry, hon, I have to stop you right there. Unless your roommate is a guy, you're out of luck." He said out of the side of his mouth, "If you're wanting to hook your friend up, try the adorable boy on your left. He's been salivating over every woman to walk in tonight."

I glanced left to find the alleged adorable boy staring unabashedly at my breasts, which made him less than adorable in my book. Since I was already self-conscious about my natural endowments, I hunched my shoulders and gave him a scowl.

"You're hot," the so-called adorable one said with a lopsided grin. I noticed then that he had peach fuzz on his chin and above his lip. I doubted he was out of high school. No wonder Ted had called him a boy.

"Shouldn't you be home doing your homework?" I asked.

"Already did it."

This wasn't working out the way I'd hoped.

Across the room, the office door opened and out walked a man I recognized instantly from his television ads — Duke Kessler. Although he had shed the royal purple robe as well as a few pounds around his middle, he still had a powerful charisma that made me feel like I was in the presence of genuine royalty. Kessler was a tall, distinguished man in his early sixties, white at the temples, but fit, tanned, and bright-eyed, with a smile that was infectious.

Hmm. Kessler wasn't supposed to return until morning, but as long as he had, wasn't this one of those opportunities I should take advantage of?

I pushed the Stop button on my machine and was nearly flung off when the treadmill came to a sudden halt. Regaining my balance, I started across the gym toward the reception counter, calling out to Duke before he disappeared inside his office again, "Mr. Kessler?"

Just as he looked around, I heard a woman call, "Abby?"

I glanced around to find the source and

saw a familiar face with long, dark hair, olive skin, and a big belly. *Yikes.* It was Marco's pregnant sister, Gina, and by the frown on her face, something was on her mind. Gina wasn't one to hold back her thoughts, either, so upon seeing her start toward me like a warship on a search-and-destroy mission, I started to sweat.

The first time I met Gina was at a dinner given by Marco's mother. The two women had spent the evening filling me with wine and lasagna, then grilling me to see if I'd make a suitable wife for Marco. I'd passed the test, and they'd been waiting for us to tie the knot ever since.

"Hi, Gina," I said with a friendly smile. "Great to see you again."

"I didn't know you were a member here, Abby."

"I have a guest pass for the day. I wanted to, um, try out the equipment to see if I wanted to join."

"Really? It looked like you were flirting to me."

And I thought Marco wasn't going to know I'd been here.

CHAPTER THIRTEEN

My face grew hot with embarrassment, and I knew my freckles were standing out like bran flakes against the fiery blush of my cheeks. "You caught me. I was trying to do a little matchmaking for a friend of mine. Her boyfriend broke up with her, and she's really depressed."

Gina studied me for a moment. "So everything is okay between you and my brother?"

"Absolutely. It's never been better between us. We have a great relationship."

At that, Gina's eyes lit up. "Then can we expect an engagement announcement soon?"

Yikes. "We're not ready to take our relationship to *that* level."

"*We're* not? Or *you're* not? Have you asked Marco how he feels about having a family?"

"Not in those exact words, but —"

"Did you know he'd like a large family?"

I swallowed. *Large?*

"Has he mentioned his concern that if he doesn't get married soon, he'll be an old father? No? For someone who professes to have a good relationship with my brother, you're sure in the dark about his feelings."

My mouth opened but no words came out. What could I say? Marco had never talked about any of that with me.

"I like you, Abby," Gina said, "and I think you're a good match for Marco, but you need to fish or cut bait, because my brother needs to get on with his life." She marched back to her group and resumed her place on the floor.

I felt as though every eye in the gym were on me. This definitely wasn't going the way I'd planned, and I was truly sorry I'd ever come up with the idea. In the future, Nikki was on her own when it came to finding a date. But at that moment all I could think about was getting out of there. Keeping my head down, my face burning with humiliation, I headed toward the door.

Moments before I reached it, however, I heard, "Young lady, did you want to see me?"

I turned just as Duke Kessler came striding up. He took one look at my face and said quietly, "Are you okay?"

I was about to tell him I'd come back

another time, but he took my arm and said kindly, "Of course you're not okay. Come with me. I'll get you some cold water."

I allowed him to usher me around the counter and through the door behind it into a plush, expensively furnished office, where Kessler took a bottle of mineral water from a built-in minicooler and handed it to me.

"Thanks," I said, and held the bottle to my flushed face to cool it down. "That was an embarrassing moment."

"I noticed."

"My boyfriend has an overprotective sister."

"My wife has one of those. Makes my life a living hell sometimes." He smiled.

Duke Kessler really was a charming man, and I couldn't help but smile back. I held out my hand. "I'm Abby Knight. I own Bloomers Flower Shop."

"It's a pleasure," he said, shaking my hand. "I've been to your shop many times over the years. When I had my realty office downtown, I always ordered my flowers there. Didn't Lottie Dombowski used to own it?"

"I bought it from her last May."

"How is Lottie, anyway? Do you ever hear from her?"

I debated about telling him of Lottie's

stomach trouble, but decided she might not appreciate my spreading around something that personal. "Lottie still works there. She taught me everything I know about the floral business." I opened the bottle and took a drink of water. Talking about Bloomers made me feel a little more centered.

"Good for Lottie. I always liked her spunk. So what can I do for you, Miss Knight?"

"Just Abby, please. I'm trying to get some information on Jonas Treat. I understand he used to work with you."

Kessler cocked his head to one side, a little wary of me now. "How are you connected to Jonas?"

"I'm the best friend of the girl who went out to dinner with him the night he was killed. The cops are questioning her in the murder and —"

He put up a hand to stop me. "Is this going to be a long story? Because if it is, I just got back from a trip and I'm beat."

"I promise to keep it short, because I'd like to ask you a few questions afterward."

"Hoping to get me to confess to the murder so your friend is off the hook?"

I blinked at him in surprise. "No! Absolutely not." At Kessler's big smile, I said,

"Well . . . maybe. Okay, yes."

He laughed. "I like you, Abby. You're plucky. Sit down, please."

He indicated a pair of beige satin-striped club chairs near a window. He took one and I sat my plucky self in the other, facing him, where I explained Nikki's situation.

"I can see why you're concerned," he said, crossing one leg over the other, "but I'm afraid I'll have to disappoint you, Abby. I didn't kill Jonas. However, don't think I hadn't considered it a few times."

I blinked at him, trying to decide whether he was being serious, only to have him break into a big smile. "Gotcha."

"Almost," I said, trying to maintain my pluckiness.

"Let me tell you a little about Jonas," Kessler said. "He was fresh out of college when I brought him into the business, an eager, attentive pupil whom I treated as a son. I taught him the ropes, gave him some of my best clients, had him outfitted by my tailor, helped him buy his first new car, and after a few years of watching him grow into a confident businessman, made him an equal partner to reward his hard work. And all the while he was cutting deals behind my back. When I learned about his treachery, I was deeply hurt, but I figured he must need the money, so I turned a blind eye to it. Basically, he was a weasel, although it took a while for me to accept it.

"Then one day Jonas announced he was leaving the partnership to strike out on his own. A week later I found out he'd secretly brokered a deal that made him a multimillionaire. You know that subdivision, Chateaux en Carnations? I negotiated with Hank Miller over that parcel of land for two years with an eye toward developing it. Hank isn't the easiest man to deal with, either. He had a list of requirements the length of my arm. And while I was in negotiations, Jonas ended our partnership, cut a deal with Hank, and snatched the land right out from under me. I never saw a dime from it.

"But that wasn't the worst part. What hurt me the most was Jonas's betrayal. I kept asking myself, After all I did for him, how could he stab me in the back? Unfortunately, all that bitterness inside caused my health to decline, until my doctor finally told me I was on the verge of a major cardiac event. I decided I had to get rid of my animosity or die, and that's how I ended up here, in the health and fitness business."

He smiled his television smile as he stood to show me his trim physique. "Look at me now. I'm healthy as a horse and have never been happier. It was the best decision I've ever made."

"I can see that."

"I'm glad to report it's been six months since I laid eyes on Jonas, a wonderful six months, I might add. He was like a poison in my system that had to be purged. And I did, by putting all my muscle, so to speak, into this gym. You saw those punching bags out there? Every time I punched one, I imagined it was him, until I was finally all punched out."

He sat down again, crossing his legs, watching me with eyes that twinkled. "You're thinking I have quite a motive for murder, aren't you?"

How was I supposed to answer that? I gave him a shrug. "You said it, not me."

"Let me tell you this. Jonas was a pathetic human being, but one to be pitied, not killed, because his greed would have eventually done him in anyway. And he didn't single me out for his dirty dealings, you know. I suspect you'll find others in town with motives as good as mine." Kessler glanced at his watch, then stood up. "And now, if you don't mind, I want to get home and say hello to my wife."

I rose. "Thanks for talking to me, Mr.

Kessler."

"Call me Duke. And you're very welcome, Abby. Good luck with your boyfriend's sister. I have a feeling you'll need it."

"Maybe I should sign up for boxing lessons."

Kessler laughed as he walked me to the door. "Try the punching bag. It works wonders."

When I got back to my apartment, Nikki was gone, the answering machine was blinking, and Simon was howling for food. "I'll feed you in a minute," I told him, as I shrugged off my coat and tossed it over a chair. "I have to check my messages."

A minute was too long for Simon. He wanted food, not excuses. He tackled my ankle and held on, forcing me to drag him along as I limped across the living room. I pushed the Play button and heard Nikki's lethargic voice: "Hi, Abby, I'm at my mom's. She wants me to stay for a few days, but I guess I'll come back tomorrow. . . . I should go to work. . . . That's all. . . . Bye."

Nikki really *was* depressed. She hadn't complained about her mother at all. I erased her message and listened to the second one: "Hey, Sunshine, where are you? No one answered at the shop and your cell phone went to voice mail. Call me and I'll give you an update on Miller."

No mention of Gina phoning him. Maybe she'd forgotten about me. I erased both messages, then raced Simon to the kitchen to feed him before returning Marco's call. But as I spooned cat food into Simon's dish, I started thinking about what Gina had said.

Have you asked Marco how he feels about having a family? Did you know he'd like a large family? Has he mentioned his concern that if he doesn't get married soon, he'll be an old father? For someone who professes to have a good relationship with my brother, you're sure in the dark about his feelings.

If Gina was right about Marco, I really *was* in the dark, because he'd never shared any of those feelings or concerns with me. *If* she was right, I was also in a bind, because I was in no hurry to get married and start a family. I liked being Marco's one-and-only, and I liked my independence, too, not to mention I was just starting to make a go of my new career. I had a good thing going. Why mess with it?

I like you, Abby, and I think you're a good match for Marco, but you need to fish or cut bait, because my brother needs to get on with his life.

If she was right about everything else, was

she right about that, too?

"I was starting to worry about you," Marco said, when I finally made the call.

"Sorry. I turned off my phone earlier and forgot to turn it on again."

"Are you okay? You sound down."

"I'm exhausted. It's been a long day. Did you reach Hank Miller?"

"Yes, at his home in the Florida Keys, as it turns out. He said he moved there toward the end of last year. He didn't seem to mind talking to me — until I asked him about the altercation with Jonas; then he got testy. He said he'd been in New Chapel on another business matter and stopped at Chateaux-whatever to see how it was coming along. He said he dropped in to see Jonas merely as a courtesy, and denied any altercation. He swore he flew home the next morning, Thursday morning, has the ticket stub to prove it, and hasn't left since. If he's telling the truth, that would place him back in the Keys three days before Jonas's murder."

"So is he off the list?"

"No way. I have witnesses who'll testify to their altercation. And his alibi was too pat. It sounded rehearsed. I'm going to check with the recorder's office to see what kind of deal Jonas made to buy Miller's land.

Maybe there's something in it that'll indicate a possible reason for their argument. Then I'll call Miller again. . . . Hold on a moment."

Marco called, "You guys want to hold it down?" Then he came back on. "Sorry. It's busy here at the bar. Tell me about your evening. Did you get your orders done?"

"All done. In fact, I squeezed in enough time to stop by Kessler's boxing gym before it closed, and you'll never guess who showed up — Duke Kessler, just back from his trip. And guess who else was there?" I took a deep breath. "Your sister, Gina. Funny story about her —"

"Wait. I can hardly hear you over the noise here. Let me pick up the phone in my office." He put me on hold and came on the line again a few minutes later. "That's better. You said you went to Kessler's gym? I thought you decided not to go."

"Actually, my decision was to go on my own so I could look for a date for Nikki without hampering your investigation."

"Hmm," was all he said. It wasn't encouraging.

"The date hunt was a bust, so I've decided to give it up. But I did talk to Kessler about Jonas — without hampering your investigation, of course."

"That's a relief," he said dryly. "Hold on. I've got another call. Looks like Gina's number."

"Wait, Marco! Before you talk to her, you should know that Gina had this crazy notion I was trying to pick up men for myself. Anyway, I hope I cleared up her misunderstanding, but if she happens to mention it, tell her you know why I went there and you're perfectly happy with the way things stand between us."

"Never mind. She hung up. So why do I need to explain our relationship to Gina?"

"Well, I just thought, in case she said anything about seeing me at the gym, you should know what happened. She's very protective of you." I didn't go further. It was too late in the evening to get into a discussion on marriage and babies.

"I guess I'll always be Gina's little brother. So tell me what you learned from Kessler."

"My impression of him was favorable. You'd like him, Marco. He's a nice guy, and he thinks I'm plucky."

"Hold on, Plucky. Gina's calling again."

CHAPTER FOURTEEN

I paced from one end of the apartment to the other, crossing my fingers that Gina's reason for phoning was something other than to lodge a complaint.

He came back on the line a few minutes later. "Sorry for the interruption. I worry when Gina calls this late. Anyway, you were about to tell me what Kessler had to say."

I was dying to know what Gina's call was about, but since Marco didn't seem concerned, I thought it better not to ask. "Kessler had quite a lot to say about the history behind his partnership with Jonas. Basically, he gave Jonas his start in real estate and treated him like a son, even when Jonas was making deals behind his back. Then Jonas left the partnership and bought Miller's land for development, after Kessler had negotiated with Hank Miller for two years for that property. Jonas became a multimillionaire selling those tracts and

Kessler got zip."

"Sounds like a strong motive for murder."

"Don't judge him just yet. Kessler, poor guy, was so furious with Jonas that he nearly had a heart attack. That's why he closed his realty office and went into the fitness business. He said he had to let go of all his animosity toward Jonas or be killed by it. So he did let it go and got healthy instead. He told me he hadn't seen Jonas in six months. So yes, there is a motive, but I don't see Kessler as a strong suspect."

"Kessler filed a lawsuit against Jonas two months ago. Does that sound like someone who let go of his animosity?"

That took me aback. Why hadn't Kessler told me? "He didn't mention the suit."

"I'm not surprised. Kessler is a great salesman, Sunshine — that was his business — and it sounds as though he may have sold you a line of bull."

"I don't think so, Marco. I got good vibes from him. You'll see when you talk" — I paused when a yawn sneaked up on me — "to him."

"Get some rest, baby. I'll call you tomorrow after I make the rounds of suspects, okay?"

"Sure. And Marco?"

"Hmm?"

"You *are* happy with the way things stand between us now, aren't you?"

"I'd be happier if we could get away together soon."

"Me, too, but that's not what I mean."

"Did Gina say something to make you doubt it?"

I couldn't think how to answer. If I said yes, he'd want to know what she'd said, and that would lead to the whole marriage/baby discussion that I wasn't prepared to have. If I said no, I'd be lying. Luckily, my silence spoke for me.

"Abby, have some faith in our relationship. And don't worry about my sister. I can handle her."

The first thing I saw when I walked into Bloomers the next morning was the ginormous bowling-pin man grinning at me from under his bowler as though he found me comical. "I'm having a bad-hair day," I grumbled, trying to smooth down my static-riddled locks. "Don't be so judgmental. You only wish you had my hair."

Grace sailed out of the parlor with a cup of coffee for me. "Here you are, dear. Conversing with our friend Homer, are you?"

I glanced around to see who she meant.

"Homer? Are you talking about *The Bowler?*"

"I find it rather unnerving to have that face staring at me, so I named him. It makes him friendly. He does resemble the cartoon character Homer Simpson, don't you think?"

"You're right! He does. But I wouldn't mention that in front of my mom."

"Wouldn't dream of it, love. One can only hope your cousin sends someone round for Homer soon. He does try one's patience."

I took a sip of coffee and closed my eyes as it glided down my throat. "You make the best coffee in the world, Grace. I wish I had time to linger over it, but I suppose a stack of orders is waiting for me."

"Did you see the newspaper this morning?" she called, returning to her duties in the parlor.

"I didn't have time. Simon batted my cell phone under the sofa during the night and it took me fifteen minutes to find it. Why? Was there more on Jonas's murder?"

"Nothing new on that front, but I thought you'd want to know that his funeral will be Friday afternoon. Also, there's an advert for Cloud Nine. Another speed-dating event is to be held tomorrow evening at seven o'clock. As you hadn't mentioned whether you'd spoken with Carmen Gold, I left the ad on your desk as a reminder. Perhaps you'll want to meet her before the event, say at six thirty? I'd be happy to set up a meeting. That would give you ample time to question her, wouldn't it?"

Grace could have been the queen's social secretary. "Thanks, but Marco already has plans to interview Carmen." I didn't say anything to Grace, but after my run-in with Gina, the last thing I wanted was to be spotted anywhere near another speed-dating event.

I took my coffee to the workroom and glanced at the spindle on my desk. No wonder Grace hadn't said anything. There were only nine orders. I hoped the drop wasn't a result of Jillian being on duty. The Cloud Nine ad was there, too, but, staying true to my word, I resisted the urge to contact Carmen.

By midmorning, I had finished three huge formal arrangements, a wreath, and an enormous funeral blanket, even after helping out in the parlor for the morning rush. I stowed the spray in the cooler and was about to head toward the parlor for a tea break when I heard Grace exclaim, "Good heavens!"

I hurried through the curtain and saw her

standing at the bay window, her hands pressed to her face. "I've never seen anything like it," she said as I joined her at the window.

In the street outside, a white stretch limousine had pulled alongside the curb. It wasn't just any stretch limo. It was a gigantic Hummer limo, so long it reached from Bloomers to Down the Hatch. It was such a novel sight, a crowd had gathered, eager to catch a glimpse of the celebrity inside.

"Is anyone famous in town?" Grace asked.

The driver's door opened, and the limo driver got out. He wore full livery — black cap, black suit and tie, white shirt, and black shoes. The throng pressed closer, many using their cell phones as cameras to snap photos as he walked around the car to the curbside and opened the door all the way at the back.

He unfolded two steps and reached inside to assist his passenger. An arm emerged clad in black leather. It was followed by a black spike-heeled boot. Then a bright copper head appeared and Jillian emerged, appearing totally shocked by the assemblage. She smiled and waved, posing for the cameras, then sashayed toward Bloomers, where she stopped to wave again.

I opened the door and nearly dragged her

inside. "What in God's name are you doing in a Hummer limo? A Hummer limo, Jillian! It barely fits on the street. Do you have any idea how much gas that thing uses?"

Jillian waved away my concern. "I can afford it." She motioned to the driver, who removed a small dolly from the vehicle and wheeled it through the doorway. I quickly shut the door, turning my back on the curious faces outside.

"It's right over there," Jillian said to the driver, pointing to Homer.

"You rented a Hummer limo to deliver your mother's birthday present?" I hissed, as the driver scooted *The Bowler* onto the base of the dolly. "Are you insane? Jillian, it's not about whether you can afford the gas. It's about *wasting* the gas. Haven't you been reading about conserving energy? Greening the country? Easing our dependence on oil?"

I paused as Grace opened the door so the driver could wheel Homer out of the shop. "Jillian, you have to stop being so self-centered. So you impressed those people out there with that monster vehicle. Maybe you'll impress your mother, too" — and wouldn't I give anything to see her face when she got a look at Homer! — "but you have to think of the big picture."

Jillian folded her arms and sighed. "I was thinking of the big picture. The limo is also for your deliveries. You want your customers to have their flowers, don't you?"

"That's why we leased the minivan."

"Who's going to drive it? You'll be busy with your orders, and Grace will be working the parlor. God knows I can't make coffee. I already told you how I feel about bugly vans, and don't even mention the words *pickup truck* in my presence. What does that leave? A limo. And you don't really think your big funeral arrangements would fit inside a regular limo, do you?"

It was hard to argue with her logic.

"So how cool would it be for your customers to have a big white Hummer pull up in front of their houses?" Jillian asked. "Wouldn't that make the flowers all the more special, not to mention the shop where they were made? Think of the publicity, Abs. Look at the big picture."

Hmm. Delivery by monster limo would be kind of cool — although it meant a temporary compromise of my principles. But I *could* accept the limo as payback for all the headaches Jillian had caused over the years.

She headed for the workroom, calling over her shoulder, "Do you have any arrangements ready to go? We might as well get

233

started."

I stared at her for a moment, still shocked that she'd done something nice for me — two days in a row. I glanced at Grace and shrugged. "Maybe Jillian is finally growing up."

"One can dream," she said blithely.

While Jillian played delivery girl, I finished the remaining orders. I hated to admit my cousin had hit on a good idea, but having that monstrous Hummer stop out front had brought in a flock of customers, some for coffee and tea, and some to browse and shop, but all of them spending money. Humming happily, I worked through my lunch hour, eating mixed nuts from a can and drinking the tea Grace supplied.

"I'm back," Jillian announced, breezing through the curtain with a white sack in her hands. "I brought you a sandwich from the deli — well, actually it's my sandwich. I couldn't finish it. I'll put it in the refrigerator and you can have it later. You'll never guess who I ran into at the bank while I was delivering that birthday bouquet to the loan officer with the handlebar mustache — who, by the way, has picked up about forty pounds of flab since he was promoted last year and is hot after a teller at least fifteen years younger than him. I mean, seriously, does *anyone* wear a handlebar mustache anymore?"

"Jillian! Stop! Who did you run into?"

"Marco's sister."

I nearly dropped my clippers. "Gina? What did she say? Did she ask any questions about me? How did she seem? Friendly? Angry? Catty? Downright hostile?"

Jillian thought about it. "She was a little flushed in the face. You know, like too much blush, maybe a little heavy-handed on the eye shadow. I mean, Vampira, here we come. Her hair wasn't too bad, though, but I guess that's one of the benefits of being preggers."

"Jillian, what did she *say* to you?"

"Well, after the normal 'how are you, great to see you' whatev, she asked how your matchmaking was going for Nikki." Jillian rolled her eyes. "Right. Like you have time for that. I told her I didn't know where she came up with that idea. You were way too busy running Bloomers to worry about Nikki's love life. You barely had time for your own — always keeping late hours, having practically no time to see Marco . . . stuff like that."

"Jillian, I *was* trying to find a date for Nikki! Oh, my God! She's going to think I really tried to pick up those guys last night."

"You? Pick up a guy?" Jillian laughed as she headed for the kitchen. "No one would believe that."

"Marco's overprotective sister would!"

Grace poked her head through the curtain. "A word, Abby, if you don't mind?"

I walked to the curtain, where Grace whispered, "I thought you'd want to know, dear. Carmen Gold stopped in to order a funeral arrangement. It appears that the Hummer caught her eye, too. Did you want to help her? It would be the perfect opportunity to have a chat about the murder."

I peered through the curtain, and sure enough, there was Carmen, perusing the gift items in one of my antique armoires. . . . No, make that looking at her reflection in the glass.

"I don't know if I should, Grace. Marco wanted to interview her."

Grace raised an eyebrow. "But Marco isn't here, is he?"

CHAPTER FIFTEEN

If the opportunity arises, of course you should make the most of it, Marco had said.

"I'll talk to Carmen," I told Grace.

"What shall we do about Jillian?"

Yikes. Grace had a point. I didn't want my nosy cousin to barge in while I was questioning Carmen and mess up my chance to help with the murder investigation.

"We'll have to send her out on more deliveries. There are three orders in the cooler, and if the limo driver can squeeze the Hummer into the alley, he can load them through the back door. Jillian won't need to step foot up front."

"Brilliant idea," Grace said. "I'll take care of it. You go talk to Carmen."

When I stepped through the curtain, Carmen stopped primping and turned toward me, her winged eyebrows raising in recognition. She was wearing a black wool swing coat with a silver-and-black scarf around her throat, her long platinum hair pulled back with a silver clip at the nape of her neck, and short black boots with silver heels. Beneath her open coat I could see a turquoise sweater and black pencil skirt.

"Nice to see you again, Carmen," I said pleasantly.

"Same here . . . Amy, isn't it?"

"Abby."

"Mmm," was her response. "Whose limo is out front?"

"My cousin hired it for the day."

"Is your cousin someone I would know?"

"Jillian Knight Osborne. She's a wardrobe consultant."

"The name doesn't ring a bell." Clearly disappointed, Carmen glanced around the shop, the silver sparkles in her lipstick catching the overhead lights. "So this is where you work."

"I own Bloomers." How I loved saying that.

"Quaint," she drawled. "I need to order flowers for a funeral."

I stepped behind the counter and pulled out the order pad. "Where will they be going?"

She opened her purse, pulled out a newspaper clipping, and squinted to read it. "Happy Dreams Funeral Home. *Happy Dreams?* Is that supposed to be a joke?"

I didn't comment. The Doves, owners of the funeral home, were good friends of mine. "And who are the flowers for?"

"Jonas Treat. T-R-E-A-T."

That was a surprise. After the hostile looks she'd given Jonas, why would she send flowers? "Did you want an arrangement, spray, wreath, or live plant?"

"An arrangement is fine."

"Are there any certain flowers you'd like?"

"You choose. Whatever a hundred bucks buys."

Why was Carmen even bothering? She certainly didn't seem to care. "What would you like the card to say?"

"Just 'Condolences.' "

"From?"

"Put 'Cloud Nine.' I didn't really know the man, other than for business."

Yet she was willing to spend a hundred bucks — anonymously — for his flowers. "How did you want to pay for that?"

"Cash." She pulled out her wallet and counted out five twenty-dollar bills.

I wrote up the receipt and handed her a copy. "It'll be delivered tomorrow morning."

"Yeah. Thanks." She folded the receipt in half, tore it into pieces, and glanced around for a place to throw it. I grabbed the small wicker trash can at my feet and came around the counter.

"Carmen, would you have time for a cup of coffee?"

She glanced at me as if she couldn't believe I'd dare ask. "I'm busy." Then she let the pieces of paper fall into the wicker can and started toward the door.

Thinking fast, I said, "Too busy for some free publicity for Cloud Nine?"

She paused, checked her watch, then heaved a bored sigh. "I hope you have espresso."

I hoped I had an idea for free publicity.

Grace made Carmen a double espresso and poured me a cup of mint tea while I gathered a tablet of paper and a pen and racked my brain for an idea. We sat at a white bistro table in the parlor with a plate of scones between us, as far as possible from a group of women having tea and chattering noisily. Since I'd eaten only a handful of nuts since breakfast, I wasted no time spreading my scone with clotted cream and raspberry jam, then chowing down. Carmen only nibbled hers, preferring to sip her espresso while gazing out the window.

Heeding Marco's advice about not making her nervous, I started with a compliment. "I was really impressed by your event last Thursday. So well organized and professional."

She glanced my way, giving me a conciliatory smile. "Thank you. What's the free publicity?"

"I, um, am planning an article for a floral magazine about women like us who own businesses, so I thought I'd feature Cloud Nine in it."

She flicked a crumb off the table. "My parents own the franchise."

Ah. Nepotism. How lucky for Carmen. "But you run it, right? When did you start?"

"A year ago. My dad thought it would be a good career for me. I suppose it's better than a boring nine-to-five job." As if to prove her point, she glanced around the parlor.

I ignored the dig. "How many events have you done in the northwest Indiana region?"

"Two."

I wrote it down, wishing she'd be a little more talkative. "Do you ever have trouble getting people to attend the events?"

"Honey, you wouldn't believe how many

people are looking for Mr. or Mrs. Right."

"Do you do background checks on the people who sign up for the event?"

"More like a Web search, and only if we make a match. Imagine the lawsuits if we sent someone out with a criminal."

A lawsuit wouldn't have been my first concern.

Carmen finished her espresso, then dug through her purse. "Look, my assistant can answer these questions for you." She slid a business card across the table. "Her name is Pamela. Give her a call."

"To be honest, I'd rather talk to you. I'll be quick, I promise." Before she could argue, I said, "Last Thursday evening you mentioned some incidents that brought about the 'no last name' rule. What kinds of incidents did you mean?"

"What, are you kidding me? I don't want that information in a magazine!"

At her shrill tone, the ladies at the other table turned to stare. "Sorry," I said quietly. "I'll stay away from that subject."

She rose and began to gather her things. "Forget it. I don't need your publicity."

Great. I'd done exactly what Marco had cautioned me not to do. "Carmen, I'm sorry. Let's move on to something more helpful to the magazine readers, okay?"

"What don't you understand about *forget it?*"

From the corner of my eye I saw Marco step into the parlor and glance around, and I breathed a sigh of relief. The cavalry had arrived! Apparently, Carmen saw him, too, as did the other women in the room, who stopped what they were doing to gape at him. In his black leather jacket and boots and slim jeans, with his permanent five-o'clock shadow and his dark hair waving onto his collar, Marco did look potently, excitingly male.

He spotted me and started toward our table, giving me that sexy little half grin. "I was hoping to find you here."

As he passed the ladies at the other table, they turned to catch his rear view, while beside me, Carmen suddenly became a purring kitten. "You did?" she asked hopefully; then her face fell when she realized he meant me.

"This is my boyfriend," I told her, as Marco put an arm around my shoulders. "Marco Salvare. Marco, this is Carmen Gold, the Cloud Nine event organizer."

He stretched out his hand to clasp hers. "My pleasure."

She forced a smile as she shook hands. "Mmm," she said in a noncommittal tone, but that was until he turned on the Salvare charm, holding her spellbound with his penetrating gaze.

"You saved me a trip to Chicago, Ms. Gold."

No female alive could resist that gaze, and it had Carmen practically drooling as she said in a throaty whisper, "Call me Carmen."

"Carmen," he said in a husky voice. "Pretty name."

She blushed like a schoolgirl and dipped her head. If she batted her eyelashes any harder, she'd fly. "I was named for the opera."

Marco widened his eyes, trying to look impressed. He wasn't an opera fan.

A tinny tune began to play, causing everyone in the room to check their cell phones.

"I have to take this call," Carmen told Marco, giving him an apologetic smile, then walked out of the room, her silver phone pressed to her ear.

As soon as she was gone, I whispered to Marco, "How did you know Carmen was here?"

He sat in the chair adjacent to mine and leaned close to say quietly, "I stopped by to check out the Hummer and saw you with her. I knew who she was from the description you gave me. By the looks of things, I arrived just in time."

"Well, watch yourself, Superman. Carmen's feisty. And so you know, she came in to order flowers for Jonas's funeral, which is odd after those looks she gave him Thursday night."

"I'm going to tell Carmen I'm investigating Jonas's hit-and-run case," Marco said, keeping one eye on the door. "If I give your hand a squeeze, play along with me . . . and here she comes."

Rather than run the risk of annoying her again, I decided to make myself scarce, although I really wanted to stay to watch Marco work his magic. We both rose as Carmen strutted back to the table, eyes glued to Marco. I said to him, "I'll get that coffee you wanted . . . babe."

Since I'd never called him that before, he gave me a quick glance, as if to say, *What is that about?* Ignoring his look, I said, "More espresso, Carmen?"

She gave me a curt nod, then sat down, angling her chair and crossing her legs so Marco would have a good view of them. As I headed toward the coffee counter, I heard her say, "Did I really save you a trip to Chicago?"

From the back of the room, I saw Marco

open his wallet and show her his PI license as he talked to her. But apparently the magic wasn't happening yet, because Carmen's face grew stony, as though he'd somehow duped her; then she slipped her purse strap over her shoulder and rose.

Instantly Marco was on his feet. As I returned with his coffee, I heard him say, "That's really a shame you have to leave now, because I was hoping you'd tell me all about Ms. Carmen Gold — who she is, and why she's in the dating service business instead of modeling for a fashion magazine." Lifting an eyebrow questioningly, he held her chair for her.

Carmen wavered and finally sat, unable to resist Marco's beguiling gaze, but gave a huff of annoyance to show she wasn't entirely pleased about it. I saw one corner of Marco's mouth twitch in amusement as he spun his chair around and straddled it, facing her. He'd have Carmen eating out of his hand in no time.

He did, too, almost as though he'd pushed her On button. Since I couldn't stand at their table without looking suspicious, I headed to the back counter to make more espresso. Unfortunately, I couldn't hear anything at all over the machine's noise, but I could see Carmen's mouth moving and imagined Marco was getting her whole life story.

I filled a clean cup with a double shot of espresso and hurried back to the table as Carmen was explaining why her parents had decided to start a speed-dating service for her.

"Daddy was hoping I'd meet my future husband at an event," she said, unable to keep the bitterness out of her voice. "He can't wait to see me married off. He says he's tired of shouldering all the responsibilities. It hasn't exactly worked out the way he wanted, though, since I'm still waiting for that special guy to come along."

Carmen was her father's responsibility? She had to be in her late thirties. Someone needed to cut that cord *yesterday.*

With a flirtatious smile, Carmen said to Marco, "So what else would you like to know about me, besides my being available?"

I put her cup in front of her, using my arm to momentarily block her view of Marco, just to remind her I was still there. "More coffee, babe?" I asked Marco.

"In a little while." Marco didn't bat an eye this time.

I checked in at the other table to see if the ladies needed refills. They requested a pot of Earl Grey, so I headed to the counter to brew more tea.

When I took the pot of tea to their table, I heard Marco say, "Let's go back to when you first learned that a car had been hit in the parking lot — and I'm assuming you've heard by now that the Ferrari was owned by Jonas Treat, who was later found dead."

Carmen put on a sad face. "Isn't it a tragedy? A man cut down in the prime of his life."

"It *is* a tragedy," Marco agreed. "Did you know Jonas?"

"Yes, through my dating service. What I mean is, he was a client."

"How did you learn about the hit-and-run incident?"

"The restaurant manager made an announcement during the mixer."

"Did you go outside to the parking lot to see what happened?"

She was ready to say no — I could see it on her lips — then she glanced around, saw me pouring tea at the table behind her, and changed her mind. "Yes, I guess I did, just about the time the police arrived."

"I don't know if you've heard," Marco said, "but there were no witnesses to the incident itself, although someone saw a sedan and a truck leaving the vicinity. We're not sure whether the incident was accidental or purposeful, but in the event it was purposeful, can you think of anyone attending the event who might have had an issue with Jonas?"

"There could be any number of people who had issues with him," she said.

"What I'm asking is if you can hazard a guess as to who might have had a reason to want revenge so badly that they would damage an obviously expensive car."

Carmen toyed with a lock of her hair. "So you don't think it was just a simple hit-and-run, like someone backing out of a parking space?"

"Excuse me," one of the ladies said, tugging on my sleeve. "We need more scones."

"Coming right up." As I hurried toward the back to refill their plate, I heard Carmen say, "Everyone knew Jonas treasured his Ferrari, so I could see how damaging it would be a good way to get back at him."

I filled the plate and took it to the women just as Marco said, "Were any of the attendees repeat customers?"

"A few," Carmen said. "The matches don't always work the first time, so we give them a second event free."

"Was Jonas Treat a repeat customer?"

Flipping her hair away from her face, she

said, "I believe he might have been."

"Would you be able to check your records?" Marco asked.

"Well, let me think. . . . Yes, Jonas did come to one other event, but that was long before Thursday night."

"How long?"

She lifted a shoulder in a casual shrug. "Maybe ten months ago."

"What was your impression of Jonas then?"

"What does that have to do with the hit-and-run?" Carmen asked guardedly.

Oops. She had him there. How would Marco talk his way out of it?

"Excuse me?" one of the ladies said, so I motioned for her to wait a minute.

Marco gave Carmen his knock-your-socks-off smile. "You'd be surprised what I can find out when I have a complete picture, and with your unique perspective, how can I miss?"

Carmen smiled, and I did, too. Marco was so smooth it was a wonder he didn't slide out of his chair.

"Could we have more cream, please?" one of the ladies asked impatiently, so I took off again, missing part of Carmen's answer.

I brought a fresh pitcher in time to catch Carmen's initial impression of Jonas. ". . .

smart, handsome, rich, charming, and, as it turned out, a big jerk. At the mixer, he worked that room like a gigolo, which makes sense, considering he was looking for a good time, not Mrs. Right."

That was a lot of information to get from observing one event.

"Did you match Jonas up with anyone ten months ago?" Marco asked, as I grabbed a wet cloth and started wiping down the other tables, trying to keep busy.

Carmen considered his question. "I believe so, but I'd have to look it up."

She remembered the other details but not that?

"I'd be amazed if you didn't have a match, given the way you described Jonas," Marco said evenly.

"Again, how does this help your investigation?" Carmen asked.

"It plays into finding someone who might have wanted to get back at him."

Carmen began to finger her mole, clearly growing nervous.

"Since you pegged Jonas as someone only looking for a good time," Marco said, "I'll bet you had reservations about matching him up with women who had come to meet their mate."

"I don't like to make judgment calls on

251

my clients," she replied. "Besides, I didn't know Jonas was a jerk at the time. It wasn't until —" She stopped, her face reddening, as though she had caught herself before divulging something she didn't want known.

Marco leaned in, watching her carefully. "It wasn't until what?"

CHAPTER SIXTEEN

A fiery blush spread from Carmen's forehead to her neck. To mask her discomfort, she reached for her cup. After taking a sip and clearing her throat, she said, "What I was about to say was, it wasn't until Jonas's date complained about him that I found out what kind of man he really was."

"So you *do* remember matching him to one of your clients?" Marco asked.

"But not the client's name," she was quick to add.

"Was Jonas's behavior bad enough to file charges?"

Carmen was now tugging on the hairs in her mole, clearly stressed. "He didn't physically hurt her or anything. What I remember was that the woman was upset because Jonas wasn't the gentleman he pretended to be. He was more interested in someone who'd buy him things and show him a good time."

Marco raised his eyebrows in surprise. "I was under the impression that Jonas was wealthy. Why would he want a woman to buy him things?"

Carmen's lips thinned ever so subtly. "Jonas was a greedy man."

"Will you look up the name of his date and get that information to me?" Marco asked.

Carmen hesitated, as though deciding how to answer. "I'll see if I can find it. We didn't keep good records back then."

Back then? It was ten months ago.

"If you find it, would you fax or e-mail it to me?" Marco handed her his card.

Carmen slipped it into her purse without replying, then glanced nervously at her watch and scooted to the edge of the chair. "I really have to be going now."

"I'm sorry if I'm keeping you," Marco said. "I suppose you want to beat the rush-hour traffic back to Chicago."

"Actually, I'm staying at the New Chapel Inn and Suites until Friday. I keep getting requests to hold an event here, so I thought I'd check out some of the local venues."

"So you're parked outside then? Tell you what: Answer a few more questions, and then I'll walk you to your car."

"If it won't take long," she said, checking

her watch.

"It won't. I promise," Marco said. "So, then, can you remember whether Jonas argued with anyone last Thursday, male or female?"

"I don't believe he did."

"Did you match Jonas with anyone that night?"

She pondered it for a moment, tapping her long fingernails on the table. "There were two matches, I believe. We didn't process them, of course, because Jonas . . . you know . . . died."

"Did any of the women attending the event act as though they recognized him or had met him previously?"

She rubbed an eyebrow. "I can't recall. The events all start to blur after a while."

"I can appreciate that. Do you remember a woman by the name of Iris?"

Carmen rolled her eyes. "Iris Frey. What a nut job. Now, there's someone who recognized Jonas . . . not only recognized him, but was hot for him. Iris even phoned me to ask if she could be put on his list."

That was surprising news. I wouldn't have guessed Iris to be that forward. Yet it did prove that she had a crush on Jonas.

"Did you put Iris on Jonas's list?" Marco asked.

"As I told Iris, we don't do that unless both parties request it. It's against our policy."

"How did Iris take the news?" Marco asked.

"She tried to convince me to give her a break. She said I could have free dry-cleaning service for a year if I'd put her name on Jonas's list. I told her it wouldn't do me any good, because I didn't live in town, so then she had the gall to offer to pay me to put her on his list."

Trying to bribe Carmen smacked of true desperation. I wondered if Iris's mother knew to what lengths her daughter had gone to hook up with Jonas. Or maybe she did know and was embarrassed. That would explain her dirty looks when I was asking questions.

"Did Iris know Jonas would be attending that night before she called you?" Marco asked.

"Oh, yes," Carmen said, checking her cup to see if any espresso was left.

"Did you see Iris converse with Jonas at any time during the evening?"

"Yes, during the mixer," Carmen said. "Jonas was talking to someone at the bar, and Iris kept trying to get his attention, until finally he got annoyed and blew her off. She turned red in the face and went to sulk in a corner."

"Excuse me?" one of the ladies called again, waving a hand in the air. "More tea?"

All that tea and not a single bathroom break? "I'll be right over," I called back.

"You know," Carmen said to Marco, "if you're looking for someone who might have wanted revenge against Jonas, I think you should take a close look at Iris. She obviously had a thing for Jonas, and after he embarrassed her in front of everyone at the bar, I could see her getting into a car and ramming that Ferrari. To tell you the truth, Iris struck me as bizarre right from that phone conversation I had with her. Here's another thing to consider: I don't ever see her type coming to these events, and I'm wondering now why she thought she had even a sliver of a chance with Jonas."

"What do you mean by Iris's type?" Marco asked.

"You saw her, Amy," Carmen said, as I breezed past with more tea. "Was Iris the type to go to a speed-dating event?"

"It's Abby," I said, putting a fresh teapot on the ladies' table. I turned my back on Carmen to say, "Anything else I can get for you?"

"Yes," one said, "Grace."

I felt my face redden. "I'll send her right in."

As I headed for the doorway, I heard Carmen tell Marco, "Iris Frey was ugh-oh-lee! I've seen bag ladies dress better. If she thought Jonas would put her name on *his* list, she's seriously delusional. If she knew anything about Jonas at all, it was that he always went for the beautiful, wealthy women."

How did she know that? Marco let her revealing comment pass, but I was certain he'd caught it.

"The ladies want you," I told Grace, as she hung up the phone behind the cash counter.

"Thank you, dear." She paused to whisper, "Your cousin returned, so I put her to work unpacking a new shipment of orchids and lilies," then glided gracefully into the parlor.

I stood just outside the parlor to the left of the doorway, trying to hear Marco and Carmen's conversation over the ladies' buzzing.

"So what do you think Iris's . . . *mumble, mumble* . . . the event?" Marco asked.

"Well," Carmen said, "how about . . . *mumble, mumble?*"

"What are you doing?" Jillian asked, startling me.

"I'm rearranging," I whispered, and quickly moved a pair of ceramic lovebirds to a different shelf. "Keep your voice down."

"You're eavesdropping."

"Go away, Jill."

She peered into the parlor, then took me by the shoulders and moved me to the other side of the doorway. "Stand here. You'll catch more of their conversation. Want some coffee?"

"No!"

With a shrug, Jillian headed into the parlor.

"Do you recall where Iris was when Jonas's car was hit?" I heard Marco ask Carmen.

How about that? I *could* hear better from the right side.

"No," Carmen replied. "It got wild in the room after we heard the crash. Everyone was running for the door and screaming. . . ."

Running and screaming? That wasn't how I remembered it.

"Seriously," Carmen said, "I think you should take a look at Iris. I could totally see her as the hit-and-run driver. Couldn't you, Amy? Oh, sorry. I thought you were Amy."

"No prob. I'm Amy's cousin Jillian, personal shopper and floral designer. And you are . . . ?"

I'd get Jill for that.

"It's *Abby*," I whispered, punching Jillian's free arm as she came out of the parlor with her latte.

"Ouch! What happened to 'the customer is always right'?" Jillian retorted smugly.

I turned back to hear Marco say to Carmen, "I'm curious about something. Considering your opinion of Jonas and the experience one of your clients had with him, when he registered for the event last Thursday night, why did you let him attend?"

"I had no idea he registered," she said. "My assistant handles that."

Hmm. Her assistant wasn't the one who handled *my* registration.

"When you saw Jonas Thursday night, did you consider sending him away?"

"Yes, of course, but I didn't want him to cause a scene. It's bad for business."

"I can understand that. Have you ever dated a client?" Marco asked.

"I don't mix business with pleasure," was her curt reply. "I really have to run now. I have another engagement."

Knowing they'd come through any moment, I dashed across to the cash register. "Have a nice day, Carmen," I called, as Marco ushered her past.

"Mmm," she replied, barely casting me a glance. "You, too, Amy."

From behind the curtain, I heard Jillian snickering.

Marco returned five minutes later, blowing on his icy fingers, his cheeks red from the cold. "I was hoping to get a look at her car to check for recent repairs to the front or back end," he said, shedding his jacket, "but Carmen is driving a rental."

Seeing Jillian head for the parlor again, I motioned for Marco to follow me to the workroom. "Do you think Carmen might be the hit-and-run driver?"

He perched on a stool at the worktable. "I wouldn't rule her out."

"Wouldn't the police have noticed the damage when they searched the restaurant parking lot after the accident?"

"Yes, if her car was still in the lot. But here's another scenario: Do you remember seeing Carmen in the room when the restaurant manager made his announcement?"

"No, but I wasn't looking for her."

"Suppose she slipped out earlier, rammed Jonas's car, hid her own at the shopping mall next door, then blended back into the crowd when the police arrived."

"And caught a ride home later with her

assistant?"

"Bingo. No one but her assistant would be the wiser."

"It's possible, if Carmen had a reason to want to damage his car."

"She had a reason for giving him hostile looks, didn't she? Maybe she decided those looks weren't enough."

I thought it over. "Maybe that's why she's sending funeral flowers — remorse. And that bit about him looking for a good time instead of Mrs. Right? And being greedy? And dating only beautiful, wealthy women? That smacked of personal experience."

"I don't know if you caught it, but Carmen got edgy when I mentioned looking for people who might want to damage his car."

"I caught it. She sure was eager to point you toward Iris after that, wasn't she?"

He held up his hand to give me a high five. "We're on the same page, baby."

Good. I liked being on Marco's page. "Carmen also contradicted herself by saying she doesn't mix business with pleasure. Before you arrived, she told me her father had started the company so she could find a husband. But how would she do that unless she dated clients?"

"Good point."

"She also lied," I said. "Carmen was the

person who took my registration information, not her assistant, and there was no running and screaming when Jonas's car was hit. It wasn't until someone from the restaurant announced that a Ferrari had been hit, and Jonas ran out of the room, that people — including me — left the restaurant to take a look."

"So why would she say that unless she wasn't there and had to guess?"

"You know what else I found interesting? Carmen had an excellent memory of the details of that speed-dating event ten months ago, except when it came to recalling the name of Jonas's date. But I'll bet her assistant would know. And guess what? I have her name and phone number." I slipped the card out of my pocket and put it in front of him. "It's Pamela."

He slid the card into his wallet. "What did you think about Carmen's revelations about Iris Frey? You've met the woman. Do you think Carmen was telling the truth?"

"About Iris trying to bribe Carmen? That surprises me, but if it's true, then my guess about Iris having a crush on Jonas was right. And when I think back, Iris definitely wasn't pleased to see Jonas talking to Nikki, so who knows? Maybe her jealousy drove her to do something irrational. She might even be the anonymous tipster."

"Exactly what I was thinking," he said, writing in his notebook. Apparently, we were on more than one page together.

"So I believe I have a kiss coming?"

Marco gave me his easy grin as he put an arm around me and pulled me toward him. "Monster," he said, then dipped his head down so our lips could meet.

"Excuse me," Jillian said loudly, clapping her hands as she came into the workroom, making me jump an inch into the air. "Sorry to interrupt your smooch-fest, but when are you going to have more deliveries for me?"

Marco gave me a look that said, *I told you to fire her.*

I twisted around to glare at her. "Did you have to clap? You took ten years off my life."

"*Someone* is jumpy today," she said. "Remember what your dad told us? If you're jumpy, that means you have a guilty conscience."

"He was a cop, Jill. He was talking about criminals."

She gave me a puzzled look. "Seriously?"

It was way too easy to bluff Jillian. "I've only got four orders to finish, and I should be able to make those deliveries myself after work, so you can have the driver take you home."

She looked so dejected that I felt bad for disappointing her, especially after how hard she'd tried to help out. I stood on tiptoe to give her a hug. "Thanks for everything, Jill. I really appreciate your hiring that limo. Enjoy the rest of your day."

"But it's only two o'clock. I can send the driver home and work the cash register for you. My fingernails are already in ruins, so it won't make any difference."

I plucked her coat off the back of my chair, put it over her shoulders, and ushered her toward the curtain. "Thanks, Jillian, but business has been slow this afternoon. Don't you have any shopping to do for your clients?"

"I'm between clients right now."

"What about your mom's gift? Have you given *The Bowler* to her yet?"

"Mom was at the country club when I dropped it off at the house this morning. I guess I should be there when she gets home and finds it, shouldn't I?"

"Are you kidding? You don't want to miss her expression when she sees it, do you? In fact, use your cell phone camera to take a picture for me, okay? I don't want to miss it either."

I watched Jillian go, then turned back with

a grin on my face. Marco merely shook his head.

"So give me your update from this morning," I urged, gathering my tools and supplies for the next order. "Did you talk to Robin?"

"She wasn't there, but get this coincidence: One of her coworkers said she had to take her car in to a body shop to have some work done."

I backed out of the cooler, a stem of lilies in my hand. "What kind of work?"

"He didn't say, but I've got the name of the shop if I need to check it out."

"I know we have to consider her a suspect in the murder because she's Jonas's ex-fiancée, but even so, why would Robin want to damage Jonas's car? She broke up with *him,* not vice versa, and seemed very glad to be rid of him."

"Do you know that for a fact?"

"I know only what Robin and Lottie told me."

"They both have it wrong," Jillian said, coming through the curtain with a cup of coffee. She dropped her coat on the back of my desk chair, sat on a stool, and put her cup down in front of her, as though she planned to be there a while.

"Robin gave Jonas an ultimatum," Jillian

said, "to either lose the woman he was cheating on her with or hit the road. So he hit the road — actually the dating circuit. Seems he never intended to marry Robin. He was a player."

"I thought you wanted to get over to your mom's house to watch her open her gift," I said.

"She won't be home for another hour." Jillian smiled at me.

"How do you know this information about Robin, Jillian?" Marco asked.

"It was all over town. You know how everyone gossips." She took a sip of coffee, looking pleased with herself.

Why didn't that kind of gossip ever reach *my* part of town? "Excuse me," I said, "but Robin told me that she was the one who did the breaking up."

"Well, Robin wasn't being honest," Jillian retorted. "She never thought Jonas wouldn't marry her, and was absolutely crushed when he backed out. She had rented a hall, lined up her bridesmaids, ordered a very expensive wedding gown, even bought him a wedding band at Bindstroms, *the* most expensive jeweler in town." Jillian sighed. "All for nothing."

"Would she have married Jonas even after he cheated on her?" I asked.

"Well, duh. After going to all that expense, wouldn't you? She could've divorced Jonas later and taken half his money, you know. Chateaux en Carnations made him a multimillionaire, and what's half of a multimillion?" She paused to calculate, then waved her hand in the air. "Well, you do the math."

My cousin, the Harvard grad. "Wait a minute, Jillian. Are you sure about that gown and wedding band? Because Robin told me she was glad she hadn't spent any money on the wedding."

"Again," Jillian said, feigning boredom, "Robin — not honest. She dropped big bucks on her gown and Jonas's wedding band — had it personalized and everything — and you know she'd get very little back if she tried to return either one. Makes you wonder what else she lied about, doesn't it?"

"Were there any rumors of who Jonas was seeing?" Marco asked.

"Are you serious?" Jillian's eyes sparkled as she shared her juicy gossip. "Too many women to list. Jonas had a new date every night — well, until he landed this aging rich chick from Chicago who couldn't do enough for him. Brioni suits, a Rolex watch — even a sports car. Then someone saw her and Jonas together in Chicago and reported back to Robin, and that's when Robin told him to lose the girlfriend or lose her. Unfortunately for Robin, it was 'Bye-bye, birdie.'

"And get this — talk about justice — turns out the rich chick used her father's money to finance Jonas's gifts, but Daddy found out and cut her off, and when Jonas discovered no more bucks were forthcoming, he said, 'Cheerio, chickadee.' "

Marco and I glanced at each other. *That had to be Carmen!*

"Do you know what kind of sports car this woman bought Jonas?" Marco asked.

"Of course," Jillian said. "A Ferrari."

"Do you know anything else about the woman?" Marco asked.

"No, but I can find out more."

"That's okay, Jill," I said, ready to shoo her out of the room. "We'll take it from here."

"How would you go about that, Jillian?" Marco asked.

"I know people who know people," my cousin answered, trying to be mysterious.

"Do you think you can find out the woman's name?" Marco asked. "First and last? Maybe an address or phone number, too?"

Jillian glided off her stool and picked up her coat. "Stand back and watch me."

■ ■ ■ ■

I waited until I heard the bell over the door jingle; then I put my hands on my hips and gazed at Marco in disbelief. "Do you have any idea what you've just unleashed? We'll never be rid of Jillian now."

Marco glanced around the workroom. "I don't see her here. Do you?"

"So you gave her that assignment to get her out of here?"

"Well, we've pretty much figured out it was Carmen, although Jillian doesn't know that."

"Aren't you clever."

He pulled me toward him, so I was standing between his knees, my arms draped around his neck. "I've been known to have a surprise or two up my sleeve."

"Really?" I tugged on his T-shirt. "Have you got any more up your sleeve?"

"I don't keep them *all* there," he said, lifting one eyebrow, which was all it took to get my blood running hot.

I nuzzled his ear, nibbling the earlobe, which I knew drove him wild. "Maybe you can drop by later this evening to show me where you keep the rest," I whispered.

"I think we're on the same page again,"

he said, and kissed me hard.

Marco's phone rang a few minutes later, but it took a while for the sound to register. He paused to check the caller ID. "It's Gina," he said, kissing me as he opened the phone to answer it. "Hey, sis. What's up?"

To give him some privacy, I moved away and began to work on my next arrangement.

"Okay, take it easy, Gina," Marco said. He listened a few moments longer, then said, "Are you really sure you want to do that? No, I'm just saying . . . Okay. I'll be there in fifteen minutes."

"Is Gina all right?" I asked, as he put away his phone.

"She's had cramps since early this morning, and she's afraid something's wrong with the baby. The doctor wants her to get over to the ER, but Gina's husband left on a business trip this morning, and little Christopher is home from preschool, so she doesn't know what to do."

"I'm sorry. I hope she's all right. Are you going to take her to the ER?"

"Yep." He got up and slid on his jacket.

I cut a hunk of wet foam with my floral knife. "What about Christopher?"

Marco zipped his jacket. "I suppose he'll have to hang out in the waiting room with me. I sure hate to expose him to all those germs, though . . . unless you'd watch him for a while?"

Me? Watch a two-year-old? "I'd like to help out, Marco, but I have orders to finish."

Marco came up to put his arms around me. "Chris is a good little kid, Abby. He'll play quietly with his toys right here. And it'll only be until my mom arrives."

The wet foam slipped out of my hands. "Your mother is coming?"

Surprise!

CHAPTER SEVENTEEN

Babysitting wasn't something I'd ever enjoyed. In fact, for several years I'd lived in dread of the next-door neighbors calling to ask if I was available that Saturday night. And between the ages of fourteen and sixteen, it seemed I was always available.

Maybe it had been the cockroaches in their kitchen, which I'd discovered after turning out the light one evening. I'd never let my feet touch the floor in their house again. Or maybe it had been their five kids, all under the age of nine, all hyperactive, and always hungry. Which necessitated a trip to the kitchen. On my skateboard. Whatever the reason, I wasn't in any hurry to repeat the experience.

But this was for Marco. How could I refuse?

"Sure. I'll watch Christopher."

"Thanks." He kissed the top of my head. "I'll bring him by on our way to the hospital, around . . ." He checked his watch. "Looks like my battery died. Probably half an hour. Okay?"

"Great!" *Just great.*

"Who is Marco bringing by?" Grace asked after Marco left.

I sighed morosely. "His two-year-old nephew."

"How delightful," Grace said. "Is the baby toilet trained?"

"You mean there's a chance he wouldn't be?"

"He's two, dear. Usually they're just beginning to wean off their nappies then."

I dropped my head in my hands with a groan. "I have to change nappies?"

"I'm here, love. I can help then, can't I?"

"Marco's mother is on her way from Ohio. Anything you can do in that department?"

"As I remember, you and she got along famously."

"That was before Gina thought I was trying to pick up men." At Grace's perplexed expression, I explained what had happened at Duke Kessler's gym and Jillian's subsequent conversation with Gina.

"Oh, dear. I can understand your concern. Well, you did survive the baby shower in good form, and this time there's no social event to attend, so perhaps you won't even see Mrs. Salvare."

From Grace's lips to God's ear.

I put together three arrangements before Marco returned with Christopher. He strode in carrying the child bundled in a blue snowsuit, with a large quilted diaper bag over his shoulder, looking every inch a suburban dad, which was as endearing as it was frightening.

"Here we are, Chris. Abby's flower shop."

The curly-haired, blue-eyed boy gazed around the room in amazement. "Abby fower sop."

"Can you say, 'Hi, Abby'?" Marco asked, giving me a wink as he stopped in front of me.

Chris opened and closed his chubby little hand. "H' Abby." He leaned forward to touch my hair, as though he'd never seen red locks before. I smelled peanut butter on his fingers and suspected I'd find sticky residue in my hair later.

"You be a good boy for Abby." Marco kissed his smooth baby cheek. The way he gazed at the child, I wondered if he were longing for one of his own — or if it was merely the power of Gina's suggestion working on my mind.

"Where should we put him?" I asked.

"There's a blanket in his bag. Maybe you can spread it in the corner."

I pulled out a cushy blue blanket with yellow and red sailboats on it and spread it in the back corner beside the cabinets. Then I began removing toys from the bag, setting them in the middle of the blanket. Marco put Chris down and squatted beside him, running his fingers through the child's hair. "Okay, Christopher Robin. Unc will be back in just a little while."

Chris immediately held up his arms to be picked up. "See Mommy."

"Mommy will be back soon, too," Marco assured him. He motioned me over, so I got onto my knees and picked up a plastic windup car, turned the key, and watched it run across the room and crash into the cooler. Chris gurgled with laughter.

Marco brought the car back. I wound it and let it go; it hit the table leg, and Chris shrieked with joy.

That wasn't so bad.

Marco brought the toy back again, leaning down to give me a kiss on the cheek and say in my ear, "You're doing great. I'll keep you posted on Gina." And then he was gone. Chris watched him depart, glanced at me in growing alarm, glanced back at the doorway, then screwed up his face, ready to cry.

"Watch, Chris!" I cried, and wound up the car again and let it run across the room. This time it ran under the curtain and disappeared.

"See Mommy!" he cried, using his hands to push himself unsteadily to his feet.

"Look what I found," Grace sang out, breezing through the curtain with the runaway toy in hand. "Someone lost a car, didn't he?"

As Chris watched, Grace wound up the car and sent it scurrying toward the blanket, where it scooted underneath and came to a stop near the child's foot. Chris instantly became intrigued and got down on his hands and knees to figure out where it went.

"I brought biscuits," Grace said quietly, placing a box of her favorite imported butter cookies on the counter. "They're always good in an emergency."

"He doesn't like me," I whispered.

"Nonsense. He's in an unfamiliar place and has separation anxiety."

Chris finally uncovered his toy and held it out to her.

"You're a love, you are," she said, and picked him up, bouncing him in her arms as naturally as though she'd done it a thousand times. Knowing Grace had never had children, I said, "How did you learn how to do that?"

"I was a nurse, don't forget." She sniffed Chris's pant leg and said, "Someone needs a nappy change." Then she glanced at me with a smile. "And someone else needs a nappy lesson."

I would have been happier with a nap.

Marco returned an hour after closing time. "Sorry it took so long," he said, when I let him in. "The ER was jammed."

"Is Gina okay?"

"She's fine. I took her home before I came here. The doctor thinks it was indigestion. She had a bowl of chili for dinner last night, even though she knows it bothers her."

All that trouble for gas.

We stepped into the workroom, where Chris was almost finished unloading a cabinet full of small plastic pots and liners, having successfully turned out two other cabinets. Marco gazed around at the mess. "I'll help you clean this up. How did he do otherwise?"

"Great," I said, throwing as much enthusiasm in my voice as possible. I wasn't about to tell him that I hadn't been able to leave Chris's side for a second since Grace left to attend her book-club meeting, and as a result, my bladder was ready to explode. "He's really a cute kid, Marco. Very well behaved." And he was, actually.

Hearing "Unc's" voice, Chris backed out of the cabinet, got to his feet, and ran into his arms. He put his chubby hands on either side of Marco's face. "See Mommy?"

"You got it. Let's get your snowsuit on, okay?"

Between the two of us, we got the wiggling child into his snowsuit and mittens, and his diaper bag loaded. "Say thank-you to Abby," Marco instructed, holding Chris in his arms.

Chris reached out to pat my face. "Tanku to Abby."

"You're welcome, Chris." I took his little hand, already showing signs of being a boy's hand, and kissed it. The kid was growing on me.

"I'll be back," Marco said, giving me a quick kiss on the cheek.

Or so he thought.

My phone rang fifteen minutes later, as I was stacking pots to put them back in the cabinet. "There's been a change of plans," Marco said quietly. "My mother just got here, and she brought Rafe with her."

"Rafe, as in Raphael, your youngest

brother?"

"You got it."

"I thought he was attending Miami of Ohio."

"The idiot dropped out with only one semester to go. Mama brought him along so I can talk some sense into him."

"Your mom didn't happen to say how long they were staying, did she?"

"She'll probably leave in a day or so. I think she just wants to be sure Gina is okay."

I hoped that was all it was. "Speaking of Gina, you explained that little misunderstanding she had about my talking to those guys at the gym, right?"

"You worry too much. Everything's cool. I'll be down soon to clean up your workroom."

"You don't need to do that. I've already got most of it cleaned up anyway." I turned my back on the mess behind me. If I couldn't see it, it wasn't there. "Stay and visit with your family." I didn't want to admit the truth, that a two-year-old had worn me out.

"Sorry about this evening, Sunshine. It wasn't what I had in mind when I told you I had a few surprises up my sleeve."

We exchanged phone kisses, then hung up. I really was beat. Chris had been a great kid, but four hours of entertaining him had taken the stuffing out of me. I couldn't imagine having to do that all day long . . . or wanting to. Was there something wrong with me?

I awoke at half past four o'clock in the morning, having slept seven solid hours. Nikki had returned, I noticed. Her bedroom door was shut and her car keys were on the kitchen counter. I showered, ate breakfast, read the newspaper, watched *The Early Show,* and it was still only six a.m.

Streetlights were still on when I pulled into the public parking lot downtown. Wrapping my scarf tighter around my neck, I hustled to Bloomers in the frigid morning air, turned off the burglar alarm, flicked on lights, and walked around the shop, enjoying the feeling of owning my very own paradise. Yep, Bloomers was *my* baby — and it didn't need diapers.

After I finished cleaning up the workroom, I turned on the computer and saw that only two orders had come in overnight. Two orders, way down from the day before, down further from the day before that. To keep from worrying, I started on one of the orders, a floral arrangement for a three-year-old boy's birthday. Remembering how much Chris had enjoyed his toy car, I dug through a stack of baby-themed containers and found an open-topped, bright yellow ceramic car with blue wheels and red trim. Then I opened the cooler to see what types of blossoms struck my fancy.

I finally settled on red carnations, yellow daisies, orange alstroemeria, dark purple alstroemeria, light purple statice, and green Kermit — crayon colors. When I finished, I was so pleased with the final product that I pulled out my digital camera and took a photograph of it. If I ever got around to designing a Web site for Bloomers, I was going to need something to put on it.

Shortly before eight o'clock, I heard the bell jingle and went up front to greet Grace.

"Good morning, love," she said, locking the door behind her. "You're here early today."

"I thought I'd get started on the orders, but there were only two."

"I'm sure more will come in," she said, heading into the parlor to prepare for the day. "Lottie should be released from the hospital today. I spoke with her last night and she couldn't wait to get into her own bed. And if she hasn't told you yet, she loved the gift basket you made."

The phone rang, so I picked it up at the

front counter. "Bloomers Flower Shop. How can I help you?"

"Abby?" I heard Nikki say, her voice rising in panic. "They're coming to arrest me!"

CHAPTER EIGHTEEN

"Are the cops there now?" I asked Nikki, who was breathing so hard I expected to hear a thunk as she fell to the floor.

"Not yet, but what am I going to do, Abby?" she wailed. "I don't want to go to jail."

"Nikki, calm down! How do you know the cops are coming to arrest you?"

"Dave just called to tell me the police lab report backs up their claim that I killed Jonas."

"How?"

"Something about the blue clay on my boots most likely coming from Jonas's property, and the blood on my sweater being Jonas's type —"

"Blood on your sweater?"

"I told you he cut his hand. I must have gotten some on my sleeve."

"How do they know it was Jonas's blood? They couldn't possibly have done DNA testing already."

"He has AB negative blood, Abby. It's uncommon."

Crap. More evidence against her.

She began to cry. "All I did was to help him clean out a wound."

"Did Dave say specifically that the cops are coming to arrest you?"

"No, but if they found blood —"

"Nikki, listen to me. If they were going to arrest you, they'd call Dave first, and he'd arrange for you to turn yourself in. If he didn't tell you that, then don't panic. Now tell me what else Dave said."

"I don't remember the rest. I was so upset I stopped listening. . . . I think maybe he said to meet him at his office in an hour."

"Okay, go see Dave in an hour; then call me and let me know what's happening."

"Abby, please find the killer."

"Marco's working on it, Nik."

"You're not working on it, too?"

"I'm doing my best, I promise, but technically Dave hired Marco for the job, so I have to be careful I don't cause any problems for him. Plus, with Lottie out, it's kind of hard for me —"

"Hard for *you?* How do you think it is for me? This is my *life* we're talking about, Abby."

She hung up.

I turned and found Grace gazing at me in concern. "More bad news?"

"The cops found more evidence incriminating Nikki."

"Oh, dear."

"She has no way to verify her alibi, and there's enough circumstantial evidence that I'm afraid the cops will stop looking for other suspects, if they haven't already."

Grace put her hand on my shoulder in sympathy.

I sighed in frustration. "I'm not supposed to be in on the investigation without Dave's approval, but honestly, Grace, it's killing me to not be actively looking for the murderer. And trying to arrange these so-called chance encounters with the suspects is ridiculous, not to mention a time waster for me. I need to get out there and search, damn it!"

"I agree with you, dear. As the saying goes, time is of the essence. Perhaps it's not a coincidence that you have only two orders this morning. Perhaps it's ordained."

Or perhaps my business was dying — another fear in the back of my mind. "Dave says I'm prejudiced on Nikki's behalf, but so what if I believe in her innocence? Why should that be a drawback?"

"Have your coffee, love; then do what you

must to help Nikki. I'll handle things here."

"There's my other concern. How can I leave you here alone, Grace? You can't manage everything by yourself."

"I won't have to. I've come up with a grand idea for assistance that happily does not involve your cousin." With a secretive glimmer in her eye, she put the cup and saucer in front of me. "Go on, then. Bottoms up. Everything looks better after that first cup."

I drank the coffee, and it did help me focus. With new resolve, I hit speed dial number two and reached Marco at his apartment. "Has Dave called you yet?" I asked.

"I just got off the phone with him."

"So you know about the blue clay and the blood on Nikki's sweater."

"Yep."

"Okay, look, Marco, I'm going to help you find the killer, so don't even think about trying to talk me out of it. This is too important."

"I'm not going to talk you out of it. In fact, Dave said Nikki called him and insisted that you be in on it."

Wow. That made things so much easier. "Fantastic. So let's divvy up the suspect list and get started."

"Will you have time to get away from Bloomers?"

"Not a problem, as it turns out."

"My notes are in my office. Meet me at the bar in half an hour. I'll unlock the alley door for you."

When I got to the bar at eight thirty, Marco was in his office talking on the phone, his chair swung to face the back wall. I walked up behind him and put my arms around him, leaning down to nuzzle his neck. "Guess who?"

"Give me a clue." He turned to face me, still holding the phone to his ear.

It wasn't Marco.

I backed up with a gasp as a younger, lankier version of Marco grinned at me, then said into the phone, "Call you later." He hung up and leaned back, clasping his hands behind his head and putting his booted feet on Marco's black metal desk. "Let's see. Red hair, freckles, and smelling like roses . . . you have to be Abby."

"You must be Marco's little brother, Raphael."

"*Younger* brother. And call me Rafe. I'm an all-American male." He opened his jacket to show me his T-shirt emblazoned with a U.S. flag on the front. "I don't go in for that Italian-culture stuff."

That had to infuriate his mother. Francesca Salvare was extremely proud of her heritage.

With a grin, Rafe said, "You made quite an impression on my nephew yesterday. All morning Chris kept saying, 'See Abby. Go Abby fower sop.'"

"How cute is that?"

As I tossed my coat and scarf on a chair, Marco came into the room, a cup of coffee in hand. "I see you've met my brother."

Even with a nine-year difference in their ages, the resemblance was striking. Rafe's face was a bit leaner, Marco's had the beginnings of crow's-feet, but both were attractive, virile men.

"Abby thought I was you," Rafe said to Marco, winking at me, reminding me even more of his older brother.

Marco scowled at him until he removed his feet from the desktop. "Did you finish bagging the empty bottles?"

"I had to make a phone call." He got up and started out of the office, pausing to say to Marco sotto voce, "You're right. She *is* hot."

That beat *plucky* any day.

Marco shut the door behind him, set his cup on his desk, and pulled me into his

289

arms. "Just so you know, I didn't tell him you were hot."

"It's okay if you did." I slid my arms around his waist. "I don't mind. Do I really smell like roses?"

He pressed his nose against the top of my head. "And vanilla."

"It's my new organic shampoo. Are you babysitting your brother this morning?"

"He's been driving my mother crazy, so I thought I'd put him to work. Rafe somehow has it in his head that he can drop out of college, laze around the house all day, hang out with his friends at night, and no one will complain."

"I'm shocked your mom puts up with that. She's such a no-nonsense person."

"He's the baby of the family. She spoiled him. So she asked me to shape him up."

"Will Rafe be staying in New Chapel then?"

"Until he realizes that school would be a hell of a lot easier than working for me." He dipped his head toward me. "You *are* hot, by the way."

Our lips met for a few long, dreamy moments. I would have happily continued down that road, but because we had more pressing concerns, we reluctantly cut it short to get to work.

Muttering, "I'll be glad when we have some time to ourselves again," Marco took a seat at his desk and pulled out his notebook, while I settled in one of the leather chairs on the other side. "All right," he said, glancing over his notes, "who would you say is our strongest suspect?"

"At this point, I'd have to say Carmen Gold."

"Motive for murder?"

"Motive. Okay, if Carmen is, as we suspect, the older woman Jonas was dating, then she'd be the one who bought him the Ferrari with her dad's money. So for motive, I'd say being used by a greedy boyfriend and then dumped when she couldn't buy him any more goodies is a good one, and also makes her a prime candidate for a vengeful hit-and-run driver, especially because she's driving a rental car now."

Marco took the Cloud Nine business card out of his wallet and lifted his phone. "Let's see what I can pry out of Carmen's assistant.

"Hi, is this Pamela? My name is Marco Salvare. I'm a private investigator working on a case involving a vehicle owned by Jonas Treat. I understand Jonas was a Cloud Nine client and — Yes, I did speak with Carmen about this case yesterday. . . . I understand, but I was hoping you could — I see. Okay, thank you." He hung up. "Pamela has orders not to talk to anyone about Jonas, but if I need the name of the company lawyer, she will provide it for me."

"That's interesting. Do you think we made Carmen nervous yesterday?"

"Seems that way." Marco pursed his lips, thinking. "Tonight is the next speed-dating event in Maraville, right? Is there a time when we could slip into the restaurant and talk to Pamela without Carmen seeing us?"

"I think so, once the first round of dating starts."

"Let's plan on it. Next up is Robin Lennox. What makes her a likely suspect?"

I listed the items on my fingers. "Jonas cheated on her while they were engaged. He backed out of their wedding at the last minute. Jillian heard Robin lost a lot of money on her gown and a wedding band for Jonas. She's having bodywork done on her car."

"You're getting good at this, Sunshine."

"I should be. I'm learning from the master."

He gave a nod to acknowledge my compliment. "So tell me how Robin knew to find Jonas at the sales office late on a Sunday evening."

"She might have known his work habits. Or maybe she phoned him earlier in the day and asked to meet with him."

"Why would he schedule a meeting with his ex-fiancée *after* his date with Nikki, or at all, for that matter? Jonas allegedly had Nikki home by midnight. That would put him back at his sales office about twelve thirty. Kind of late to set up a meeting. Besides, how would he know in advance what time his date with Nikki would end?"

I scratched my forehead, thinking. "We did discuss an angry ex tailing him, didn't we? Maybe Robin followed him that evening, waited until after Jonas took Nikki home, then called him from her car and asked to see him."

"Still, why would Jonas agree to meet with her?"

"That would depend on the reason Robin gave for wanting a meeting."

"What we need is a copy of Jonas's phone records. Dave was expecting the prosecutor's discovery information to come this morning, and the phone records should be in that package, so I'll give him a call when we finish here." Marco glanced at his watch, muttered something about the battery, then unstrapped it from his wrist and laid it aside. "Let's keep going. What about

Iris Frey?"

"All signs seem to indicate Iris had a crush on Jonas, and her feelings clearly weren't reciprocated, so maybe she found out about his dinner date with Nikki, then, in a jealous rage, confronted him afterward and stabbed him."

"If Iris had a crush on Jonas, why kill him? Why not go after Nikki?"

I pondered that for a moment. "If Iris can't have Jonas, no one can?"

"It's weak, considering she never even dated him. Why would she think she had a chance?"

"Maybe Jonas flirted with her at the dry cleaner's."

"Still weak."

"You're right. Plus, Iris doesn't seem the violent type, although, as you've pointed out, people swept up in the heat of the moment can do bad things. Don't look so surprised. I actually do listen to you."

With a sly grin, Marco said, "Okay, Fireball, then how would Iris have found out about Jonas's date with Nikki?"

"Follow him to Nikki's house." I shrugged. "Iris doesn't really seem the stalker type to me, but as you've also told me, we can't count someone out until we can."

Marco's eyes widened. "You *are* a fireball today."

"I do my best," I said, flipping back my hair to make him laugh.

"We need photos of our suspects. If someone's been stalking Jonas, the staff at his sales office might be able to identify the person."

Somewhere in the bar, glass shattered. Then Rafe called, "I'm okay. I just dropped an empty beer bottle. I'll clean it up."

Marco went to the doorway. "Rafe!"

His brother appeared a few seconds later, a sheepish look on his face. "Sorry. It slipped out of my hands."

"Forget that for the moment. You're computer savvy. I need photos of these people." He tore off a page in his notebook and handed it to his brother. "See what you can dig up."

"Yes, master," Rafe said, pretending to be Dr. Frankenstein's assistant. "Igor get photos." He hunched his back and dragged one leg as he headed toward the desk, glancing at me as he passed. "How do you stand him?" he whispered.

"It takes practice," I whispered back.

Ignoring his brother's antics, Marco vacated his desk so Rafe could sit down, then took a seat in the chair next to mine and propped his notebook on his lap. "Next up is Hank Miller. What do we know about him?"

"Miller sold his land to Jonas. He had an altercation with Jonas three days before Jonas was killed. Miller claimed he was in Florida when Jonas died."

"I tried to reach Miller at his home in the Keys earlier this morning to get more information, but no one answered. I asked a friend of mine at O'Hare to check the passenger manifests on all flights in and out of the Miami, Key West, and Marathon airports around that date to see if by chance Miller did any flying. I should hear back from him today."

Marco turned the page in his notebook. "Last up is Duke Kessler. What do we know?"

I ticked the items off on my fingers. "Jonas made deals behind Duke's back. Jonas left the realty business to cut him out of a multimillion dollar deal. Duke filed a lawsuit two months ago over it."

"Losing out on that kind of money is a strong motive. Do we know where Kessler was when Jonas was killed?"

"Sorry. I didn't ask him."

"No problem. Kessler was probably interviewed by the cops, so that information should be in the discovery package, too. I still want to get over to the gym to talk to him myself."

"Here's your photo of Iris Frey," Rafe said. "It's from an archived article in the *New Chapel News* from last year. Is the picture quality okay? It's kind of grainy."

We went around the desk to look at the monitor screen. "It's clear enough," Marco said.

"That is one unattractive woman," Rafe said, shaking his head. "I've never seen anyone with a face shaped like an hourglass. It's like her head got caught in a vise."

"At least Iris has a good sense of humor," I said. "You should meet her mother." Then, as I skimmed through the article, I said to Marco, "This is sad. According to the paper, a fire destroyed part of the second floor of their building and severely injured Iris's father, William, while he slept. I don't remember it, but I was in law school. I didn't have time to read the back of the cereal boxes, let alone newspapers."

"I was a rookie cop then," Marco said. "I recall a concern about arson being raised, but the cause was finally determined to be from an unattended candle in one of the bedrooms."

Rafe's fingers flew over the keyboard.

"Here's something about Cloud Nine."

I stood at Rafe's shoulder, watching the monitor as he scrolled down the Cloud Nine Web site searching for a photo.

"While you're finishing that, I'll call Dave," Marco said, and picked to the phone.

"Here we go," Rafe said. "Damn! Carmen Gold is a babe."

"She's too old for you," I said.

He cast me a decidedly Marco-like flirtatious glance. "Not a problem. I like older women."

"Just print the photo." On second thought . . . "Hey, Rafe, how would you feel about going out with a very attractive twenty-six-year-old?"

Rafe gave me a skeptical glance. "Well, okay, if my big bro doesn't mind."

"Not me! My roommate, Nikki."

Rafe reached for the paper coming out of the printer. "The murder suspect? Pass."

"Nikki didn't kill anyone," I said, snatching the print from his hand. "She was in the wrong place at the wrong time."

Marco ended his call and picked up his notebook, reading from it. "Okay, here's what Dave told me. He received the discovery package, but the phone records were omitted, so he's expecting to get them shortly by fax. The only interviews he has knowledge of were conducted with Hank Miller, Duke Kessler, Nikki, and Jonas's employees at the sales office. No one has been called back for a second interview."

"I can't believe they didn't interview Carmen," I said. "From talking to Nikki, the detectives knew Jonas attended a speed-dating event. You'd think they'd want to find out who Jonas met and what transpired that evening, especially since it took place a mere three days before he was murdered. They're ignoring the obvious. Do they know something we don't?"

"We don't have time to speculate," Marco said, gathering the photos from Rafe. "We've got a lot to accomplish and it's already . . ." He glanced at his wrist, remembering belatedly that he had removed his watch. "Damn. I keep forgetting."

"Toss your watch my way," Rafe said. "If that jewelry store is still on the corner, I'll take it down and get a battery put in."

"Thanks," Marco said. "All right, let's get to work. Abby, do you want to see what you can get Iris Frey to tell you about her whereabouts Sunday night?"

"I'm on it," I said, slipping on my coat. "I'm also going to stop at Betty's Bridal Shop to see if there's any record of Robin ordering a gown. I want to know if she told me the truth about her wedding expenses."

"We also need to get over to Dunn's Body Shop later today to see if we can get a look at Robin's car," Marco said. "Right now I'm going to make a few phone calls to see what I can find out about Miller's and Kessler's alibis; then I'll head over to Dave's office to pick up the discovery information. Meet me here when you're finished, and we'll head to Jonas's development to show our suspects' photos to his employees."

"Sounds like a plan," I told him. But not a complete one. I needed a reason to go to Frey's. I picked up Marco's coffee cup and saw a few drops left. "Got a spare shirt?"

Marco opened a sleek black cabinet beneath his wall-mounted TV and pulled out a light gray T-shirt with black script on it that said, DOWN THE HATCH BAR AND GRILL.

"Dude," Rafe said, "can I have one?"

Marco tossed it to his brother and gave me another one. I tipped his cup, spilling the last sip of coffee onto one sleeve. "Now I have a reason to go to Frey's."

When I stepped inside the dry-cleaning shop, I was instantly assailed by the chemical odor. There was a line of people waiting to drop off clothing, but no Iris behind the counter, only a high school–aged girl sporting short black hair with purple tips. Because of time constraints, I bypassed the line, walked up to the counter, and said to the girl, "Is Iris here?"

"Hey! No cuts!" the last woman in line yelled, clearly believing she was in third grade.

"Iris will be in at noon," the girl told me, taking payment from a senior citizen who didn't seem at all bothered by my standing beside her. "She comes in late on Thursdays."

Noon? *Damn.* Half the day would be gone. I glanced through the doorway behind the counter and saw Iris's mother working the huge pressing iron, wearing the same drab smock she'd had on before. *Hmm.* Maybe she would tell me where Iris was Sunday evening.

"Can I speak with Mrs. Frey?" I asked the girl.

She glanced behind her, through the doorway, then said quietly to me, "She doesn't like to be bothered."

"Get in line," someone else called.

"I just need to talk to someone," I called back, then whispered to the girl, "This is really important."

"Why are you carrying a shirt with you

then?" Ms. No-Cuts called snidely, starting others grumbling, too.

"Fine!" I said loudly. I stuffed the T-shirt in my purse, flipped up the counter gate, and darted through the doorway into the back room.

"Wait," the girl yelled. "You're not allowed back there. You might —"

Fall into a laundry cart?

CHAPTER NINETEEN

In my haste to reach Mrs. Frey, I didn't notice the canvas cart parked just inside the doorway. I was too busy wishing I'd brought a bouquet of flowers, because it always made the questioning easier. My knees hit the soft side of the cart, and I tumbled face-first into a pile of soiled clothing.

As I struggled to find purchase to push myself out of the smelly clothes, a strong hand reached in, grabbed my upper arm, and pulled me to my feet. "Thank you," I said, straightening my coat and smoothing down my hair. "I usually make a less dramatic entrance."

Mrs. Frey's sunken-cheeked face seemed to be formed into a permanent frown, so I couldn't tell whether she was smiling or scowling, but my bet was on the scowl.

"What are you doing here?" she said in a decidedly unfriendly tone.

"I don't know if you remember me, but I

was in the other day to drop off some laundry." *Good job, Abby.* Like that would make me stand out from all the other customers.

She went back to the big presser and removed a pair of men's slacks. "I remember you. The nosy florist. What do you want?"

"I'm helping my friend, an investigator, with a" — might as well use Marco's gambit — "a hit-and-run accident that happened in the parking lot of the Wild Boar Steak House in Maraville after the Cloud Nine speed-dating event last Thursday night, and I thought maybe —"

"I wasn't there," she snarled.

"Yes, I know that, but did Iris mention anything about the accident to you?"

"Iris isn't here."

"I know that, too, but she *was* at the restaurant that night."

"That stupid girl. I told her not to go there. Men are nothing but trouble anyway. Why would she want to meet someone and get married? What is marriage but misery? I had nothing but misery for thirty-seven years. Misery and hard labor. But has Iris ever listened to me? Ha! Do you listen to your mother?"

"Most of the time." Fingers crossed behind my back.

"Iris doesn't listen to nothing I say." Mrs. Frey put in another pair of pants and closed the machine. "I don't know what I can tell you, except how stupid that girl is. Now look what happened. We get nosy investigators poking into our business."

"Has someone been around to question Iris?"

She glared at me. "Looks like Iris ain't the only stupid girl around here."

It wasn't going to be easy to get useful information from this nasty old woman, but I was determined to find a way, even if I had to be sneaky. "So you're not in favor of Iris dating then?"

"Iris? Why would she want to date? Where does it lead except to a miserable marriage?"

"I hear you loud and clear," I said, playing along. "It's hard to find a decent guy out there. At least Iris has her comedy-club gig to keep her socially active."

Mrs. Frey turned the pants in the presser. "Comedy," she said, scoffing. "Is there anything funny about life? Misery, that's all it's ever been. Misery and hard work."

"Maybe you need to try something new, like taking up a hobby," I said, but at her fierce scowl, I figured that boat wasn't about to sail anytime soon.

"I got my bingo night. I don't need a hobby. Iris, she don't care for bingo. Says it's for the geezer gals. Says that's why she needs her comedy club." Mrs. Frey ended with a snort of disapproval.

"You and Iris lead a very quiet life then."

"What of it?"

"Nothing! Quiet is good. Everyone needs a little quiet." As Mrs. Frey put the pants on a hanger and reached for the next pair, I cast about for some way to broach the subject of Iris's alibi, but couldn't think of a damn thing. "So, this past Sunday evening, another quiet night at home for the two of you?"

Mrs. Frey's eyes immediately narrowed. "I thought you wanted to know about Thursday night."

I smacked myself on the forehead. "I meant Thursday night, not Sunday night."

I could tell by her clenched jaw that she wasn't buying it. "You're a nosy girl. I've had enough of your questions. Get out of here."

"Okay, no problem. I'll drop by some other time."

She started toward me, yelling, "Not some other time. Not ever! You hear me? I don't want you coming around here ever again. Get out!"

I backed quickly out of the room, nearly falling into the cart again, and turned toward the shocked face of the counter clerk and her one remaining customer, Ms. No-Cuts, who was watching with a smug grin.

Regaining my composure, I called back, "Thanks for your help, Mrs. Frey." Then I returned No-Cuts' smile and strolled idly toward the door.

"Don't forget your free newspaper," the girl called, but I was halfway out the door and not about to go back.

Just as I was about to cross the street, I heard, "Hey! Wait up."

I turned to see the young clerk scoot out the door behind No-Cuts and hurry up to me with a newspaper. "Take this, please," she said, and thrust it at me. "I needed a reason to talk to you. You're the florist, right? The one who was in the newspapers for helping to solve some murders?"

"That's me," I answered with some hesitation.

"Are you investigating the Jonas Treat murder?"

"Why?"

"Isn't that why you wanted to see Mrs. Frey? Look, I can't talk long. I don't want her to see me. Besides, it might not mean anything, but after I read about Mr. Treat's murder, I figured someone should know."

I was all ears now. "Know what?"

"That Iris had a crush on Mr. Treat, and ever since his murder she's been acting really weird — weirder than usual, I mean."

"Have you talked to the cops about Iris?"

"No way. I've had a few run-ins with them, and . . . well, you know, why remind them of it, right?"

"Maybe Iris is grieving over Mr. Treat's death."

"I guess that could be it. Iris *was* in love with the guy. She even went to that speed-dating thing Thursday night because he was going to be there. Iris never does anything like that."

This girl knew much more than I expected. "Do you have any idea how Iris knew Mr. Treat would be at that event?"

"She came across an invitation in his suit coat pocket. She always went through his pockets. She wouldn't let anyone else wait on him or handle his clothes."

"How do you know Iris found the invitation?"

The girl darted a nervous glance back at the building. "I saw her take the envelope out of his suit and open it."

"What did Iris do after she opened the

envelope?"

"She took it over to the window to read it — her eyesight isn't real good — and then got all flushed in the face, like she does when she gets angry or excited. Then she went to the restroom and started talking to herself. She does that a lot."

The girl smiled sheepishly. "My friend and I, we like to make fun of Iris and her freaky ways, and sometimes we listen at the bathroom door when she practices her comedy routines. She hates being overheard. We only do that after Mrs. Frey leaves, though."

"What did Iris say or do after she saw the invitation?"

"She said Mr. Treat — well, she called him Jonas — would be her captive audience for nine minutes, and she'd have to be really on her game so he'd see the person behind the fright mask."

Iris seemed to be a realist about her appearance, which made it even odder that she thought she had a chance with Jonas. "Did you see the invitation?"

"Just for a second. It was black with silver writing on it, in a silver envelope."

That sounded like something Carmen would use. "Did you happen to see a return address on the envelope?"

"No. Iris put everything back in the

pocket and took the suit into the back room, and then I got busy and forgot about it." The girl glanced over her shoulder, saw a customer enter the shop, then said, "Oops. Gotta go," and darted back.

Puzzling over the new information, I headed for the courthouse square. At least the girl had solved the riddle of how Iris had known Jonas would be at last Thursday's Cloud Nine event. How frustrated Iris must have been when Carmen refused to put her on Jonas's list, not to mention how embarrassed when Jonas blew her off during the mixer.

I'd walked two blocks when I suddenly remembered Marco's soiled T-shirt still in my purse. Oh, well. I'd just launder it myself.

As I approached the corner of Franklin and Lincoln, I happened to glance through the big plate-glass window of Bindstroms Jewelry Shop and saw Rafe waiting at the counter, probably on his mission to repair Marco's watch. *Hmm.* If Robin had purchased a wedding band locally, this would be the place to do so, yet I didn't dare make inquiries if Mrs. Bindstrom was in the shop. She was one of the biggest gossips in town. Who knew what story she'd concoct from my questions? I'd hate to start any rumors about Robin.

Trying not to be obvious, I glanced inside twice more as I strolled past. No sign of Mrs. Bindstrom. So, on impulse, I joined Rafe, deciding to take advantage of the opportunity to do a little extra sleuthing.

"Hey, Freckles," Rafe said, as I joined him in front of a long glass case filled with diamond rings. "What's happening?"

Two customers stood just a few feet away, looking at a display of watches, so I moved closer to him and said in an undertone, "I'm investigating."

"May I show you a ring?" a saleswoman asked, sliding open a glass door on her side of the counter. I'd never seen her before, so I doubted she knew who I was.

"Actually . . ." I began.

The eager saleswoman set a tray full of diamond rings in front of me. "I'm not sure what style of engagement ring you're looking for, but the emerald cut is always classic."

Engagement ring? As the woman held out a ring for me to slip over my finger, Rafe said, "Go ahead, Freckles, try it on."

I gave him a scowl, but he merely pressed his lips together to keep from laughing.

"Stop joking around, Rafe," I said, elbowing him as I smiled at the woman. "I'm sorry. I'm not here to look at engagement rings."

At that moment, a loud rapping sound made everyone in the jewelry store turn to look toward the window, where, outside, my aunt Corrine and three of her friends were waving at me. I gave them a quick wave back, then, when they kept waving, motioned them on.

"Your fan club?" Rafe asked, as another clerk walked up and handed him a case with Marco's watch inside.

"Right, my fan club, all four of them." I leaned close to whisper, "Don't you have work to do back at the bar?"

"Subtle." Giving me a devilish wink, he sauntered toward the door in perfect Marco style.

"What kind of ring *are* you interested in?" the saleswoman asked.

"Actually, a man's wedding band. I'm not sure how long ago it was ordered, but it would be under the name Robin Lennox. Could you look that up for me?"

"I'm not quite clear on this, Robin, if I may call you that. You've ordered the band and want to know if it's ready?"

"Well . . ." Did I really want to waste more time explaining? "Yes."

She went to the office and returned a few

minutes later to report that the wedding band had been returned for a partial refund: "By Robin Lennox." She gave me a skeptical glance. "What did you say your name was?"

Nice going, Abby. "It doesn't matter." I backed toward the door. "Thanks for your help."

So Jillian's gossip was correct: Robin had been more invested in the wedding than she'd wanted me to believe. I had a feeling I'd find she'd dropped a few bucks on a wedding gown, as well.

I stepped out the door and glanced up and down the sidewalk but saw no sign of my aunt and her friends, luckily. As I started across the street, I noticed a cop car waiting for the light to change. At the wheel was my buddy, Sergeant Reilly, pretending not to notice me. Like that ever worked.

At forty years old, Sean Reilly was a nice-looking man, with intelligent hazel eyes, good facial structure, and brown hair starting to show a bit of white at the temples. As a rookie cop, he'd trained under my dad, and had later become Marco's buddy, which eventually made us friends of sorts, although Reilly wasn't always thrilled about it.

I darted up to the car and tapped on his window. "Reilly, I need to talk to you!"

Frowning in concern, he pointed to the cross street. When the light turned green, he made a hard left turn and pulled to the curb. I dashed to the passenger side of his car as he released the lock, letting me slide in.

"Thanks," I said, rubbing my hands to warm them. "It's really cold today."

"Did something happen? Are you okay?"

"I'm fine. I just need some information about the Jonas Treat investigation."

"*That's* what this is about?" His face darkened like a thundercloud as he pointed toward the sidewalk. "Out."

"Seriously, Reilly, I need to know if the detectives have been investigating anyone besides Nikki, because it seems to me they haven't."

"First of all, don't put me in this position again. You know I can't give you information. Second, don't come running up to my car unless it's an emergency. Got it?"

What was it with men and positions? I sat forward on the seat. "I didn't mean to scare you, Reilly, but Nikki's in big trouble. Can't you just give me a hint of what the DA has in mind?"

"Do you have any idea what would happen to me if —"

"I know the drill. Come on, Reilly, you've

gotten to know Nikki. Is she a murderer? So just give me a nod or a shake — yes or no, have they looked at anyone else as a serious suspect?"

"I don't have any information about the case, Abby."

"Then I'll tell you about it. The detectives are focusing on Nikki because of circumstantial evidence. But if they haven't looked at anyone else, of course they don't have other evidence. They've stopped processing it. They could be sitting on a big fat clue that would point straight to the real killer, and they wouldn't even know it."

"What can I say? The DA calls the shots."

With my fingers on the door handle I gave it another try. "Why would the DA set his sights on Nikki without taking a hard look at anyone else? Is Darnell that sure of a conviction? He must realize Nikki would present a sympathetic figure to a jury."

"Abby!"

"Okay!" I opened the door and put one foot on the ground, but my mind was still racing. "Do you think Darnell has an ulterior motive? Is he getting pressure from city hall to wrap up the case? Have I angered him by helping to solve other murders? Wait! Elections are coming up, aren't they? Please tell me he's not trying to make himself look good by scoring another conviction."

Reilly sighed.

I hit my fist against the seat. "Damn it, Reilly, that's the reason, isn't it? I can't believe Melvin Darnell, the so-called man of the people, would put an innocent young woman in prison to help himself get reelected. Where is his conscience?"

Reilly's radio squawked. He reached for the button, pausing to say, "You need to get out now, Abby."

"We need to stop Darnell, Reilly."

"Out! Now!"

Frowning at him, I climbed out and shut the door, then watched with a sinking feeling as he pulled away. When a prominent person was murdered, the public got nervous. So the faster the DA could bring an indictment, the bigger a hero he was, even if the person indicted wasn't guilty. It happened all the time — one of the many flaws in our judicial system.

So if Darnell had his sights set on Nikki to further his own career, the only way to stop him was to find the real killer. But that would take time, and how much time did we have? It sure would have helped to have Reilly working with us.

All around me, lawyers, judges, and clerks

were descending on the courthouse to start another workday. Among them was Deputy Prosecutor Gregory F. Morgan, briefcase in hand, walking in an easy stride that said he was in no rush to get to his office. Morgan and I had gone to high school together, and he'd reluctantly helped me out on a few investigations by passing along pertinent information. He was also Darnell's right-hand man, just the guy I needed to see.

"Greg," I called, hurrying toward him. "Got a minute?"

Although bundled in a beige wool topcoat, Morgan could still pass for a *GQ* model. He wasn't tall, but he was good-looking in an angelic, little-boy sort of way. Women had been falling for Morgan since he was in high school. Even now, the women he worked with adored him, treating him more like a pet than a prosecutor, which merely reinforced his belief that the world started and stopped at his feet.

"A minute for my favorite florist?" He flashed his camera-ready smile. "Always."

Yeah, right. Back in high school Morgan had treated me as though I were transparent, looking through me rather than at me. But that was before I grew breasts.

"Are you working on the Jonas Treat murder?" I asked, catching my breath.

"Abby, Abby," Morgan said with an exasperated sigh, "you know I can't talk about my current cases."

Did he realize he'd just answered my question? "Look, Greg, I don't know how aware you are of what's happening —"

He scoffed. "Of course I'm aware of what's happening."

"Then you know Nikki Hiduke has apparently been singled out as the prime suspect, which is so completely ludicrous I'm ashamed to admit my father was ever a cop on this police force. Truly, Morgan, the detectives seem to have totally ignored everyone else, and I'm talking about people with actual motives —"

"Whoa, Abby. Nikki was singled out because of the evidence."

"It's circumstantial. Every bit of it. You remember Nikki, right? Tall, blond, pretty? She went on her very first date with Jonas the night he was killed, Greg. She had no reason to want him dead."

"Come on, Abby. They found blue clay on her boots, the victim's blood type on her sweater, her fingerprints in his office . . . she even admitted to being there."

"They found her fingerprints and no one else's? Are you saying they didn't find the prints of the people who work with Jonas?"

"Look at it from the detectives' viewpoint. Nikki was the last one known to have seen the victim before he died, she lied about the events of that night, and she has no way to prove where she was when the murder took place. Can you blame them for thinking she might have done it?"

"As I keep trying to tell you, Greg, Nikki doesn't have a motive, but at least three other people do, and if you'll give me a chance to —"

"I have to stop you right there, Abby. The DA is convening a grand jury tomorrow, and I expect they'll come back with an indictment."

"Tomorrow? For God's sake, Greg, Darnell's going to put an innocent woman behind bars!"

"Lower your voice, will you? People are staring. Besides, it isn't my call. I told you, the DA is convening them."

"Then stop him! He'll listen to you. Tell him you know there are credible suspects the detectives have overlooked."

"Do you have proof tying any of these so-called credible suspects to the murder?"

"Not yet, but if I had a few more days —"

"Then I'm sorry, Abby. I won't stick my neck out until I have something solid to take to Darnell. But if you do get that proof today, come see me."

He walked away as though he didn't have a care in the world.

I stared at Greg's back, my fists clenched in frustration. I'd get that proof somehow.

A strong gust of cold wind reminded me I was shivering, so I turned up my collar and headed north. I had one more stop to make before returning to Down the Hatch to share the bad news with Marco.

Betty's Bridal Shop was located in a beautiful old home three short city blocks from the square. The last time I'd been there was to be fitted for a bridesmaid's gown for Jillian's wedding, and it hadn't been a pleasant experience. The other bridesmaids were tall and willowy, whereas I was . . . well, not. But when I stepped inside, the first thing I saw was a mannequin about my size wearing a dazzling, pearl-encrusted, off-white satin wedding gown that accentuated her curves and actually made her look taller at the same time, which I hadn't thought was humanly possible.

I stepped up to the mannequin to see if we were the same height. Not quite, but pretty damn close.

"A stunning gown, is it not?" a buttery smooth voice said. I turned to find a woman in her sixties with upswept silver hair and huge fuchsia earrings smiling predatorily. "It would look spectacular on you, darling. Would you like to try it on?"

"Oh, no, thank you," I said, moving away from the mannequin. "I'm not here to buy a gown."

"I see." The butter turned to ice. She probably worked on commission.

In my most professional voice, I said, "I'm helping with a murder investigation, and I'm hoping you can tell me if Robin Lennox ordered a wedding dress a few months ago."

She arranged a fold in the mannequin's gown. "Sorry, no can do."

"Not even to help catch a murderer?"

"Sorry, not even then."

Sorry, she was lying. "Look, I just need to know whether the dress was purchased here."

The saleswoman cast a nervous glance over her shoulder, then whispered, "The owner would kill me if I divulged customer information to a stranger. . . . But to a customer?" She grinned slyly. "That's different."

Ah, so that was how the game was played. "You know, maybe I will try on that gown."

With a conspiratorial smile, the woman

led me into one of the salons. She searched through a rack of gowns, located a size she thought would fit, and ushered me into a roomy, curtained dressing room. "I'll go see what I can find about the Lennox gown."

"Thank you so much."

I was planning to only pretend to try on the dress, but once I was inside the dressing room, standing in front of the three-way mirror with the beautiful gown in my arms, I had a change of heart. Quickly I shed my coat and clothes and pulled the layers of satin over my head.

Wowsers! The gown was gorgeous, fitted at the waist with a heart-shaped neckline that didn't give me Dolly Parton boobs. I really did seem taller, too. In fact, I really liked the dress.

I turned to the left, then to the right, then stepped back and twirled in a circle. I imagined a veil over my hair, pearl earrings on my lobes, satin heels, and sighed wistfully. Maybe someday I'd be ready.

"How are we doing?" Butter Voice called from outside the curtain. Before I could reply, she parted it and stepped inside. "Oh, darling! This is the gown for you."

"It is lovely." I gave the dress another glance, then turned away from my reflection. "Did you find that information on

Robin Lennox?"

"Yes, and yes, she did order a gown."

"Can you tell me how much it cost?"

"Sorry, no can do. That wasn't part of the deal. Now, about *this* gown?"

"Sorry. No can decide so quickly."

"I see. Well, I'll leave you alone, then. Let me know if you need help."

I waited until she left, then gazed at myself in the gown one more time. Nikki had to see this. Knowing what a chicken I was about marriage, this would definitely make her laugh. I pulled out my cell phone and snapped a picture of myself pretending to scream, then sent it to Nikki with a message that said, "Bridezilla lives!"

Sent to Portia, the phone duly reported.

Portia? Oh, no! I'd missed Nikki's entry in the address book by one line. Quickly, I sent my sister-in-law a text message that said, *Disregard previous msg.* Then I re-sent the photo to Nikki. That goof would earn me some ribbing at the next family gathering.

When I walked into his office, Marco was watching the computer monitor over Rafe's shoulder, the phone pressed to his ear. He lifted an eyebrow to let me know he'd seen me.

"Thanks, Steve. I'll see you then." Marco hung up and clapped Rafe on the shoulder. "Good job, man. Hey, Sunshine. Why the frown?"

"Greg Morgan told me the DA is convening the grand jury tomorrow."

"Damn," Marco muttered. "I was hoping for more time."

"Elections are coming up," I said, "so obviously Darnell's going after an easy conviction. You know what that means, Marco."

"Don't even think about it." Marco grabbed his leather jacket from a bar stool. "Let's go out to Jonas's development. I'll fill you in on some surprising information on the way."

"How surprising?"

"It just might break this case wide open."

Chapter Twenty

"Hank Miller," Marco said, as we headed toward Chateaux en Carnations in his green Prius, "lied about being in Florida when Jonas was killed. If you remember, he told me he was at his home in the Keys on Sunday night. But I've got flight manifests from my friend at O'Hare and a car rental receipt that show he flew into O'Hare airport on Saturday, the day before Jonas died, rented an SUV, returned it Monday morning, then flew back to the Miami International Airport Monday afternoon."

"Marco, you just poked a big fat hole in Miller's alibi!"

"You got it. Now we need to know why he lied to me and, more important, what his reason was for flying to O'Hare and renting a vehicle."

"He must have been coming back to New Chapel."

"Even so, that doesn't make him a murderer. After all, he still has a home here. He might have come back to check on it."

"Then what did you find out that might break this case wide open?"

"Rafe stumbled across an item in the crime section of the *News*'s online edition about problems builders at Chateaux en Carnations were having with thieves stealing copper wiring. I called the development's general contractor to find out what steps they'd taken to stop the theft, and, as I suspected, security cameras have been installed in strategic locations. I spoke with Steve, the general contractor, just now, and he said he'll meet us at the sales office in half an hour to let us watch the videotapes from Sunday."

"Marco, that's wonderful! If Miller shows up on the video at the right place and time, we've got our killer. But why don't the police have the tapes?"

"They apparently didn't know about the security cameras. When I mentioned it to Steve, he said he hadn't even considered that the cameras might provide evidence. It's an oversight that shouldn't have happened, but did. Obviously, we'll have to turn the videotapes over to the police after we view them, but we'll deal with that later. So, tell me how it went with Iris."

"I didn't get to talk to her. She wasn't due at the dry cleaner's until noon. I tried to talk to Mrs. Frey instead, but she got hostile and chased me out. But it wasn't a total waste of time. I learned from one of the employees that Iris found an invitation to Thursday's speed-dating event in Jonas's suit pocket. That answers the question of how Iris knew he'd be there. The girl said Iris was so excited when she read the invitation, she ran to the washroom and rehearsed how she was going to wow Jonas.

"So think about it, Marco. Even though Carmen wouldn't put Iris on Jonas's list, Iris still went to the event with high expectations and ended up being rejected. It's not a terribly strong motive, but it's still a motive."

"I thought people had to sign up for the event."

"Someone sent Jonas an invitation in a silver envelope — and silver just happens to be Carmen Gold's favorite color . . . or metal. The problem is, though, why would Carmen send Jonas an invitation to a speed-dating event after the shameful way he used her?"

"What's even more interesting is why Jonas would accept her invitation."

"I can answer that one. Jonas was a womanizer. What better way to meet lots of women than a speed-dating event? And so what if Carmen was there? I don't see him caring how it affected her."

Marco nodded. "And Carmen would know he'd jump at the opportunity to attend."

"Exactly, which would indicate she had an ulterior motive for inviting him, such as revenge. Maybe she damaged the Ferrari, then decided it wasn't enough."

"Or maybe Jonas figured out she hit his car and threatened to press charges."

"She was so enraged, she stabbed him," I said, "then called in an anonymous tip about Nikki to throw the cops off her trail."

"I'm still having trouble with that scenario," Marco said. "To make it plausible, Carmen would've had to know Jonas was with Nikki Sunday evening."

"Let's hope Carmen's assistant can shed light on that problem tonight."

"Who knows?" Marco said, as he made a right turn into a subdivision marked by a huge stone arch etched with the words *Chateaux en Carnations*. "Depending on what we learn here, we might not even need to go to the speed-dating event."

Just beyond the arch was a wooden sign that said MODEL HOME/SALES OFFICE, with an arrow pointing up the street. The development was laid out in a giant oval pattern, with one main road circling around it and small cul-de-sacs shooting off from it. We drove up the main drag, Lily Drive, past five empty lots, and stopped at the only house on the block, a beautiful brick-and-cedar home with a wooden sign in the yard that said SALES OFFICE.

"There's the footbridge," I said, pointing out the quaint wooden walkway that spanned a small creek alongside the house. "That's where Jonas cut his hand."

"Let's see if we can find an area designated as a park."

"Why is that important?"

"One of the phone calls I made this morning was to the recorder's office. A clerk there informed me that, in addition to the purchase price, the deal was that Jonas was to turn the south meadow into a park named after the Miller family. He also was to keep the woodland that encircles the acreage undeveloped and use only what had been farmed to build on. In light of the altercation between Jonas and Miller, I want to see how closely Jonas kept to the agreement."

We drove slowly around the oval, finding all lots undeveloped except for two, where huge homes were under construction, but saw no signs of a park. We circled a second time until finally Marco turned onto Camellia Circle. "If the park was supposed to be built on the south meadow, this is as south as it gets."

At the end of the cul-de-sac was a huge tract of meadowland on which a sign had been placed: FUTURE SITE OF THE JONAS TREAT GREENS AND CLUBHOUSE.

"That's not a park," I said.

Marco pointed straight ahead. "Look way out there."

I shielded my eyes to gaze across the hard-packed ground. In the distance, dozens of stumps jutted from the bare earth. "My God, Marco, there must've been hundreds of trees out there. I can't believe he destroyed the woodland."

"More lots for him to sell."

"No wonder there was an altercation. Miller must have been livid when he saw that."

We drove back to the model home, parked in the driveway, and walked across the lot to reach the footbridge. As we passed the side of the house, I noticed the landscape shrubs had been set in what appeared to be blue-gray mud. I stopped to examine it.

"Marco, this is what Nikki must have had on her boots, the dense blue clay Jonas had trucked in that got him in trouble with the environmental agency."

Marco crouched down to see it, then stood to glance around the property. "It seems to be only here in the landscaping."

"Jonas was stopped before he could bring in more. It kills the plants."

At that moment, the front door of the model home opened and a real estate agent in a blue blazer, black skirt, and black heels stepped onto the porch. "Can I help you?" she called.

I certainly hoped so.

We stepped into a travertine-floored foyer and were directed through the kitchen to the door that led to a three-car garage. The garage had been converted to an office and display area where I saw samples of wood flooring, countertops, and cabinetry. Two men in pants and casual shirts sat at desks near the door, one on the phone and another doing paperwork. The second man immediately jumped up and came to greet us.

"Hi, I'm Bob Turk," the thirty-something man said, extending his hand. "Interested in some property here?"

Marco showed his ID, then introduced us and explained that he'd been hired to track down suspects in the Jonas Treat murder case. He didn't offer any more information, such as who had hired him, but Bob didn't seem to need it.

"What can I do to help?" he asked. "We're all eager to find Jonas's killer."

Marco spread the five photos on Bob's desk. "Take a look at these people, if you would, and tell me what you know about them."

Bob touched the first photo. "That's Hank Miller. Everyone around here knows him — and also knows not to cross him. Hank is used to having his way about things."

The other salesman ended his phone call and came over to introduce himself as Norm Krazinsky, Jonas's sales manager. He had been put in charge of the development until Jonas's heirs decided what to do. Norm seemed to be an easygoing middle-aged man who did way too much sitting at his desk, if that spare tire around his middle was any indication.

"Miller?" he said, looking at the photo. "Yes, sir, I've gotten to know old Hank well over the years, but he hasn't been a happy camper lately, not that I blame the guy."

"Why is that?" Marco asked.

"You have to understand, the Miller family goes back three generations on this land, so Hank was very particular about what he wanted done with it. Now, I don't know the details of their agreement, but I do know that when Hank dropped by one day last week, he had quite a burr up his butt, shouting about Jonas welshing on their deal and threatening to get his shotgun and put a few holes in Jonas's hide. See, Hank firmly believes a man is only as good as his word. He didn't take Jonas's deceit well."

"Did you tell the detectives about the incident?" I asked.

"Yes, sir. I sure did."

"Was it common for Miller to stop by here?" Marco asked.

"He used to come around a lot at first," Bob said, "but then he moved to Florida and hasn't been up much since. His wife died about a year ago, and his family is all gone from this area, so he didn't feel the need to make the trip as often."

"Now, he did come back around Christmas," Norm said, "to see how the development was going, but it wasn't a good meeting. I heard him threaten to file a suit to halt the development, but Jonas was able to get him calmed down, telling him everything would be taken care of just as he'd promised. I don't think he ever intended to keep his promise, though."

Marco was writing in his notebook. "So Miller came by at Christmas, got some assurances from Jonas, then didn't come back until last week?"

"Yes, sir. That we know of, anyway," Norm said.

The real estate agent stepped into the garage, her eyes wide with curiosity. Bob waved her over, introduced her as Anita Burnett, then explained what we were doing.

Anita pointed to Kessler's photo. "I worked for Duke until he closed his realty office."

"Was there any animosity between Kessler and Jonas?" Marco asked.

"Sure there was," Anita said. "Jonas cheated him out of a lot of money. Poor Duke, after all he did for Jonas, he never could understand how Jonas could stab him in the back. Personally, I don't think Jonas knew what loyalty meant."

I was betting Robin would have the same complaint.

"Is it possible Kessler came here Sunday night to confront Jonas?" Marco asked.

Anita shook her head. "Not Duke. I got to know him really well during my twelve years with him. He was always fair and generous. If he was going to get back at

Jonas in any way, he'd take legal action."

"Are you aware that Kessler filed a lawsuit against Jonas?" Marco asked her.

"Jonas wouldn't reveal anything like that to me," Anita said, "and I don't see Duke anymore. I'm just saying that's how Duke would have reacted. It isn't in him to hurt anyone."

"I've met Kessler several times," Bob added. "He's always been a nice guy."

I gave Marco a tiny nudge, as if to say, *I told you so.* Then I couldn't help saying to Anita, "You seem to have a pretty low opinion of Jonas. Why did you work for him?"

She shrugged. "I have kids in college, and the pay's been good. What can I say?"

"Have any of you seen Duke Kessler here at the development?" Marco asked.

All three said no, so Marco pointed to Robin's photo. "Do you know her, or have you seen her around?"

The men shook their heads, but Anita hesitated. "She looks familiar."

Marco said, "If I told you that was Robin Lennox, would you know the name?"

The men didn't, but Anita smiled. "I remember her now. She's Jonas's former fiancée. I met her last summer when she came into Duke's realty office to go to lunch with Jonas. Her hair was different then — blond; I think."

"Anything you can tell me about Robin?" Marco asked her.

"Just what everyone in town knows, that Jonas was seeing other women behind her back while they were engaged."

Boy, I sure felt out of the loop. Clearly, I needed to stop burying myself in my work.

"And her?" Marco asked, pointing to Iris's photo.

Bob grimaced. "Was she in a car accident?"

"She works at Frey's Dry Cleaner," Norm said. "The owner's daughter, right?"

"Do you patronize Frey's?" Marco asked.

"Not me, no, sir, but Iris waited on me once when I had to pick up Jonas's dry cleaning. She got all bent out of shape because I came to get his suits. Said it wasn't their policy to give out someone else's garments, and next time Jonas would have to come himself. I just looked at her like, 'Lady, what are you talking about? I have the ticket.' "

"When was this?" Marco asked.

"Maybe two weeks ago," Norm replied. "I told Jonas, and he thought it was funny."

Anita tapped Iris's photo. "One evening, about nine o'clock, when I left to go home,

I saw a woman drive by very slowly. It could have been this woman."

"How long ago did this happen?" Marco asked.

"Several weeks ago. I know it was a Wednesday night, because that's my long day. We take turns working the evening hours."

"Iris does her comedy gig on Wednesday nights," I reminded Marco. "It might not have been her."

"Do you remember the car?" Marco asked Anita.

"It was a dark color, maybe navy blue? Black? I'm not sure. I'm color-blind at night."

"Sedan? Convertible? SUV?" Marco asked.

"Sedan. It had a low, boxy shape."

Marco noted it. "Did Jonas mention anything about attending a speed-dating event to any of you?"

After all three said no, he pointed to Carmen's picture. "How about the woman in this last photo? Anyone recognize her?"

Anita shook her head; Bob frowned in thought, as though trying to place the face; and Norm's eyebrows lifted in surprise. "Come with me," he said, and led us through the kitchen into a beautifully furnished den. "This was Jonas's office."

As Marco and I took in the surroundings — cherry wainscoting, built-in cabinetry, cherry executive's desk, and green silk–upholstered furniture — Norm walked across the room to a large armoire-style cabinet and opened one of the doors, revealing a bulletin board inside. Pinned to the cork was an eight-by-ten piece of thick white paper with pinholes scattered over the surface. Norm unpinned the paper and turned it over, revealing a glamorous black-and-white head shot of Carmen Gold, riddled with holes.

I moved closer to study the glossy photo. "What happened?"

Norm reached inside the cabinet and pulled out a box filled with darts. "Target practice."

"Jonas did this?" I asked.

Norm nodded. "Yes, ma'am. He called it his stress buster."

"Did you show the cops?" Marco asked.

"No, sir. I didn't think about it until just now."

"Do you know what this woman's relationship to Jonas was?" Marco asked.

"Former girlfriend, as far as I know."

"How do you know about Carmen being a former girlfriend?" Marco asked.

"When Jonas opened the envelope, he commented about how he couldn't seem to get rid of his former girlfriends."

"Did the photo come in the mail?" Marco asked.

"Yes, sir, about a month ago, in a big silver envelope," Norm said.

"Just like the invitation in his suit pocket," I said to Marco.

"Did Jonas keep the envelope?" Marco asked.

Norm shook his head. "No, sir. It went right into the shredder with the junk mail."

We returned to the garage, where Marco gathered up the photos. "Is there anything else you can think of that might help us find the killer? Anyone Jonas mentioned having trouble with, someone he was afraid to see, any threatening phone calls or letters?"

"Jonas was fearless," Anita said. "Like there were no consequences for anything he did."

"Do any of you stand to inherit anything from Jonas's estate?"

"No," they said in unison, seemingly surprised by the question. I knew Marco only wanted to rule them out as potential suspects.

Marco glanced at me. "Anything you want to know?"

I thought he'd never ask. I showed Anita the picture of Iris again. "When you saw someone who might be this woman drive by, what happened? Did she see you? Did she keep driving or slow down in front of the house?"

"I came out and locked the door," Anita recounted, "then turned to find her watching me — or, rather, frowning at me — from the car. She didn't stop, just kept driving slowly past."

"Has she been back?" Marco asked.

"Not that I've noticed," Anita said.

"Excuse me?" a deep voice behind us said.

I turned toward the door to see a tall, sturdy man in a heavy down vest, thick flannel shirt, work pants, and dirty yellow boots, carrying a yellow hard hat and a paper bag.

"Hey, Steve," Bob said with a smile. "What's happening?"

"I'm supposed to meet a Marco Salvare here."

"I'm Marco." He stepped forward to shake Steve's hand. "Thanks for coming over."

"Glad to help." Steve held up the paper bag. "I've got one video for you to see, taken from under the stone arch. It's the only one that shows this building. I have to warn you, though, after sunset you won't see much. We don't have streetlights yet, so except for

340

the security landscaping lights around the sales office, all you're going to see are headlights and taillights of vehicles driving through. The other two cameras are positioned on the roofs of the houses under construction, but they're over on the east side and won't help you here."

"Let's hope it shows enough to catch a killer," Marco said.

"Hey, Norm," Steve said, "this sounds tacky, but is it okay to use the VCR in Jonas's office?"

While Marco inserted the videotape into the machine, Norm, Bob, Anita, Steve, and I grouped chairs in front of Jonas's new wide flat-screen television set, a purchase made two weeks before Jonas's death, Norm informed us. That a person's life could end so abruptly, even violently, was a sobering and chilling thought, and for the next few minutes no one spoke.

Marco used the remote to start the video, affording us a view from beneath the arch up Lily Drive to just beyond the model home. As Steve warned, once the sun set at five o'clock, it became nearly impossible to see anything but the model home, and only then because of the lights placed around the house to illuminate the shrubbery.

"How are people made aware of the security cameras here?" Marco asked.

"We posted signs all around," Norm said. "Anyone driving through would know."

We continued to watch for a while, and when nothing happened, Marco said, "I'm going to fast-forward the tape to . . . Abby, what time did Nikki say Jonas brought her out here?"

"Around eleven o'clock," I said. What I didn't say was, *If Nikki told the truth.*

"We'll be coming up to eleven o'clock Sunday night shortly," Marco said, watching the timer in the lower right corner. He slowed the video to a normal speed, and within five minutes, a car came out from under the arch, drove up Lily Drive, and pulled into the driveway. Marco hit the Zoom button. "It looks like a silver Audi."

"That's what Jonas rented after his Ferrari was damaged," Norm said.

"There's Nikki," I said as a woman got out of the car. *Right on time.*

We watched as Jonas opened the front door of the model home, turned on floodlights, then took Nikki by the hand and led her to the wooden footbridge over the creek. I almost glanced away when Jonas kissed her, but then he yanked his hand from the railing as though he were hurt. Nikki examined it; then they went straight into the house.

"It happened just like she said," I told Marco, feeling my shoulders sag in relief.

Within ten minutes they left the house, with Jonas switching off the floodlights and locking the front door before getting into the car. As he backed out of the driveway, Marco paused the tape, then pointed to something on the upper left side of the screen. "Do you see that? Jonas's headlights picked up something. What does it look like to you?"

"The front end of a car?" Bob asked.

"I think you're right," Anita said. "You can just make out a reflection on the head-lights and a little bit of a shine where a bumper would be."

"It appears to be parked on the opposite side of the road, along the curve about two lots beyond this house," Norm said, "and facing this direction." He got up and went to a window. "You can see the curve from here."

"Any reason for a car to be parked in that area at night?" Marco asked.

"None," Steve said. "As I mentioned, the houses under construction are on the east side of the development and aren't even close to being habitable, and the construction trailer gets locked up when I leave at five o'clock. There's no reason at all a car should be there."

Marco rewound the tape to just before Jonas and Nikki arrived; then we watched closely as Jonas turned in to the driveway. "No reflection," Marco said, "so we know the vehicle wasn't there when Jonas first arrived."

He fast-forwarded to when the floodlights went on. "And now the vehicle is there. The light is reflecting off the headlights and bumper. Can anyone tell what kind of vehicle it is?"

"By the shape, I'd guess an old Nissan or Toyota," Bob said, as we squinted at the screen.

"Does it look like the car you saw driving past?" I asked Anita.

"I really can't tell," she said.

"How could that vehicle have gotten into the subdivision?" Marco asked. "We didn't see it come out from under the arch. Is there another way in?"

"There's only one entrance," Anita said. "It's designed to be a gated community with limited access."

"I know another way," Steve said. "I saw it when I walked the land with the county surveyor. There's a trail through one of the lots on the south side. It leads toward an old barn behind the Miller farmhouse on Rollercoaster Road," he said, referring to the hilly road's local name. "It was probably a tractor path at one time."

"How do I find it?" Marco asked.

"Continue on around Lily Drive," Steve directed, "past Camellia Circle; then turn onto Tulip Court and drive to the end. The trail comes out there."

"Could someone drive the trail from Rollercoaster Road straight into the subdivision without anyone knowing?" Marco asked.

"If he knew how to find it," Steve said, "although I don't know how easy it would be to get a car down that path. It's narrow and rutted. It'd be a bumpy ride."

"Outside of the county surveyor and all of you, who else would know about it?" Marco asked.

"One person for sure," Steve said. "Hank Miller."

Marco thought for a moment, then said, "I'm going to ask you all a question that might make you uncomfortable, so if you'd rather not answer, or would prefer to answer in private, feel free to do so. Do you believe Hank Miller could have killed Jonas, either by accident or design?"

Bob said, "I don't have a problem answering that. Yes, I believe Hank Miller could have killed Jonas."

The others nodded in agreement.

"Have any of you seen Miller around town in the past several days?" Marco asked.

No one had, so he asked, "Does Miller have any relatives in the area, do you know?"

"I got the impression he was the last of his family in Indiana," Bob said. "He mentioned cousins living in the Florida Keys. That's why he relocated there."

"Hank Miller's son, his only child, died in an accident on Rollercoaster Road many years ago," Anita volunteered. "The boy was struck and killed right in front of their house. And Mrs. Miller passed away last year. My friend Kaye worked at the hospice center when Mrs. Miller was brought in for end-of-life care. Kaye said Hank donated a large sum to the hospice center in her name and wanted the park in Chateaux en Carnations dedicated to her and his son."

"That's so sad," I said, and Anita nodded in agreement.

"Is that the land Jonas labeled as the greens and clubhouse?" Marco asked.

"Yes," Anita said. "And now, with Jonas's passing, I'll bet Miller Park will be built after all."

I met Marco's gaze and knew what was

going through his mind. Perhaps that was exactly what Hank Miller had decided.

CHAPTER
TWENTY-ONE

Hank Miller was beginning to look like our man. Unfortunately, what we had on him was still circumstantial. I knew it wouldn't convince Greg Morgan to talk to the DA. I crossed my fingers, hoping something on the video would reveal the true killer.

On the television screen, the Audi came toward the arch, then disappeared, obviously to take Nikki home. I turned my attention back to that indistinct shape farther up the block, expecting to see headlights come on to follow the Audi. Instead, the shape seemed to vanish.

"What happened?" I asked.

Marco backed up the tape and we watched that portion again in slow motion. Amazingly, the vehicle was there when Jonas left, and then it wasn't.

"It might have backed up," Bob suggested. "Too bad the taillights aren't visible."

We continued to watch the video until the

silver Audi returned shortly after twelve thirty in the morning. At that point, Marco slowed the tape to watch for the other car to reappear. Sure enough, as Jonas turned into the driveway, his headlights reflected off the vehicle's front end.

"I'll bet it never left the subdivision," I said.

All eyes were on the screen, expecting to see an interior light come on as someone emerged from the mystery vehicle, but instead, after another ten minutes, the car seemed to vanish again. We spent another half hour searching the tape, right up until the moment the first police car arrived on the scene at four in the morning, but the vehicle never appeared.

"I'll need to turn the video over to the police as evidence," Marco said. "They can get someone to lighten and sharpen it, and hopefully reveal more. If there's anything on it that helps solve the case, I'll certainly let you know."

"It's yours," Steve said. "Good luck."

Back in the Prius, we headed up Lily Drive, found Tulip Court, and turned right, following it to the end. We got out of the car and walked along the curb until Marco stopped and pointed out two narrow ruts in the frozen ground where dead grass had been flattened.

"This must be the tractor path. It heads toward that old red barn way out there — and look, these tire tracks were laid down fairly recently."

I gazed across the field, following the tracks as far as I could see them. "That must be Miller's barn. He could have driven this path Sunday night, Marco."

"Let's take a drive around to the Miller homestead and see what we find."

We got back into the car, drove out of the development, and headed south to Rollercoaster Road. Marco turned east and drove up the hilly road until he saw the old Miller farmhouse on the left. He pulled onto the shoulder of the road a short distance from the house, and we both got out.

"Why didn't you park in the driveway?" I asked, as we hiked along the road. "The house is empty, isn't it?"

"I don't like to take chances or announce my presence. Remember, I haven't been able to reach Miller."

As we crossed the lawn, passing a FOR SALE sign in the yard, I said, "What a shame Miller didn't have any family to leave this quaint old house to. Look at that great wraparound porch and the gingerbread trim in the attic dormers. The house must date back to the late eighteen hundreds. I'll bet it exudes charm inside."

"Along with a leaky roof and a rotting foundation. See those old timbers? I'll bet they're infested with termites. And see how the shingles are curled back? Some are missing entirely."

"It'd be a great fixer-upper."

"It'd be easier to tear it down and start fresh."

Clearly, we weren't on the same page now.

Avoiding the gravel driveway, we circled the shuttered house, where I saw raised garden beds, dormant now, with flagstone paths winding through them, a grape arbor, and white trellises. On the side porch were pots that I imagined had overflowed with petunias and geraniums in the summer, and hanging baskets that might have held impatiens. Mrs. Miller had obviously loved growing things.

Behind the house was the old barn, its red paint faded and peeling off the weathered boards. Marco walked to where the driveway ended, then pointed out tire tracks that continued on around the barn and set off to follow them. Because the ground was mushy from melted snow, I stayed behind, keeping to the flagstone path that ran from the back door of the house to a small service door in the barn's side wall.

I spotted a white wrought-iron bench beside the door with an old bucket underneath and decided to take a look. Inside the pail was a rusty trowel and a pair of faded, moldy green gardener's gloves. Beside the bench, an old blue boy's bicycle leaned against the barn as though the owner had left it there only hours ago. The bike had old-fashioned balloon tires, rusted fenders, a worn black leather seat, crusty handlebars with dirty white rubber grips, and faded, multicolored plastic streamers hanging from the ends. A shudder ran through me when I realized I had probably stumbled upon Hank Miller's son's bike.

Had the boy been struck while riding it? I wondered. Perhaps Mrs. Miller had insisted it be kept as a remembrance. Perhaps Hank hadn't been able to throw it out after she died.

"Abby," I heard, and turned to find Marco striding toward me. "Those tire tracks lead straight across the field into Chateaux en Carnations. I also found five headstones near the edge of the property, with Miller family names on them."

"A family cemetery?"

"I'll bet that's why Miller specified the

land be kept as a park, so the graves would be undisturbed."

"What are the odds those are Miller's tire tracks?"

"Without making casts of the treads, it's damn near impossible to say. We'll have to report it to the police and hope they follow up."

"So what do we do now?"

"Let's go have a look at Robin's car. With any luck, we'll be able to cross one person off the list."

On the way to Dunn's Body Shop I phoned Nikki to update her on our progress, only to find her in tears. "What happened?" I asked.

"I've been laid off."

"Why?"

"My supervisor at the hospital told me to stay home until my case gets resolved . . . but when is that going to happen?"

"Soon, Nikki. We've turned up three very strong suspects."

"When will you know which one it is?"

"That's hard to say. We're still gathering evidence."

"I hope it doesn't take long, Abby. Dave said the grand jury is convening tomorrow. If they come back with an indictment —"

Before she could finish that thought I said, "You're not going to be arrested, Nikki. I won't let that happen."

After I calmed Nikki's fears, I phoned Grace to see how things were at the shop, only to hear an unfamiliar male voice on the other end. "Bloomers Flower Shop. May I help you?"

"This is Abby. And you are . . . ?"

"Oh, hey, Abby. It's Joey Dombowski."

"Joey! Why aren't you in school?" I held my hand over the phone to whisper to Marco, "It's one of Lottie's quadruplets."

"Don't worry," Joey said. "I'm not ditching class. Today's an in-service day for teacher training. Wait. Hold on. Miss Bingham wants to talk to you."

In a moment, I heard Grace's chipper voice. "Hello, dear. How is everything?"

"We're making some progress, Grace. We've got it narrowed down to three suspects. Why is Joey answering the phone?"

"Lottie mentioned the boys being off today, so I enlisted them as my assistants."

"All four of them?"

"Yes, dear, Jimmy, Joey, Johnny, and Karl. And you needn't worry about wages. I bartered for their help. They have free passes for a week to the bowling alley, compliments of my dear Richard."

Richard Davis was Grace's beau, a silver-haired Texan who owned the Mini-World Sports Center. I liked Richard, not only because he treated Grace like a princess, but also because he drove a 1971 fire-engine red El Dorado Cadillac convertible. Anyone with a car like that got high marks from me.

"Please thank Richard for me, Grace. And I really appreciate your handling everything for me today — efficiently, as usual."

"You're entirely welcome, love, and I shall certainly pass along your message, but it's nothing, really. We're happy to help out. And you'll be pleased to know Lottie's boys have been perfect gentlemen, charming the ladies in the coffee shop all morning. Lottie is quite the proud mum, too. But perhaps you'd like to speak to her?"

"Lottie is there?"

"Herman brought her in just for a bit. She's definitely on the mend, because she was bored silly at home and insisted on coming. She's quite eager to get back to work, too. She's in the parlor with him now. Shall I put her on?"

Lottie was back! What a relief. "Yes, in just a minute. How is business? Do I have orders waiting?"

"Well," she said, "it's been rather quiet."

"So no orders or no business — or both?"

"Two orders for delivery tomorrow. We also had a customer come in to buy a silk arrangement, and another bought a pair of candlesticks. Do remember, love, it's January. Nothing much happens until Valentine's Day, so don't worry about business being a bit stodgy."

Don't worry? Maybe Grace had money tucked away to pay her bills, but I didn't.

"By the way, dear, your mother called only a moment ago to remind you of dinner tomorrow night, and she said to invite Marco."

"Wait. What? Are you sure she said Marco, not markers or markdowns or —"

"No, love, she distinctly said Marco."

I was shocked. Marco had never been invited to a Friday-night dinner. Except for one rare occasion, when she tried to arrange a reconciliation between me and my former fiancé, Mom insisted it was for family only. Knowing what a stickler she was for tradition, I couldn't help but wonder what she had planned. The unveiling of another one of her sculptures, perhaps? Since she was also a big fan of surprises, I wasn't sure what to expect. Luckily, Marco would be occupied with his own family, so he would be spared any potential public embarrassment that one of her pieces of art was likely to produce.

"Okay, thanks, Grace. I'll see you around noon."

"Hold on, love. I'll put Lottie right on."

"Lottie's sons are helping out at Bloomers," I told Marco while I waited.

"Has to be better than Jillian," he said.

"Also my business is slowing."

Marco glanced at me. "Are you worried?"

"Grace said it's normal for January, but yes, I'm worried. She also said my mom called to remind me of dinner at the country club tomorrow night."

Marco chuckled. He knew I wasn't a fan of those dinners, during which my acclaimed doctor brothers and their übersophisticated wives got to show off their affluence, while I struggled to select the proper fork for my salad and tried to hold my wineglass by its stem without spilling the contents in my lap.

"Don't laugh," I warned him. "Your presence has been requested."

He glanced at me as though I'd just spoken in Chinese. "What?"

"That's right. You're invited."

"I feel honored."

"I wouldn't be too hasty about that. She's got something cooking, and that's never good."

"What do you think it is?"

"Mom loves surprises, so who knows? My best guess is that she's created artwork to bequeath to the country club. So don't feel bad about missing the dinner. You'll probably be glad you did."

Marco gave me a puzzled glance. "Why will I miss it?"

"Your mother is in town, remember? You can't skip one of her homemade Italian meals."

"Not a problem. She's supposed to leave tomorrow morning."

Damn!

In a moment, Lottie came on the line. "Hey, sweetie, how's it going?"

"You first. Tell me how you're feeling."

"Not bad. The pain's gone but my belly is still achy. You know me, sweetie. I'm too tough to keep down. Is Nikki doing okay? Catch me up."

I gave her a speedy rundown of everything we'd discovered since I'd last talked to her, including my visit with Mrs. Frey, my conversation with Greg Morgan, and the mysterious vehicle caught on video. Lottie followed with her assessment.

"From the sound of it, the cops ought to be hot on Hank Miller's trail. Hank was always an ornery old coot. He once got into a fistfight with his mailman for delivering junk mail. Now, Iris Frey, there's an odd duck, practically a copy of her mother, Dalva. I see Dalva at bingo every Sunday evening, and let me tell you, the woman never smiles, not even when she wins. Didn't know her husband, Bill, but by the way Dalva talks about him, I didn't miss out on anything. Had to feel sorry for the guy, though, trapped up in his bedroom when that fire broke out. He never did recover from it, probably from inhaling that smoke.

"Carmen Gold . . . well, I don't know the woman, so I probably shouldn't say, but if it's true she spent her daddy's hard-earned money on a fancy car for a younger guy — a playboy at that — she ought to get a swift kick in her heinie. It's reckless and disrespectful behavior, which makes me think she'd be capable of other impetuous acts. I think you know what I mean by that.

"Duke Kessler — now, there's a peach of a man, and a good husband, according to his wife, who should know. Quite a salesman, too, but he never took advantage of people. You're right to cross him off your list. And Robin Lennox, poor thing, should have gone after Jonas with a switch for leaving her at the altar, but she wouldn't have killed him, and she's not brash enough to ram his car in a restaurant parking lot. Takes a hothead to pull a stunt like that."

"We're heading to Dunn's Body Shop right now to see if you're right about Robin."

"Keep me posted," Lottie said. "And tell Justin hi. I'm going home now. I'm plumb tuckered out."

I was plumb tuckered out, too, just from listening to her. But it sure was good to have her back, even for a little while.

At Dunn's Body Shop, we found Lottie's nephew working on the underside of a car. He rolled out and grinned at us, his face, hands, and shirt covered in oil.

"Hey, little Abby! How's the Vette? Still rockin'? Hey, Marco. Good to see you, man."

It was due to Justin Dombowski that I had my beloved Corvette. The 1960 convertible had been tucked away in a barn out in the country by a farmer who indulged his lifelong dream to own one, then couldn't bring himself to drive it for fear of looking foolish. As a result, it sat neglected for decades, becoming a home for various barn denizens until the man died.

Only last year the farmer's wife hauled out the Vette and took it to their mechanic to see if it could be salvaged and sold. That mechanic happened to be Justin, who happened to know I was desperate for transportation and had very little money. It helped that Justin also had a crush on me. He took the Vette off the widow's hands, got it running, painted it my favorite color, bright yellow, and sold it to me for a price that fit my meager budget. And in return, I went out to dinner with him — at a truck stop — and found a dead fly in my undercooked hamburger.

But when I was tooling down the highway with the top down and the wind in my hair, who cared about a little food poisoning?

After Marco explained our mission to Justin, he had no problem showing us Robin's car, a 2001 dark green Hyundai with a sleek body style and no front- or rear-end damage. Apparently, Robin had hit a deep pothole and mangled the undercarriage.

"I'm moving Robin to the bottom of the list," Marco said as we drove back to town. "Unless her name turns up on the phone records, I don't see any reason to keep her on it."

My cell phone buzzed and Jillian's name

appeared on the screen. "Hey, Jill, what's up?"

"I know for certain who bought Jonas the Ferrari," she said excitedly. "Carmen Gold. I have her address in Chicago, if you need it. I even have the name of the salesman at the car dealership who sold the car to her."

"That's amazing. Good job, Jillian!" I whispered to Marco, "Jillian has proof Carmen bought Jonas the Ferrari."

Marco gave me a thumbs-up.

"How did your mom like her birthday gift?" I asked my cousin.

"Abby, she's crazy about it! I wish you could have seen her expression when she pulled off the wrapping paper. I thought she was going to cry."

I could believe that.

Marco's cell phone rang. He answered it with his usual "Salvare."

"So when do you want me back at Bloomers?" Jillian asked. "I've cleared my schedule for the entire afternoon."

"As it turns out, I have help today. Lottie's boys are there." Lucky for me.

"Okay, let me get this straight. You chose four pimple-faced high school boys over me? Thanks a lot. Now what am I supposed to do? I have a whole afternoon blocked off for you."

"Go shopping. Valentine's Day will be here in a few weeks, and I'll bet you don't have anything for Claymore yet." I glanced over at Marco and saw worry lines between his brows as he closed his phone. "Jillian, I need to hang up now. Jillian? Are you there?"

"Sorry. I had another call. Your mom, as it turns out."

"My mom? What did she want?"

"I won't know that until I call her back, duh!"

I had a feeling Mom was rounding up the extended family for her country-club dinner surprise, but I didn't go into it with Jill because I was concerned about Marco's phone call. I hung up with Jillian and said to him, "Bad news?"

"That was Gina calling from the hospital. My mother slipped on the steps going out to get the mail and hurt her ankle. The ER doctor said she may have broken a bone."

"Oh, Marco, your poor mom!"

"She's in a lot of pain, but Rafe and Gina are with her. They're waiting for the orthopedic surgeon, so I'll head over there after I drop you off, to see what the surgeon has to report."

"Did Gina say who the surgeon was?"

"No. Hey, maybe it's your brother Jordan."

With any luck, maybe not. My brother was a highly competent doctor, yet if anything went wrong, I didn't want to think what it would do to the relationship between our families. "The speed-dating event starts at seven o'clock tonight. Will you still be able to make it?"

"I'll find a way. As soon as I know something, I'll call you from the hospital."

"I guess your mom won't be going home tomorrow, will she?"

"She'll probably stick around until she's comfortable enough to travel. Rafe will have to drive her back."

"So . . . looks like you won't make our family dinner tomorrow night."

"Probably not." Marco pulled into a parking space near Bloomers and leaned over to kiss me. "Sorry, Sunshine."

Hmm. That broken ankle might not be such bad news after all.

CHAPTER
TWENTY-TWO

It was almost noon when Marco dropped me off in front of Bloomers. In spite of the worries hanging over me, I felt revved up, as if the solution to the murder were right around the corner. I attributed part of my buoyancy to the fact that whatever Mom had up her sleeve for tomorrow night's dinner, Marco wouldn't be there to witness it.

Inside the shop, I found Grace behind the cash register, two of the four quadruplets entertaining several tables of women by juggling oranges, and one playing waiter with a towel over his arm, sweeping around the room with a coffeepot in one hand and a teapot in the other.

"Aren't we missing a quadruplet?" I asked Grace.

"I sent Karl to the deli to get sandwiches for lunch. Here are your messages, love. When you have time, would you give me a progress report on the murder investigation?"

"Sure." I shuffled through the slips of paper as I headed toward the workroom. Three were from my mother, apparently believing she needed to remind me about the Friday dinner, and one was from my aunt Corrine, Jillian's mom, asking me to call her ASAP. I dialed her cell phone number on the spot and caught her shopping with her friends in town.

"Abby," she whispered, "I know you have a lot going on right now, but you have to help me. Jillian gave me the most ghastly gift for my birthday, and I don't want to hurt her feelings. Would you please take it off my hands? Maybe sell it at your shop? Please?"

"I can't, Aunt Corrine. Mom made it, and Jillian has been helping out at Bloomers, so both of them would spot it if I put it on display. It's not like I can tuck it behind a plant."

"What am I going to do?" my aunt whispered desperately. "It's sitting right in the middle of my grand foyer, grinning at everyone who enters my front door. The UPS driver refuses to step inside to pick up a package. How can I invite guests over? What was my daughter thinking?"

"If I ever figure that one out, I'll let you know."

"Please, Abby, think of a way to get that thing out of my house."

And then inspiration hit me — a way to help my aunt out of a jam and keep Jillian out of my hair without offending either my mom or my cousin. My brain was firing on all cylinders today! "There might be a way, Aunt Corrine, but you'll have to do something for me, too."

"Anything, Abby. Name it. Want an expensive shower? I'll be happy to throw one for you."

A shower? What was she talking about? "All you have to do is keep Jillian away from Bloomers for the next four days, until my assistant comes back to work, and then I'll take *The Bowler* off your hands."

"It's a deal," my aunt said in relief. "Just let me know when to send it over."

As soon as I hung up, I sought out Grace and explained the situation. She called her beau, then came back to the workroom beaming.

"Richard would be delighted to take *The Bowler.* He said it would fit in perfectly at the bowling alley. He'll even place a brass plaque on it to display the artist's name and the donor. That should please your mum and your cousin."

Two worries eliminated in less than an hour. The day was really looking up. I actually began to hum as I started pulling flowers for the first order. Because luck always ran in threes, I couldn't wait to discover what my next lucky break would be.

Karl arrived bearing a variety of sandwiches — ham, turkey, and tender sliced beef, smothered with spicy mustard and melted Swiss cheese on fresh ciabatta bread. We ate in two shifts, Karl, Johnny, and I on the second, when Karl managed to spill mustard down the front of his blue shirt.

"Mom is going to kill me," he said, trying to blot the spill with a paper napkin. "This is my Sunday dress shirt."

"You're toast, bro," Johnny said, clearly enjoying his sibling's suffering.

As I watched Karl's feeble attempt to wash out the mustard, I had another inspiration. I pulled Marco's Down the Hatch T-shirt from my purse, rinsed the coffee spots off the sleeve, and used a hair dryer to dry it. "Take off your shirt, and put this one on," I told Karl, handing him the gray T-shirt. "I'll run it down to the dry cleaner's after work."

Now I had a new reason to talk to Iris.

Shortly before three o'clock, Marco

phoned to tell me his mother hadn't needed surgery, and Rafe and Gina were taking her home. "I'm heading up to Chicago. I got another call from my buddy at O'Hare. It seems Hank Miller flew into Chicago this morning and, from what I was able to uncover, he booked a room at the O'Hare Hilton."

"Why would Miller stay at the Hilton and not his house here in town?"

"That's what I want to know, among other things. I'll stop by Dave's office afterward to see if he received those phone records yet."

"Keep me posted. As soon as I close up the shop I'm going to Frey's to see if Iris will talk to me. Are we still on for the speed-dating event tonight?"

"You bet. I'll pick you up at six thirty."

At five o'clock, with a light snow falling, I locked up the shop and drove to the dry cleaner's, intending to go straight home afterward so I'd have time to eat before Marco arrived. The parking spaces in front of Frey's were occupied, so I used the side driveway to get to the small lot in the rear. There was only one space free and it was beside a huge brown Dumpster being used for the second-floor renovations.

I pulled cautiously into the parking space, then, with Karl's shirt in hand, I locked my Vette and started toward the driveway that ran along the side of the house. At the sight of a bicycle propped near the building's back door, however, I stopped short. By the distant glow of a streetlight in the alley, the bike appeared to be blue, with rusty fenders, handlebars with faded tassels, and a black leather seat. I went over to the bike for a closer inspection. It certainly looked like the one I'd seen against Miller's barn. But how could that be possible?

Puzzled, I went inside Frey's and found five people in line, none of whom resembled the photo of Hank Miller or seemed damp or cold enough to have used the bike. Iris, with her bright spots of pink on her cheekbones and drab smock, was chatting with the first customer while writing up a ticket.

When my turn finally came, Iris greeted me with her usual, "Well, look who's here. It's the underground florist!" then went straight into a comedy routine. "Hey, Florist Gump, any big *plants* for the weekend? Seen your *stalkbroker* recently? You can tell me. My *tulips* are sealed."

"Ha! Pretty funny, Iris."

She shook her head, her misshapen mouth curving crookedly, as though she cracked herself up. "What have you got there?"

I placed the blue dress shirt on the counter. "A shirt with a nasty mustard stain."

She stuck a paper marker near the stain, then handed me a ticket to fill out. As I wrote in my information, I said, "Are you going to the speed-dating event tonight?"

"No, ma'am. Not going to make that mistake again. Yourself?"

Okay, Abby, here goes nothing. "Actually, yes. I'm helping investigate Jonas Treat's murder, and I need to talk to Carmen Gold's assistant."

At the mention of Jonas's name, a small shock went through Iris. Then she glanced over her shoulder, as though concerned someone might be listening, leaned her hands on the counter, and said in a hushed, angry voice, "I know Carmen. That bitch killed Jonas. Don't you think so?"

Her vehemence stunned me. "I can't really divulge any information."

Iris nodded knowingly. "I understand. But that's all right, because I know she did it. She set a trap for him."

"Seriously?"

Iris glanced around again, then whispered, "She sent Jonas a personal invitation to the last speed-dating event."

"Are you sure? I thought people had to sign up for it. I know I did."

With a perfectly straight face, Iris said, "Jonas *showed* it to me."

"Really?"

"Oh, yes. He often took me into his confidence."

Sure he did. "Jonas must have been surprised Carmen sent him an invitation."

"Surprised — and very, *very* displeased. He told me he couldn't abide Carmen. He thought she was pushy and arrogant and rude. That's why he wanted me there — to show her the kind of woman he really liked, someone who had depth and character and could make him laugh. But that wily Carmen sensed what we were up to and kept us apart all evening."

"No kidding! That must have infuriated Jonas."

"Indeed it did infuriate him. Indeed it did. He read her the riot act, that's for sure."

"Wow. I was right there and didn't even notice! When did he confront her?"

"Right after the dating session ended, just before the mixer. I don't know if you're aware of this, but Carmen left shortly afterward, and then *bam!*" Iris hit her fist against the counter, making me jump. "Jonas's beautiful Ferrari was hit. You know what I'm thinking, right? That Carmen is the hit-and-run driver as well as the murderer."

"Really!"

"It makes sense, doesn't it? Carmen wanted revenge against Jonas for choosing me over her." Iris lifted her eyebrows, clearly expecting me to be impressed.

"I see. But if she smashed his car for revenge, why would she need to kill him?"

Iris blinked rapidly, clearly not expecting that question.

A customer came in, so Iris tore off the ticket, handed me the stub, and clipped the rest onto the shirt. "This will be ready Tuesday morning. Anything else I can do for you?"

"No, that's it. Thanks for your help."

"Anytime. And don't forget your newspaper."

I walked back to my car, mulling over what Iris clearly wanted me to believe: that Jonas had taken her into his confidence, and had chosen her over Carmen, prompting Carmen's vengeful acts of hit-and-run and then murder. Did Iris believe that herself?

As I approached my car, I again noticed the bike. Were there really two old-fashioned blue bicycles around? Since my curiosity did not like to be denied, I went back inside to ask Iris about it.

She had just finished ringing up the customer and glanced at me in surprise when I stepped up to the counter. "Did you forget something?"

"I was wondering whose blue bicycle is parked around back."

"Mine."

Hers? Now I was really confused.

"Why do you ask?"

Yikes. She'd caught me off guard. "It, um, reminded me of my brother's bike. He sold it years ago, and I always wondered what happened to it." That sounded plausible. "Isn't it kind of cold to use a bike in the winter?"

"I bundle up, but I don't ride it much, only if Mother has the car when I need to be somewhere. With these ridiculous gas prices, I save lots of money, I'll tell you that."

"I believe you. If gas prices climb any higher, I might have to get one for myself."

I thanked Iris and left, stopping for a newspaper to make her happy. I made the trek around the house to the parking lot, then couldn't resist taking another look at the bicycle. Rusty fenders, balloon tires, handlebars with dirty white rubber grips, streamers — was it the same bike I'd seen propped up against the barn or not?

I checked my watch and decided I had enough time to squeeze in a quick stop at the Miller homestead. On the way, I phoned Marco, but got his voice mail, so I left a message telling him what I'd learned from Iris, where I was headed, and why. Shortly before I turned onto Rollercoaster Road, he returned the call.

"Where are you?" he asked.

"About two minutes away from Miller's house. Where are you?"

"Stuck in traffic on the Borman Expressway. You shouldn't go there alone in the dark, Abby. We can check for the bike in the morning."

I pulled into the driveway. "Too late. I'm already here. I'll just take a quick look and hop right back in my car."

Marco sighed in exasperation. "Do you have a flashlight with you?"

"No, but I should be able to tell if the bike is there or not."

"Then keep me on the line."

"I can do that. Did you find Hank Miller?"

"No, damn it. I struck out again. The hotel manager told me Miller made his reservations yesterday but hasn't checked in yet. I slipped the guy a twenty to alert me when Miller shows up."

I got out of the car and started toward the back of the house. My boots crunched loudly on the gravel, so I hopped onto the frozen grass. "It's creepy here," I whispered into the phone. "It's so dark and still."

"I really don't like your being there alone, Abby."

"Didn't your friend at O'Hare tell you Miller's plane got in this morning?"

"Correct."

"You'd think he would have checked in by now," I mused, "unless he drove back to New Chapel instead."

"Which is why I'd rather you weren't on his property," Marco said in exasperation.

"I'm being extremely cautious, Marco," I said quietly. "Don't worry. Remember, I learned from the master. So let's try to reason out why Miller would make hotel reservations if he were coming back here."

"Here's a reason — to establish an alibi. Now, would you please get back in the Vette and go home?"

"I'm almost at the barn. Okay, I can see the wrought-iron bench now and —" I stopped. "Marco, the bike's not here."

CHAPTER
TWENTY-THREE

"I don't see it anywhere," I said quietly, making my way around the house.

"Forget the bike, Abby. Just get out of there. I don't have a good feeling about your being there."

Neither did I. My scalp was prickling, as though an unseen presence watched me. I glanced at the shuttered windows of the house, half expecting to see a ghostly visage peering out. "I'm heading for my car right now. But I'm still puzzled by the bike. If it was Iris's we saw this morning, what was it doing here?"

"There could be more than one blue bicycle in town, Abby."

"Two old-fashioned blue bikes with rusty fenders and handlebar grips with streamers? And both connected to two of our suspects? That's too freakish, Marco."

"Maybe a Realtor came by to stow the bike out of sight before showing the house to prospective buyers."

In the background I heard horns honking.

"Concentrate on driving, Marco. We can talk on our way to the Wild Boar."

Back at the apartment, I found Nikki under a blanket on the sofa watching a rerun of *The Cosby Show,* with Simon asleep on her stomach. Nikki had always had a slender face, but now it appeared hollow-cheeked, almost gaunt. I could tell the stress was eating her up.

Hearing me come in, Simon lifted his head, then leaped off the sofa and galloped toward me, meowing his urgency to be fed.

"I gave him food an hour ago," Nikki called.

I scratched Simon behind the ears. "Sorry, buddy. You were ratted out. Nikki, have you eaten yet?"

"Nothing sounds good. Tell me what happened today."

"Come to the kitchen and I'll give you the rundown while I make supper for us."

Over a hastily thrown-together supper of black-bean-and-cheese burritos, I gave Nikki the information we'd gathered that day. "We're closing in, Nikki. I can feel it in my gut. I really think that by tomorrow, we'll know who the killer is."

She rested her chin on her fist. "And if you don't, you'll come visit me in jail?"

"Have a little faith, Nik. We're both due for some good luck."

Marco arrived ten minutes early, just as I was dabbing on peach-colored lip gloss. Luckily, I didn't have to fuss with my hair. Along with my black boots, dressy black slacks, a yellow sweater, and my peacoat, I'd decided to tuck my red locks under a rolled-brim wool hat, hoping to remain incognito at the speed-dating event. People tended to notice me because of my hair color, and I certainly didn't want to draw Carmen's attention tonight.

"Sorry if I rushed you," Marco said, as he escorted me across the parking lot of my apartment building. "I thought we'd swing by Miller's property and have a fresh look around before we head to the Wild Boar."

"To see if the blue bike is back?"

"Ideally, to find out who owns it. I was thinking about what you told me earlier — how Iris fixated on Jonas and about the coincidence with the bicycles — so, on my way to pick you up, I stopped at Frey's."

"Wasn't I right? The bikes are identical, aren't they?"

"I don't know. The bike was gone. At the

same time, the hotel manager hasn't heard from Miller, and that makes me uneasy."

"Maybe he's staying at his house."

"I guess we'll find out. By the way, I read through some of the discovery information, specifically transcripts of interviews with Hank Miller, Duke Kessler, and Robin Lennox. Kessler's and Lennox's alibis were verified, but not Miller's, so it's possible he's still being investigated. I gave Dave the flight manifests to pass on to the DA, and Dave felt sure it would guarantee Miller a callback, if they haven't done so already."

"So it's possible Miller came back to town for that reason and is with the detectives right now."

"Possible, yes."

"If that doesn't pan out, will those flight manifests be enough to convince the DA to hold off on convening the grand jury tomorrow?"

"I wouldn't count on it."

"Did you see the phone records, by the way?"

"Yes, but they weren't much help. In the month before the murder, none of our suspects communicated with Jonas. He received four calls on the day he died, all pertaining to his business, and placed one to Nikki an hour before he picked her up.

That was his last call."

"That's not good news."

Marco reached across the seat to squeeze my hand. "Don't lose hope, Sunshine. We'll find the killer."

As we headed west through town, I flipped down the visor to make sure my hair was tucked inside. "What's our game plan for interviewing Pamela?"

"Give me a time frame for the speed-dating event."

"From six thirty to seven o'clock, the attendees sign in and pay. At seven, Carmen goes over the rules with the women. That takes about five minutes. Then the guys enter and find their tables, Carmen reviews the rules once more, Pamela presses a buzzer, and the first nine-minute date begins. That's when Pamela should exit."

"Let's sit at the bar in the main dining area and wait for Pamela to come out. If she takes a seat at a table in the restaurant or a stool at the bar, you approach her first, since she might remember you from last week and be more willing to chat. If she leaves the restaurant, we'll have to catch her outside and try to convince her to talk to us. We just need to make sure Carmen doesn't see us talking to Pamela."

I tucked in a strand and flipped up the visor. "That's why I wore my hat."

Marco glanced at me. "You're kind of cute in that hat."

"I'd rather be sexy, but cute is fine."

"You'd be sexy if that hat was *all* you had on."

"Say the word, hotshot, and I'll make it happen."

He gave me a glance with those bedroom eyes that made me tingle way down deep inside. "You know what we're going to do after we wrap up this case?"

"I can think of a few things I'd like to do."

"Like go back to Key West?"

With a sigh of pleasure, I said, "Oh, yeah. That'll do."

A half mile down Rollercoaster Road, the farmhouse came into view. Marco pulled onto the shoulder and got out to study the house. "No car in the driveway, no lights showing from behind the shutters. It sure doesn't look like Miller is there."

"So what should we do first?"

"Let's go check around back and see if we can find the bike."

The sky was an ugly charcoal gray, still spitting snow, and the wind had picked up, swirling leaves and debris around our boots. While Marco retrieved his heavy-duty flashlight from the trunk, I turned up the collar of my coat and stuffed my hands in my pockets, still with the feeling of being watched.

Leaving his flashlight off, Marco guided us up the road and in a wide circle around the house, where he spent a few minutes observing the back before moving on down toward the barn. In the distance, across the barren fields and stripped woodland, I could see the model home at Chateaux en Carnations illuminated by the cheery glow of the landscaping lights.

As we approached the barn, Marco switched on the high-powered beam, then swept it along the side of the old weathered building. There was no sign of the bicycle.

"It might be in the barn," Marco said.

Shivering, I asked, "Is it possible Miller came back for it?"

"Anything's possible. The problem is, why would he wait until now? He moved to the Keys last year. If it was important to him, why wouldn't he have taken it then?"

"In that case, maybe it *was* Iris's bike we saw here."

"But what would bring her here? What connects her to this farm?"

I gazed out across the field and saw the answer right in front of me. Pointing toward the model home, I said, "There's the connection, Marco. She could watch Jonas coming and going from here." I walked to the end of the barn and pointed to an opening cut high into the siding. "Look. A hayloft. The perfect place for her to spy on Jonas."

My cell phone rang, startling both of us. I grabbed it and answered quickly, "Hello?" just as Marco took off toward the big double doors on the broad side of the barn.

"Abby?" Lottie said. "Sorry to bother you, sweetie, but ever since I talked to you this afternoon, something's been eating at me. Got a minute?"

"Sure," I said, hurrying after Marco.

"You said Dalva Frey told you Iris was at home with her the Sunday evening Jonas was killed, right? But I know for a fact that Dalva was playing bingo that night. She sat across from me."

"Do you know how late she stayed?"

"We usually quit by ten, and we all leave together. In fact, I remember seeing her drive away. She's got an old black clunker of a car. Anyway, I thought you should know."

I thanked Lottie for the tip, then ran to help Marco, who was trying to open the heavy doors. "Mrs. Frey lied about being at home with Iris the night Jonas was killed," I said breathlessly. "She was at bingo. Lottie sat across from her."

"Unless she played until one o'clock in the morning, Abby, it doesn't really prove anything, other than that she lied. Give me a hand here. The doors are barred from the inside."

Marco managed to get enough play on one door to pry it open a few inches; then he had me slide my arm through the gap and lift the bar. He opened the door and stepped inside, sweeping the flashlight across the straw-covered floor. Hearing things skitter about, I moved close beside him. I wasn't afraid of mice, but rats, roaches, snakes — not a fan.

The high-powered beam showed a cavernous room with stalls along one wall, a wooden trough in the middle, low pens along the opposite wall, and a hayloft above, with a tall wooden ladder propped nearby for access.

I pointed toward the loft. "Let's climb up to see what the view looks like."

Marco maneuvered the tall, unwieldy ladder around so it leaned against the loft floor. "These rungs are old. You'd better let me go up first."

"So you can fall on top of me? I don't think so. Hand over the flashlight, hotshot."

"Then test the rungs before you put weight on them."

I climbed cautiously up the ladder, then shone the light on the loft floor to make sure I wasn't stepping into a snake's next, if snakes had nests. But except for a thin layer of dirty straw, all I saw were old gray boards. I tested the boards before stepping onto them; then, as Marco joined me, I shone the beam around the loft, illuminating a few bales of old hay along one side. But it was the opening at the end I was interested in.

"Look! It faces Chateaux en Carnations. Could Iris find a better place to spy on Jonas?" I picked my way across the floor, stopping a few feet short of the opening. "She even left a blanket up here."

Marco crouched near the brown wool blanket, felt along one side, then lifted a corner. "Look at this." He flipped the blanket back to reveal a pair of black binoculars.

"Iris was quite the little spy, wasn't she?"

"Let's get these things to the police." Marco slipped on a pair of gloves from his pocket, put the binoculars onto the blanket, then folded up the corners and tied them at the top.

Carrying the flashlight, Marco climbed down first, then had me drop the bundle into his arms. After I descended, he shone his light around the barn again, halting the beam at a small wooden service door, where I could see a black wool coat hanging from a peg. As I remembered, the door faced the house, and outside it was the wrought-iron bench.

Marco moved the beam from the coat down onto a three-legged milking stool. Next to the stool was a pair of large black rubber boots. And beside the boots was an old blue bicycle with rusty fenders and handle grips with streamers.

"You were right," I said. "Someone did move it inside. But who? Iris? Miller? A Realtor?"

A chill went up my spine as I glanced around. If it wasn't the Realtor, then it must have been moved by the bike's true owner. And where was he or she now?

To think I'd told Nikki barns weren't scary. Right.

"Take this," Marco said, and handed me the wool bundle. He strode across the barn floor to crouch in front of the bike, aiming the beam at the tires. "Look. Blue clay."

He crumbled a piece with his fingers for me to see, then propped the flashlight on the floor and picked up one of the boots, turning it over in front of the light to reveal more blue clay on the soles. Someone had worn those boots to the model home. Were they the killer's?

"They're large boots, Marco. I don't think they're Iris's. She has tiny feet."

"Let's take these with us, too. Finger-prints, DNA — something will tell us who used them."

He picked up the boots by the top edge and reached for his flashlight.

"Don't move a muscle!" an angry voice shouted.

CHAPTER
TWENTY-FOUR

With a gasp, I turned to see a hunched figure with a large head and spindly legs standing in the doorway. "It's Iris," I whispered to Marco. As he snatched up the flashlight, I called, "Don't be alarmed. It's me, Abby, the underground florist."

At that moment, Marco directed the beam toward her face. But it wasn't Iris after all. It was her mother, Dalva Frey — and she was aiming a shotgun at us.

The woman held up one hand to shield her eyes from the beam, revealing a knee-length pink flannel nightgown under a bulky down jacket, skinny bare legs, and black mules. "Put that light down!"

"Stand behind me," Marco whispered. As he leaned down to put the flashlight on the floor, he whispered again, "Text Reilly an SOS."

Oh, no! I must have lost my cell phone when I climbed up to the loft. "I don't have my phone," I whispered back.

He patted his back pocket as he called in a calm voice, "No need for the shotgun, Mrs. Frey. We're not here to harm anyone."

As Marco continued to talk to her, I put the bundle down, slid his cell from his pocket, opened it, and hunted for Reilly's number.

"I'm looking for Hank Miller, Mrs. Frey. This is his property, isn't it?"

"Not while I'm renting here. Put them boots down, I said, and get your hands in the air."

My cold fingers fumbled on the keypad, but I managed to type; *SOS.* But just as I was about to hit Send, I realized Reilly would need a location.

"I'm a private investigator," Marco said, raising his hands in compliance. "I'll be glad to show you my ID. It's right here in my wallet. Let me just reach into my pocket and get it out for you."

"Keep those hands in the air!" Mrs. Frey snarled. "Don't try to trick me. I know you're after Iris. Miss Nosy-Pants there has been snooping around her all week."

Oh, great. Our predicament was all *my* fault.

Concentrate! that little voice of reason

ordered. Trying to block out Mrs. Frey's ranting, I began to type again: *M-I-L-L-E-R-S —*

"Hey, stupid girl, I can see you back there. I want both of you on your knees now!"

My fingers froze. On our knees? Why? So she could kill us to protect Iris?

"Mrs. Frey," Marco said in his cop's voice, moving slowly toward her, "put the shotgun down. We didn't know you were renting here. It's Miller we're after, not Iris."

B-A-R-N, I typed hastily.

Before I could hit Send, there was an explosion directly overhead, showering us with bits of hay and stinging splinters of wood. Marco dived for me, pulling me down to the ground beneath him, making me lose my grip on the phone. I felt it slip from my hands, but at that moment, with my ears ringing from the blast, all I could think about was covering my head.

When the dust cleared, I looked up and saw a jagged hole in the loft floor. Then I glanced at Mrs. Frey and saw her swing the weapon in our direction. "See what happens when you don't listen?"

The woman was insane. I had to find the phone before she shot us! My heart raced wildly as I searched the floor, shards of wood pricking my fingers.

"Now, for the last time, get on your knees!"

I found it!

"Get ready to run," Marco whispered.

I pressed Send just as he gave the three-legged stool a hard kick, sending it tumbling noisily across the wooden floor toward Mrs. Frey. He grabbed my arm and pulled me in a dash toward the open door. But our escape came to a halt just as we reached the first stall, when a match flared in the dark. Instantly, Marco pushed me into the stall and crouched down beside me, just as a lantern began to glow.

"There's nowhere to go," Mrs. Frey called in a singsong voice, as the light got brighter. "You might as well come out."

Suddenly, there was a heavy crunch of gravel outside, and thin shafts of light filtered through cracks in the barn wall, as though a vehicle were approaching. It couldn't be the police, I thought, not that fast.

Instantly, the lantern light went out. Then, as a car door slammed, I heard rapid shuffling, as though Mrs. Frey were hurrying along the straw floor. What was she afraid of? Who did she think was in the car?

"Marco, what should we do?" I whispered. He put his hand on my shoulder to keep me down. "Wait."

The ancient door hinges creaked, and I heard footsteps stop just inside the barn. "Mother? Are you in here?"

Iris! I squeezed Marco's arm as the lantern light grew bright again. Now we were really trapped.

"For God's sake, Iris," Mrs. Frey called, "you scared the living daylights out of me."

"There's a car parked up the road, and I saw light in here. . . . Why do you have the shotgun?"

"I heard something and came to see what it was. Go on, now; get out of here. I can handle it. Go back to the house."

In a voice heavy with suspicion, Iris said, "Who moved the ladder? Were you up in the loft?"

"Don't worry. Your secret hidey-hole is safe. Now get out of here."

Footsteps came closer to the stall. I held my breath and curled my body into a tighter knot behind Marco. "Is that my blanket on the floor?" Iris demanded.

"Oh, for Pete's sake!" her mother cried. "I knew I should've burned this barn down and put an end to your perverted pleasures."

Iris marched past the stall, grumbling to herself. Then something hit the floorboards with a loud thunk. "My binoculars? You took them from the loft? I told you to leave my things alone!"

"I didn't touch your damn things." Shuffling footsteps came toward us; then she was standing at the open stall door, pointing the muzzle of the shotgun at us. "They did."

A moment later, Iris was gazing down on us, too. "Abby? What are you doing?" She turned to gaze at her mother. "What the hell's going on here?"

Marco signaled for me to follow his lead by quickly squeezing my hand, then prompted me to rise with him, hands in the air.

"My name is Marco Salvare," he said in that quiet, confident voice of authority. "I'm a private investigator looking for Hank Miller. Abby came along only to keep me company. I removed the blanket and binoculars from the loft because I thought they belonged to Miller. No harm done, though." He put his arm around me to lead me out of the stall. "We don't need them. So we'll just be on our —"

Mrs. Frey blocked our path. "Get down on your knees, hands behind your head. Iris, go get that gray duct tape off the shelf."

As her mother set the lantern on the floor, keeping the weapon aimed at Marco's chest, Iris gazed first at us, then at her mom, as though in a daze. "What are you doing, Mother? Didn't you hear what the man said? No harm done. Let them go."

"What I'm doing is trying to protect you, Iris. Now, they have to be dealt with, so go get that tape."

Iris grabbed the gun's muzzle and shoved it to the side. "You're not going to *deal* with anyone. What's the matter with you?" To us she said, "You can leave."

She didn't have to tell me twice.

We'd just stepped out of the stall when Mrs. Frey tried to yank the muzzle of the shotgun out of Iris's grasp. "Stupid girl! You can't let them get away. They'll ruin everything."

As the women struggled for the weapon, Marco took my hand and we ran. But before we could reach the door, a shot rang out, and this time thick pieces of wood from the rafters rained down on our heads. Before another shot was fired, Marco pushed me behind a fat post, doing his best to shield me with his body, while Iris screamed, "Mother, have you lost your mind?"

"They have to be stopped, Iris. They know about Jonas."

"What are you talking about?" Iris cried. "What about Jonas?"

"Don't question me now. Just get the

tape." Then to us Mrs. Frey yelled. "You take a step out that door, and I'll blast you to bits."

"What do they know about Jonas?" Iris ground out.

"Not now, Iris!"

"I'm not moving until you give me an answer."

There was a sharp sigh; then Mrs. Frey said in a tone of exasperation, "I made sure Jonas wouldn't hurt you anymore. But these people will, Iris, if we don't stop them."

"Wait a minute," Iris said, her voice registering confusion. "What do you mean, you made sure he wouldn't hurt me? What are you saying?"

What the heck *was* Mrs. Frey saying. *She* killed Jonas?

"Make a run for it while they're arguing," Marco whispered, his voice so faint I could barely hear it. "Wait for my signal."

"You don't need to know everything, Iris! Isn't it enough that we're free of the misery now? Free of their abuses?"

"Whose abuses?" Iris cried. "No one abused us. Are you talking about Father again?"

"Are you gonna help me or are you gonna stand there with that stupid look on your face?"

"Answer me first!" Iris demanded, stamping her foot.

"For pity's sake, where have you been, Iris? Didn't we suffer enough hell from that man?"

"From Father?" Iris cried hysterically. "What did he ever do to me? You're the one who made my life hell!"

I peered around the post just as Mrs. Frey hit Iris on the side of her head with the butt of her shotgun. "Don't talk to me like that," she sneered, as Iris crumpled to the floor, holding her head. "I'm the one who always protected you. I'm the one who put an end to his abuse. No more suffering for us, Iris. No more misery."

Iris appeared dazed as she stared up at Dalva. "*You* set the fire? It wasn't an accident?"

I clapped my hand over my mouth in shock.

"I did what I had to do to protect you, Iris, just like I did with that no-good Jonas Treat."

Iris began to sob, rocking back and forth in misery, holding her injured head. "You killed Jonas! Oh, my Lord! You killed him! You killed the man I love."

"What was I supposed to do, let you keep stalking that idiot?" Mrs. Frey shouted, as

Iris keened in grief. "Watch you throw yourself at him? Flirt like a hussy every time he came into the shop? Go through his pockets, making believe he was in love with you while he ridiculed you every time your back was turned?"

"Stop it!" Iris screamed. "Don't say that! He loved me!"

"He didn't love you, and you know it. I saw you that night, huddled in the car crying while he smooched his date outside that model home. You sat there like a whipped puppy, wishing it were you with him. What a pathetic sight you were. I had to put an end to it."

Mrs. Frey had to be talking about Jonas's date with Nikki.

"You followed me!" Iris cried.

"You think I was about to let you throw your life away for a shallow little man who'd treat you like a slave and use you up until you were nothing but a dried-up old crone?"

With a roar of fury, Iris leaped at her, and the two began to struggle. I glanced at Marco, expecting him to give me a signal, and saw him sagged against the post, blood streaming down the side of his head.

"Marco," I whispered in fright, as the women battled just yards away. "You're hurt!"

He touched his fingers to his temple, then looked at them as though he couldn't understand why blood was there. "Go, Abby," he said weakly. "Now."

"I'm not leaving you here!"

"Do it!" Then he slumped over.

I started to reach for him, only to feel the barrel of the shotgun between my shoulder blades. "Don't move," Mrs. Frey commanded in a snarl.

Trying to keep the fear out of my voice, I said, "He's wounded. I need to help him."

"Doesn't matter. You'll both be dead soon anyway."

I swallowed hard and glanced around for Iris, only to see her out cold on the floor.

"Mrs. Frey, please," I begged, as panic rose in my throat. "I love him."

"Love," she said with a scoff, then jabbed me in the back again. "I'll be right back. Stay there."

Without seeming to shift position, I turned my head enough to keep her in my peripheral view. With the shotgun aimed at me, she backed toward a shelf stacked with supplies, a roll of gray tape among them. If she tied us up, we'd be at her mercy, and I couldn't let that happen. I desperately groped for the right words to keep her mind engaged, even as I prayed that Reilly had received my message and was on his way.

"You fell in love once, Mrs. Frey. You got married, had a baby. You loved that baby, didn't you?"

She felt along the shelf for the roll of gray tape, never taking her eyes off me.

"You love Iris, don't you, Mrs. Frey? Look how you've protected her all these years. Only a good mother does that. Only a mother who loves her child goes to those lengths."

"Like she ever appreciated me," Mrs. Frey said snidely, snatching the roll of tape.

I cast a glance at Marco and saw blood pooling beneath his head and a sickly pallor coming to his face. Moving very slowly, I reached for his wrist and found a pulse, weak but steady. I had no way of knowing how badly he was injured, but it didn't matter. I wasn't about to let him die.

"I'll bet Iris just never told you she appreciated you, Mrs. Frey. That's how it is with me. I appreciate my mom but I forget to tell her. She protects me just like you protect Iris."

"Iris didn't understand," the woman said, shuffling toward me. "She was too young to know how cruel her father was to me. I suffered until I couldn't stand it anymore; then one night I found a candle burning in Iris's bedroom, and it came to me just like that, how to make Bill's death look like an accident. It almost didn't work, though. The damned firemen got there too fast. Iris doesn't know how lucky we were that the old bastard died anyway."

She was standing above Marco now. "Pull his hands behind him."

My mind raced. I had to do something fast. "He's unconscious. What's the point of tying his hands? He can't hurt you."

At that moment, Marco groaned. Quickly, Mrs. Frey raised the butt of the shotgun, ready to slam it down on his head. Every hair on my body stood on end as I imagined the outcome, and at once I was filled with an almost blinding rage.

Before she could act, I lunged at her, lifting her off the floor with newfound strength before taking her down, landing on top of her with a hard thud that drove the air out of my lungs. As I gulped for breath, she used the heels of her hands to shove my chin up, then with startling might wrestled me onto my back and pressed the shotgun barrel across my throat until I thought my Adam's apple would be crushed.

I pushed frantically against the weapon, trying to break her hold as my strength waned. In the background I heard Marco groan again. With one last burst of adrenaline, I slid my hands along the woman's bare legs until I could pinch her thighs hard. As she bellowed in pain, I broke her hold on the weapon and pushed her off. Dragging air into my starved lungs, I got to my knees and reached for the shotgun just as she grabbed the other end. Then we began a deadly tug-of-war I was not about to let her win.

Suddenly, gravel crunched outside as vehicles came toward the barn, with a multitude of red and blue lights flashing through the slits in the boards. I wanted to shout for joy. The police had come! Reilly had received my message. It was my third stroke of luck.

When Mrs. Frey realized what was happening, her eyes widened in fear. She let go of the shotgun, sending me sprawling backward onto the straw as she glanced around in a panic. Her gaze focused on the small wooden door at the far end of the barn. And then she fled, half loping, half shuffling, toward it.

I scrambled to my feet to stop her, but as she passed her daughter's prostrate form, Iris's hand shot out and grabbed her ankle, causing her mother to fall on her face. Before Dalva could get up, Iris sprang on top of her and began pummeling her back, sobbing, "Murderer! You killed the only men I ever loved! You're going to rot in hell for what you did."

At once the room was filled with shouts, and thundering feet, and the beams of many flashlights, as the cops swarmed in, weapons drawn. I immediately put the shotgun on the ground and raised my hands, but they ignored me and aimed their guns at Iris.

With a gasp, she raised her hands, her crooked mouth agape in terror. "Don't shoot me! I'm innocent!"

As the cops took control of both women, I quickly ran to Marco's side and knelt down, smoothing back his dark hair, sticky now with blood, trying to see where he was hurt. Talking soothingly even while I trembled in fear, I said, "Marco, the cops are here. We'll get you to the hospital now. You'll be fine." But there was no response.

And then Reilly was beside me, feeling Marco's neck for a pulse. At the sight of our cop buddy, tears of relief spilled out of my eyes. Reilly waved over the EMTs, then glanced at me. "Marco's going to be fine. Are you okay?"

I nodded, wiping the wetness off my face, as the medical technicians checked Marco's head for injury and took his vital signs.

"How is he?" I asked them, sniffing back tears.

"Seems to be a superficial wound," one of them said, as the other began wrapping his head with gauze. "Scalps bleed a lot. He might need a transfusion, but he'll be okay."

As the cops brought Iris and her mom past, both in handcuffs, I pointed out Mrs. Frey to Reilly. "She murdered Jonas. She planned the whole thing. The blue bike over there is what she used to get to Jonas's office and back. Her daughter didn't know anything about it. Don't let them put Iris in jail, Reilly."

"I'll do my best," he said.

The techs lay Marco on a rolling stretcher, raised it, then wheeled him out of the barn toward the ambulance waiting farther up the driveway. I followed behind, exhausted emotionally and physically. As we walked, Reilly asked questions. I told him everything I could remember; then, before climbing into the back of the ambulance, I said, "I'm going to stay at the hospital until I know Marco's okay. Would you call his family? And my parents?"

"I'll take care of everything," he promised; then the doors were shut and we were off.

CHAPTER TWENTY-FIVE

By midnight, Marco was sitting up in his hospital bed, sipping water and making jokes about wimping out on me. He had two stitches on his head, cuts and bruises on his face and hands, and a headache, but his color was good and so were all his vital signs.

"Come on, Sunshine, smile. I don't look that bad, do I?"

For at least the twelfth time that evening, I put my arms around him and leaned my head on his shoulder, sitting beside him on the bed. "I'm sorry, Marco. I'm just so relieved you're okay. You don't know how close you came to not being here."

He wrapped an arm around me and kissed the top of my head. "Isn't it lucky for me I have a fireball for a girlfriend?"

The nurse came in and scowled at the sight of me on the bed. Sheepishly, I slid off and went to the other side while she checked

Marco's blood pressure and took his temperature. At a knock on the door frame, I glanced over and saw Reilly, out of uniform now.

"How's it going?" Reilly asked me, with a nod toward Marco.

"He's cracking jokes," I replied. "That tells you something."

As the nurse left the room, Reilly walked up to the bed. "Hey, man. You're looking better than last time I saw you. How's your head?"

"A little sore, but thanks to Abby, I kept it. That's the important thing."

"I wanted to give you an update," Reilly said, pulling up a chair. "We got a confession from Mrs. Frey on the murder of Jonas Treat, and full cooperation from her daughter."

"Good," I said. "That old woman is insane. They're not charging Iris with stalking or anything, are they?"

"Who's going to file charges?" Reilly asked. "Jonas? Besides, she's been through enough, what with losing her dad and putting up with that nutcase of a mother. Mrs. Frey's being charged in her husband's murder, too, by the way. So I'd say her life is over. And just so you know, she was also the anonymous tipster."

I scooted back onto the bed beside Marco. "How did Mrs. Frey explain Jonas's murder?"

"She's been renting Miller's old place since October, when the renovations on the second floor of the dry cleaner's started, which is when Iris began spying on Jonas. Mrs. Frey was disgusted with Iris's behavior, but it wasn't until that Sunday night that she decided to put an end to it.

"Apparently, after Mrs. Frey got back from bingo, Iris took the car and was gone a long time. Mrs. Frey became suspicious, fearing Iris was up to her tricks of stalking Jonas, and biked over to the subdivision to see Iris sitting in the car in tears over 'that pervert,' as Mrs. Frey called Jonas. She went back home, waited until Iris went to bed, then rode to the model home and had a showdown with Jonas that ended with her pulling a knife and stabbing him. Naturally, she claims it was in self-defense, even though she stabbed him from behind."

"How did Mrs. Frey know Jonas was at the office?" I asked.

"Iris wasn't the only one spying from the loft," Reilly said.

"Do you buy her story?" I asked.

Reilly shrugged. "Not for me to decide. By the way, Marco, Abby mentioned that

407

you'd been trying to reach Hank Miller, so I thought I'd let you know one of the detectives told me Miller came into town today for a second interview. It seems you weren't the only ones to doubt his alibi. Anyway, he was able to satisfy their questions, so they let him go back to Chicago. He's set to fly back to Miami in the morning."

"That solves one mystery," Marco said. "But we still have a hit-and-run driver out there somewhere. You might want to suggest the detectives talk to Carmen Gold about that."

"Done," Reilly said. "After the cops put a little pressure on Carmen's assistant — I think her name is Pamela — she was more than happy to give a statement about her boss's act of vengeance against Jonas."

I noticed Marco's eyelids starting to droop. "Are you okay?"

"Just tired. You must be, too, Sunshine. Why don't you go home and get some rest?"

Knowing Marco would be okay now, I decided to take him up on it. I lowered the head of the bed, then kissed him on the cheek. "I'll be back in the morning. If there's anything you need, call me, okay?"

Barely awake, he said softly, "What I need is you. But that'll have to wait."

With a blush, I turned to find Reilly staring at his shoes, as if embarrassed to have overheard. "So," he said, "need a ride home?"

A persistent buzzing dragged me from a deep sleep. After staying up half the night explaining everything to Nikki, who was so relieved she insisted on making big, gloppy chocolate sundaes for us, it took me a full minute to realize the noise was coming from my cell phone. I groped for it on the nightstand, then croaked, "Hello?"

"Rise and shine, Fireball," Marco said in his husky voice. "It's eight in the morning."

Eight? Oh, no! I'd overslept. "Marco, you sound better. How do you feel?"

"A few bruises, still have a headache, but not too bad, considering. The doctor released me, so I'm going home to rest. Rafe is picking me up in ten minutes."

I sat up, rubbing my eyes. "That's great!"

"Does Nikki know what happened yet?"

"I gave her the whole story last night. She's so relieved, Marco, and so appreciative. She wants to take us out to dinner next week."

"Okay by me. What do you want to do about your family dinner tonight?"

"I'm sure you're not up to going."

"I know how important this is to you,

Abby. I'll rest up today. It'll be fine."

It wasn't fine with me. "What about your mom? Won't she be hurt if you miss a meal with her?"

"She said I should go. She practically insisted."

"You're kidding." That wasn't the Francesca Salvare I knew.

"She said it would be an insult to turn down your parents' invitation, especially after what you and I went through. So what time should I pick you up?"

"Six o'clock, but I'll pick you up. You need to take it easy."

I hung up with a feeling of dread in the pit of my stomach. My mother was planning something awful; I just knew it. Why had Mrs. Salvare chosen today to be so gracious?

That feeling stayed with me while I showered, ate breakfast, drove to the flower shop, and filled Grace in on the events of the previous day.

"Oh, Abby, love! You brave, dear girl, the ordeal you went through! I never would have suspected Iris's mother. But it all makes sense now, doesn't it? And then to rescue the man you love!" She gave me a hug. "I'm so proud of you, dear, and so very glad you weren't hurt."

As tears misted her eyes, Grace straightened her shoulders. "Right, then. Have a seat and I'll bring you a nice cup of my special coffee."

Under Grace's tender ministrations, I felt much better, until my mom and dad called for a full report at noon. After what seemed like an interminable grilling, Mom ended our conversation with a happy, "See you and Marco tonight. Don't be late. You're in for a surprise."

And then my feeling of dread returned.

That feeling grew stronger still when Jillian stopped by, having heard the news about Mrs. Frey's capture through the Knight family grapevine. "Wittle Abs! I'm so glad you're safe," she cried. "Oh, look, your hands are cut." She picked up my hands and turned them over. "Hmm," she said, then dropped them. "Oh, well. See you tonight."

That was it? No questions about how I got the cuts on my hands? No questions about how I helped capture Jonas's murderer or even what I was wearing at the time? Who was this woman impersonating my annoying cousin?

"Jillian, wait," I called. "Exactly why did my mom call you yesterday?"

She merely wiggled her fingers at me and

hurried out.

When I got home after work and wanted to share my feelings of impending doom with Nikki, I found her dressed for a date.

"You'll never guess who asked me out," she said, putting on her earrings at the mirror.

I stopped sipping my tea. "If you say Scott, I'll banish you from my life forever."

"Scott? Scott who?" she said, then laughed. "Don't worry. I've gotten a lot smarter about men since that fiasco. It's Greg Morgan."

I nearly spit tea all over her. "Seriously, Nikki, no jokes. Who is it?"

She turned toward me, putting her hands on either side of my face. "Greg. Morgan. He called today to tell me I've been cleared and to apologize for what I went through. Then he asked me out. He wants to take me to the Italian Village in Chicago. Isn't that exciting?"

I shuddered, remembering my disastrous date with Morgan at that very restaurant, where I not only suffered through dinner with a horrendous sunburn, but also had to pin up the hem of my dress with clear tape that had crackled throughout the evening as it slowly came undone. And Morgan had been oblivious to everything. I still had nightmares about the experience.

"Nikki, this is *Morgan,* remember? Mr. Hey-Look-At-Me? Are you certain you want to go out with him?"

She smiled and nodded, her eyes bright and clear, her skin glowing. Her mojo was back. Who was I to spoil it for her?

"Go for it, girlfriend." I gave her a hug and ran to get ready for the calamity that awaited me.

At six o'clock I pulled up in front of the big, two-story house where Marco had an apartment on the second floor. He came out moments later, his stride strong, his face cleanly shaved, looking as handsome as ever in his black leather jacket, a light blue mock turtleneck sweater underneath. Instead of jeans and boots, though, he had on black pants and shined shoes.

He got into the passenger side and leaned over to give me a kiss. "I missed you today."

"I missed you, too. How are you feeling?"

"Fine." He tipped his head forward. "Stitches don't show much, do they?"

"Not at all. Your hair covers them."

Taking a deep breath, he buckled his seat belt and said bravely, "Let's do this thing."

"Are you sure? We can still cancel. I can

tell my family you weren't feeling well."

"Come on, Abby. This is only dinner with your family. As long as you're with me and there's food involved, it can't be all bad."

"Even if my mom unveils a hideous work of art?"

"Even then."

I held on to that thought as we headed for the country club. I held on to Marco's hand, as well, when we walked into the sprawling modern brick building and the hostess said to me, "You're in the library this evening, Miss Knight."

Hmm. That was a surprise. The library was a private dining room usually reserved for special events. I sincerely hoped it didn't tie in with some sort of unveiling.

I led Marco toward the cozy room off to the side of the main dining room, where bookshelves lined the walnut wainscoted walls, a fire in the stone hearth crackled invitingly, and a black baby grand piano sat regally in a corner. We walked into the room and saw my family seated at the long banquet table.

At the foot of the table, nearest the door, was my dad in his wheelchair, with Mom beside him. Next were my brothers, Jonathan and Jordan, sisters-in-law Portia and Kathy, and thirteen-year-old niece, Tara, looking particularly fetching — or was that because she was a younger version of me? Beyond them were Jillian and Claymore, Aunt Corrine and Uncle Doug, and dear God! Sitting at the far end were Marco's mother, brother, Rafe, and sister, Gina. I glanced at Marco in bewilderment. He returned my look.

My mom jumped to her feet and cried, "Here are our heroes!"

At once, all but my dad rose, cheering and clapping. "We're so proud of both of you," Dad said, beaming at me from his wheelchair. "You're a chip off the old block, sweetheart — and Marco, fine job, man! You brought in another murderer. I couldn't be prouder if you were my own son."

"Thank you, sir," Marco said, shaking his hand.

I stepped up to give my dad a kiss on the cheek, then saw the huge sheet cake in the middle of the table that said in giant yellow letters, CONGRATULATIONS!

Then Jillian called, "It's a doubration!"

Everyone stopped clapping and turned to stare at her.

"Double celebration," she said, rolling her eyes. "Duh!"

Double celebration? I glanced back at Marco and saw his brows knit. He was

415

clearly as befuddled as I was. He gave me a look that said, *What the hell is going on?* As if I had a clue.

"Okay, you two lovebirds," my mom said, "tell us your other news."

"What other news?" I asked.

"Isn't she coy?" Mom said to the group. "Okay, honey, I'll break the ice by being the first to congratulate you. I'm truly happy for both of you."

I put my hand on my dad's shoulder and whispered, "What's going on?"

"Sweetheart," he said, patting my hand, "I hope we're not spoiling your surprise too much, but we know about your engagement."

"Our *what?*" Marco asked, as my mother drew us toward the head of the table.

"Stop pretending you don't know what we're talking about," Mom said, wagging a finger at us. "We're not the only ones who can follow clues, you know."

"What clues?" I asked, growing exasperated.

"Let's start with last weekend," she said. "According to Jillian, you and Marco slipped away together, and that's when Marco popped the question."

"Jillian!" I cried. "I never told you that!"

She propped her chin on her palm and

smiled. "You didn't deny it, either."

"In the first place," I ground out, "I remember the exact moment you asked me about the weekend, and if you'd stopped complaining about the cash register mangling your fingernails long enough to let me speak —"

"So deny it now." She gave me a smug smile. "Tell us you two didn't go away together."

I glanced at Marco for help, but he merely shrugged. Surrounded by a pack of gossip-hungry females, he was out of his element. "Okay, look, there was a reason we didn't say anything."

"Of course, dear," Mom said, "because you wanted to surprise us. I know how you love surprises."

Oh, God, I hated surprises. "Mom, no, you've got it wrong."

"Your aunt Corrine even saw you and Marco picking out a ring at Bindstroms."

"What?" I asked, turning toward my aunt. "When was this?"

"Yesterday," Aunt Corrine said. "Remember when I waved to you?"

"That was Rafe!" I pointed at Marco's brother, who seemed to be enjoying the mix-up. "Tell them why I was there, Rafe."

"As I remember it," he said, a devilish

twinkle in his eyes, "you did look at the diamond rings."

Before I could splutter out an explanation, Portia said cannily, "Then there's the wedding gown you tried on."

"Wait a minute," I said. "That was supposed to be a joke, Portia. I meant to send the photo to Nikki, not you."

"So why were you trying it on in the first place?" Portia asked.

"I was investigating!"

"Right," she said, "by trying on a wedding gown." Everyone snickered. Okay, I'll admit it did sound a bit far-fetched.

"When can we see your ring?" Jillian clamored, clearing up the mystery of why she'd wanted to examine my hands.

As I gave her a scowl, Mrs. Salvare said, "And what about your honeymoon plans, eh?"

"What honeymoon plans?" Marco asked, frowning at her.

Rafe gave us a sheepish grin. "I found some Key West brochures on your desk and took them home with me."

"Why would you do a stupid thing like that?" Marco growled.

"Hey! It wasn't stupid!" Rafe shot back. "Can I help it if Gina and Mom came to that conclusion when they saw the bro-

418

chures?"

"So naturally I called your mom to find out if we were on the right track," Gina said.

"Of course, I didn't know a thing at the time," Mom said. "But then Corrine called to tell us about seeing you at Bindstroms, and then Portia called about the wedding dress photo, and that's when I put two and two together and came up with the idea of a surprise party, because, well, you love surprises so much."

Right. Surprise! No engagement! They were so determined to believe their own version of the events, they weren't listening to a word I was saying. How could I get through to them?

"Looks like they put the pieces together," Marco said quietly.

"It sure does," I said. "Too bad it was the wrong puzzle."

Mrs. Salvare hobbled toward us on her crutch and held out her free arm. "Come here, both of you, and let me hug you." She wrapped her arm around me first and gave me an exuberant hug. "*Bella,* you saved my boy's life. And may I be the first to welcome you to the Salvare family." Then she let me go to pinch Marco's cheek and say proudly, "My boy, eh? He's a good man. He'll make you a fine husband."

"So, Abby, have you two set a date?" Gina asked, her eyes holding a hint of a challenge. *Ah, yes. Fish or cut bait. Very clever, Gina.*

As I gazed at all the faces watching us expectantly, waiting for my answer, I had a sudden inspiration. I squeezed Marco's hand. "Sorry to disappoint you, Gina, but we haven't set a date just yet. When we have one, I promise you'll be one of the first to know."

"Actually," Marco said, "I'm partial to September. How about you, Abby?"

I darted a glance at him, trying not to show my surprise. He hadn't squeezed my hand. What did he mean? *Oh, my God!* Did he really want to get married? Was Gina right about him after all?

What if she was right? Was I ready for marriage? And babies? And diapers? What would I do with Bloomers?

What's wrong with you? the little voice of reason in my head asked. *You're crazy about Marco. Would you rather lose him than marry him?*

Of course I didn't want to lose him. I loved Marco with all my heart. And, truthfully, why wouldn't I want to marry him? Had any other man ever come close to being what I wanted in a husband?

Still . . .

I took a deep breath and said, "I'll get back to you on that."

Marco's mouth curved up at the corners and his dark eyes twinkled mischievously. And then he squeezed my hand.

ABOUT THE AUTHOR

Kate Collins, a former teacher, lives with her husband in northwest Indiana during the mild months, then hightails it down to Key West for as much of the winter as possible. She's also the author of several romance novels under various pseudonyms. Visit her Web site at www.katecollinsbooks.com.

The employees of Thorndike Press hope you have enjoyed this Large Print book. All our Thorndike, Wheeler, and Kennebec Large Print titles are designed for easy reading, and all our books are made to last. Other Thorndike Press Large Print books are available at your library, through selected bookstores, or directly from us.

For information about titles, please call:
   (800) 223-1244

or visit our Web site at:
   http://gale.cengage.com/thorndike

To share your comments, please write:
   Publisher
   Thorndike Press
   295 Kennedy Memorial Drive
   Waterville, ME 04901